ninth witness

BOOK NINE

A.D.CHRONICLES®

ninth
witness

Tyndale House Publishers, Inc.
Carol Stream, Illinois

BODIE & BROCK
THOENE

Visit Tyndale's exciting Web site at www.tyndale.com

TYNDALE and Tyndale's quill logo are registered trademarks of Tyndale House Publishers, Inc.

A.D. Chronicles and the fish design are registered trademarks of Bodie Thoene.

Ninth Witness

A.D. Chronicles series designed by Rule 29, www.rule29.com

Interior designed by Dean H. Renninger

Edited by Ramona Cramer Tucker

This novel is a work of fiction. Names, characters, places, and incidents either are the product of the authors' imaginations or are used fictitiously. Any resemblance to actual events, locales, organizations, or persons, living or dead, is entirely coincidental and beyond the intent of either the authors or the publisher.

Library of Congress Cataloging-in-Publication Data

Thoene, Bodie, date.
   Ninth witness / Bodie & Brock Thoene.
     p. cm. — (A.D. chronicles ; bk. 9)
  ISBN 978-0-8423-7531-3 (hc)
  ISBN 978-0-8423-7532-0 (sc)
   1. Jesus Christ—Fiction. 2. Bible. N.T.—History of Biblical events—fiction. I. Thoene, Brock, date. II. Title.
  PS3570.H46N56 2008
 813'.54—dc22   2008020072

Printed in the United States of America

15   14   13   12   11   10   09
 7   6   5   4   3   2   1

*This story is dedicated to our dear friends,
fellow writers, and prayer partners of YWAM,
especially in Kona and Harpendon!
Trusting ever in the promises of Joshua 1:5-9!*

Jesus said to him, "Today salvation has come to this house, because this man, too, is a son of Abraham. For the Son of Man came to seek and to save what was lost."

LUKE 19:9-10

Prologue

The courtyard of Zachai the Publican was quiet now as guests wandered off to find sleeping pallets beneath the shelter of the portico. Zachai sighed with contentment. Forgiven, fixed in his resolve to make restitution, eager to begin atoning for his sins against others, the once-most-hated man in Judea sat on the broad railing of the fountain. He leaned his back against a stone lion and began to make a mental list of what he must repay: a confiscated vineyard that had to be restored to its rightful owner; a slave, sold to satisfy a debt, who must be redeemed and set free . . . so many others.

Zachai was determined to fulfill his pledge to right every wrong he had done.

Dawn was only hours away. How dramatically Zachai's life had changed between yesterday's first light and now. Was it only yesterday the despised tax collector of Jericho had climbed the sukomore fig tree in order to catch a glimpse of the passing Prophet from Nazareth? Zachai had caught much more than he had bargained for. Yeshua had passed the synagogue, then stopped beneath the tree. Looking up, He had called Zachai by name: "Come down! I'm coming to your house today!"[1]

And so Yeshua had shocked and angered the religious rulers of the city by entering the home of a publican. But Zachai's heart had been transformed from darkness to light, from sorrow to joy, from disgrace to honor.

Zachai felt truly happy for the first time in his life. From his perch he watched as his servants cleaned up the wreckage of the banquet. Knots of hangers-on spoke in quiet tones as they clustered round the bases of the dimming torches. Three of Yeshua's talmidim faced their Master in a half circle. They seemed to be arguing some point while Yeshua studied them with an amused expression.

It was late—well into the third watch. Most of Jericho slept now. In the shadow of Jericho's ancient sukomore fig tree a trio of Jerusalem's elite Pharisee sect, cloaked, as if in disguise, waited to speak with Yeshua. Had they come to the home of Zachai the Publican after the banquet in order to entrap the great Rabbi? Would they use Yeshua's presence in the home of the infamous Zachai to discredit Him?

Nakdimon ben Gurion, bull-like in physique but known for his acts of mercy, was the youngest member of the ruling council in Jerusalem.

Nakdimon's uncle Gamaliel, of late middle age, was an aristocratic lawyer and member of the Sanhedrin. In his youth, Gamaliel bar Simeon had studied Torah under the great Rabbi Hillel.

The third man Zachai recognized immediately. The sharp, angular profile of the wealthy youthful merchant, Joseph of Arimathea, was familiar to the tax collector.

Had these Jewish rulers supped at the banquet Zachai held for Yeshua, among the other followers and sinners? Zachai wondered. Had they been somewhere at the long tables with the other guests all evening long? Or were they latecomers, bribing Zachai's gatekeeper for entrance and only now seeking audience with Yeshua?

In the flickering light of the torches Zachai could scarcely believe his eyes. Rabbinic law declared that if a Pharisee entered the gates of a publican's house he would become unclean. Yet for this meeting with Yeshua they had come by night into defilement.

Zachai smiled ruefully at what deeds could be accomplished by night. "Ah, well. Don't hold it against them, God. They're only in my garden. Not technically beneath my roof, eh? The branches of the fig tree are the roof over their heads."

Minutes passed until Yeshua finished hearing the argument between His talmidim. The Master replied with a few softly spoken phrases. At His answer His followers sniffed and shuffled and, looking everywhere but into His face, sheepishly wandered off to find a bed.

Only then did the three rulers of Israel dare step out of the shadows for a word with the Rabbi from Nazareth. Once again, as He had with His talmidim, Yeshua listened intently to their words as they questioned Him.

Zachai strained to hear the exchange, but the splash of water in the fountain masked Yeshua's words.

Nakdimon gestured toward the gate and shook his head.

Gamaliel seemed to agree with whatever his nephew said.

Zachai overheard Joseph of Arimathea speak two words clearly: "Danger . . . Yerushalayim."

Zachai leaned forward, hoping to catch the full implication of Joseph's warning.

Yeshua nodded, thanking them for coming but gently refusing the advice of the esteemed counselors. "Passover . . . my Father's business . . ."

A man's voice behind Zachai spoke bitterly. "You see, Mother, he will not be dissuaded from Yerushalayim."

A woman answered with sad resignation. "Yes. It is Passover."

Zachai cleared his throat and stood, alerting the speakers to his presence.

Peniel, the man born blind, now sighted and among Yeshua's followers, raised his hand in greeting and approached the fountain with Yeshua's younger brother and His mother. Peniel saluted Zachai. "Shalom be with you."

"And also with you." Zachai held his hands palms up in greeting.

Yeshua's mother added, "May the name of Zachai of Jericho be blessed for his kindness to my son and all of us. May Zachai have peace at his going out and coming in."

Yeshua's younger brother, a short, swarthy man in his late twenties, scowled at Zachai as if he were an intruder instead of master of the estate. "All your household is sleeping."

"There is a time to sleep. I will sleep after I awaken from my dream."

Zachai motioned for the trio to sit beside him. "Sit. Sit, please." And then, "I was making certain I would never forget . . . the Son of David holding audience beneath my fig tree. The honor of such a night, eh? And never before have the walls of this house enclosed members of the Sanhedrin."

Peniel, following Zachai's gaze to the three rulers, closed his eyes and appeared to listen to their voices. "My ears see them well. Those three? Gamaliel, who is counted a wise man. And his nephew, Nakdimon ben Gurion, who is a good man. Being a good man he is also counted as wise. And Joseph of Arimathea, who is a rich man. Wealth makes him also good and wise by the standards of the world. I would know their voices anywhere. I've heard them discuss the Law often as I sat at Nicanor Gate and begged. Those three are as upright as that fig tree, with roots planted deep in the righteousness of Torah."

Zachai inhaled deeply. "Until today I would have argued that Righteousness could not enter the gates of a publican like myself. Not in my home."

"We all heard what Yeshua said: 'Today *Yeshua*, Salvation, has come to your home, Zachai,'² Peniel countered. "As for seeing a vision of three Pharisees planted there beneath your fig tree, the part that might be mistaken for a Pharisee is only their outward bark."

Mary did not take her eyes from Yeshua. "They came to warn him. Those men from Yerushalayim."

"The foolishness of this journey," muttered Yeshua's brother. "See, Mother? They are talking, but he isn't listening. No one can tell him anything. And Peter, James, and John as well."

Mary put a gentle hand on her son's arm to silence him. "He told us once that he must be about his Father's business. The shepherd . . . finding lost sheep." She sighed. "You don't remember. You were so young. We were there, you see. Passover in Yerushalayim. The bar mitzvah. Zachariah and Elisheba and young Yochanan. And then here . . . in Jericho. Inside the city gates . . . your father and I turned back to search."

Suddenly energized by the possibility of learning more about Yeshua, Zachai urged Mary to tell the story. "When he was a boy?"

Mary fell silent for a moment. "Our first pilgrimage with him. Yerushalayim. The year Archelaus was banished."

"The year of the census revolt," Yeshua's brother added sullenly.

Peniel hugged his lanky legs and studied Yeshua's face from a distance. "So we're going. No turning back, eh? Well then. Never again will we say: 'Next year in Yerushalayim.' It's this year."

Mary did not reply; neither did she look away.

Yeshua's brother grimaced as if pierced with a sudden pain. "The census revolt. Has he forgotten? See there, Mother. The look in his eye. He has set his face toward Yerushalayim . . . set it like flint."[3]

the middle east

FIRST CENTURY A.D.

Mount Hermon +

GALILEE

Caesarea Philippi

Mediterranean Sea

Chorazin
Capernaum · Bethsaida
Magdala · Sea of Galilee
Sepphoris · · Tiberias

Beth Shan

Jordan River

SAMARIA

Jericho ·
Jerusalem · + Mount of Olives
· Bethany
Bethlehem ·
· Herodium

PEREA

JUDEA   Dead Sea

IDUMEA

N

← to Alexandria, Egypt

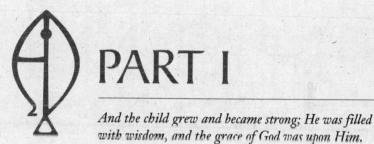

PART I

And the child grew and became strong; He was filled with wisdom, and the grace of God was upon Him.

LUKE 2:40

JERUSALEM

FIRST CENTURY A.D.

KIDRON VALLEY

Josephus' Third Wall

Gate

Golgotha
(Gordon's Calvary)

Tower of
Psephinus

TYROPOEON

Bezetha

Josephus' Second Wall

Sheep Pool
(Pool of
Bethesda)

Fish Gate

Antonia
Fortress

Israel
Pool

Gethsemane

Sheep
Gate

Temple
Mount

Garden Gate
Solomon's Porch
Horse Gate
Beautiful Gate

Golgotha
(Church of the
Holy Sepulchre)

Warren's Gate
Wilson's Arch
(bridge)

Altar

Temple

Tower's
Pool

First Wall

Tombs

Tower of Hippicus

Josephus'

Xystus

Barclay's
Gate
Royal Porch

Pinnacle of
Temple
(traditional
location)

Gate

Tower of Phasael
Tower of Mariamne
Praetorium
Herod's Palace

Gennath
Gate

Herod
Antipas'
Palace

Hulda
Gates

Robinson's
Arch (stairs)

Herod's
Family
Tombs

Upper
City

aqueduct

Valley
Gate

Serpent's
Pool

House of Caiaphas,
the High Priest

ESCARPMENT

Gihon Spring

MT. OF OLIVES

aqueduct

Essene
Quarter

Lower
City

Water
Gate

Hezekiah's
Tunnel

Solomon's
Pool

Upper Room
(traditional site
of Last Supper)

Siloam
Pool

Essene Gate

Gate

HINNOM VALLEY

S unset was quickly approaching. The appearance of three stars and the inability to distinguish white thread from black would usher in the Feast of Purim. It was the fourteenth of Adar in the 3767th year of Creation and one month before Passover.

Rabbi Mazzar, standing before the Scripture cupboard in the Nazareth synagogue, drew forth the scroll of Esther, the reading mandated for tonight's celebration. Tonight and tomorrow all Jews would celebrate the miraculous deliverance of the Jews of Persia from the clutches of the evil Haman. While reviewing the megillah of Esther, the congregation would revile Haman and extol the courage of the heroine and her uncle Mordechai.

It had been almost five hundred years since the events recorded in Esther had taken place. In the centuries following, empires had risen and fallen; Israel had been restored to greatness and had withered again.

The aged rabbi reflected on the passage of time. Esther's story had been read when the land of Israel was a province of Persia; when it had been annexed by Alexander the Great; when it had belonged to the Ptolemys of Egypt; when it had been under the thumb of the Seleucids of Syria; when it had enjoyed the brief sunlight of the Maccabees.

Tonight a Roman governor ruled the land. Though the empire had held sway over Judea for close to a hundred years, now, for the first time, Rome ruled Jewish affairs directly, instead of through a puppet king.

The rabbi stroked his wispy beard as he cast his mind back over the turmoil of more recent years. This year marked the eleventh anniversary of the death of King Herod. Interesting connection that: The remembrance of Esther's heroism and the death of Herod were two occasions when it was forbidden to fast or to mourn.

Herod's death, coming at the end of a string of murders, persecutions, and tortures, was acknowledged each year throughout Jewry. In the Galil they rejoiced quietly, for Antipas, son of the Butcher King, ruled here.

The rabbi shook his head sadly and peered out at the gathering darkness. Recent futile attempts to reestablish Jewish independence had failed miserably. After some initial success, including surprising the Roman garrison at Sepphoris, the Zealots had been defeated. Even now they were being hunted down. Like pinching out candle flames, the remaining pockets of Jewish resistance were being crushed.

All day today Roman legionaries, recruited from hereditary Jewish enemies like Idumeans and Samaritans, wielded hammers. They were not widening the Imperial highways or building another aqueduct or even repairing fortifications damaged in the revolt. They were crucifying the latest batch of captured rebels.

Though the executions were conducted along the main roads and not beside Nazareth's winding lane, the rhythmic thump of mallets, punctuated by anguished shrieks, echoed up and down the hillsides of the town.

The families would come to the synagogue tonight because it was their custom to do so. Mazzar would supervise the reading of Esther, because it was the right thing to do. What no one could instill in the occasion was any feeling of celebration. Where was the provision of the Almighty on this night? Where was there a Mordechai for this age? Where an Esther?

Herod Antipas reclined at a table amid a host of laughing, smiling guests. It was the Feast of Purim, which Antipas also celebrated as his birthday. Because of the commandment to rejoice on the anniversary of the heroic deliverance of the Jews, some took the holiday as license for extreme drunkenness and revelry. It was, as one rabbi said, the most easily filled religious requirement for those who were never pious at any other time of year.

Antipas never required an excuse, religious or otherwise, for debauchery. Though he was only about thirty years of age, his face already showed the sagging jowls and furrowed ravages of excessive pleasure-seeking.

Moreover, this year's holiday and birthday offered him no reason for mirth, but even more excuse for drink. The celebration was taking place in the moldy, dark, drafty halls of Jerusalem's crumbling Hasmonean Palace. The Roman governor, Quirinius, had graciously allotted the old pile to Antipas as a Jerusalem residence, while the upstart, arrogant civil servant paraded around in the grand chambers and marble-lined corridors built by Antipas' father, Herod the Great.

There was no justice in the world—none at all.

After successfully conspiring with his brother Archelaus to eliminate their half brother Antipater as heir, Antipas had been shuttled off to be tetrarch of Galilee, as if that hick province would satisfy him.

Archelaus was an idiot, pompous and easily flattered. It had been Antipas' plan all along to let Archelaus prove how incompetent he was—that much of the plan had worked—and then be named in his place as the king of the Jews, like old Herod.

Antipas had even denounced Archelaus to Caesar, siding with the religious types he despised with the notion that they would support his claim to the throne.

Instead, now a Roman occupied the royal palace. . . . A Roman sat in the chair of state. . . . A Roman laid down the law in Judea as if there were no proper King of the Jews. And the religious establishment, from the newly appointed high priest on down, toadied to the Romans.

It was more than enough reason to be drunk.

The foolish rebellion in Antipas' tetrarchy had cemented the fact that he would not be named king, but Antipas blamed the uprising on Rome. If the Empire had only waited awhile before launching their stupid census. Rome's heavy-handed presence had sparked new calls for a mythical messiah and summoned forth the revolution that would usher in a glorious, resurgent Jewish kingdom.

Ha! Rome's presence had prompted a torrent of executions and condemned Antipas to celebrate his birthday slobbering into his cups. His wife, a princess of Nabatea, had long since abandoned her husband's side at dinner with no pretense of humility. She despised him when he was sober; she abhorred him when he was drunk.

So be it! She was only a temporary expedient until a better partnership presented itself.

Antipas shook his head ponderously and wine slopped out of the jeweled goblet. A servant attentively refilled it while studiously avoiding his master's drunken glare.

Just let anyone claim to be the Messiah—that Anointed One! Antipas would crush him utterly . . . and anyone who dared speak well of him or even the dream of him! If old Herod had been a suspicious, bloodthirsty tyrant, Antipas was fully prepared to out-Herod Herod!

The full moon rose in the constellation of The Virgin. Its bright gleam illuminated a colorless landscape. It created a ring in the sky from which all the other nearby lights, save The Lord of the Sabbath, were banished.

The reading of Esther proceeded as planned. Despite the unavoidably somber tone of the evening, the Scripture portions designed to be spoken in unison by the assembly and the roaring and hissing that accompanied each mention of the villain Haman's name were louder than Rabbi Mazzar had ever heard.

It took little pondering to realize the noise was not celebration but an earnest desire to drown out the screams of the crucified.

The square chamber of the synagogue was packed. Likewise, the Women's Gallery was full. No one wanted to be home alone tonight. If there was no joy in numbers, at least there was less terror because of being with all your friends and neighbors.

Other Purim feasts were given to drunkenness and revelry.

Not this night.

If the congregation was drunk with anything, it was apprehension.

The cantor chanted the words: *"And the king said, 'Hang him on that.'"*

Loud cheering, much applause, and the stamping of feet succeeded this decree.

"So they hanged Haman . . ."

Even louder applause, mixed with hisses, groans, and shouts of derision followed this use of the villain's name.

". . . on the gallows that he had prepared for Mordechai."[4]

Looking around the congregation, Rabbi Mazzar saw strained hopefulness on each face: Would the Almighty ever intervene again in Jewish affairs? Haman's plan to slaughter Jews had failed, yet just out of sight—around the bend, down the canyon—Jews were being slaughtered.

True, some of the crucified were brigands and bandits, but some were patriots, eager for Israel to live again.

The story had passed its climactic moment: Esther had triumphed; Haman was dealt with; the rest was a song of victory.

Mazzar's eye lighted on the screen of the gallery where the women and children sat. What had attracted his attention was the face of his student Yeshua. It was pressed into a gap in the lattice, eager to hear every word.

The cantor arrived at another Scripture portion to be spoken in chorus, and the audience took up the refrain:

"Then Mordechai went out from the presence of the king in royal robes of blue and white, with a great golden crown and a robe of fine linen and purple, and the city of Susa shouted and rejoiced."[5]

Mazzar saw Yeshua's face beaming as He chanted . . . as if He were viewing the story as a present reality—not an oft-repeated legend or a far-off promise, but a contemporary truth.

Why was that?

The Jews had light and gladness and joy and honor.[6]

What a contrast this life of Yeshua was now compared to the gloomy expectations Rabbi Mazzar had when he'd first learned Yeshua's mother, Mary, was pregnant while still only bethrothed to Yosef. The dark thoughts and gossip of the villagers of Nazareth had been turned to light by Yeshua's kindness as He was growing up. The sorrow of His grandparents had been transformed to gladness and joy in the presence of Yeshua's laughter. The disgrace predicted for Mary had instead become honor through the virtue and wisdom of her son.

It seemed like few even remembered the questions that had swirled around Yeshua's conception. The villagers simply accepted Him as one of them.

Mazzar turned to look out the window of the synagogue. A frown of surprise added to the wrinkles on his lined face. A shadow crept across the moon . . . but there were no clouds in the sky.

By the time the cantor sang, *"The Jews struck all their enemies with the sword, killing and destroying them,"*[7] others in the assembly had also noticed the celestial event.

It was impossible to miss: The eclipse was turning the moon to blood.

"Exactly what occurred just before the death of Herod eleven years ago," Mazzar murmured aloud.

When the reading neared its completion, the chorus was loudest of all:

"For Mordechai the Jew was second in rank to King Ahasuerus, and he was great among the Jews and popular with the multitude of his brothers, for he sought the welfare of his people and spoke peace to all his people."[8]

Another glance at his pupil brought yet another surprise to the rabbi. Now Yeshua's face looked grave, somber.

What was he failing to grasp that his student obviously perceived? Mazzar wondered.

What did the blood on the moon mean this year?

CHAPTER 2

The smoke from burning huts in the Zealot camp west of the Sea of Galilee mingled with the stench of burning flesh. The confines of the outpost were littered with dead Galilean rebels. Those who had fallen in this final battle with the Romans were the lucky ones.

The Roman legionaries collected their own dead and carted them away. They who worshipped Caesar as the son of a god, as a new incarnation of the god Jupiter, looked at the bloodred moon with pleasure. The eclipse on the Jewish holiday of Purim, they believed, was an omen of ill fortune for the Jews and a sign of yet another victory for the Empire of mighty Caesar.

The old woman crept on hands and knees to the opening of the narrow crevasse above the devastation. The cleft was wide enough for a child to squeeze through, and for the frail old woman who was their nurse. In the search for fugitives, the Romans had overlooked this hiding place a dozen times.

"Judah! Betrayed," she whispered. "All of them! Betrayed."

The crone had hidden here with the commander's two children for a day and a night. The children slept in the exhaustion of terror and grief. Come morning they would be hungry and in need of water. Was it safe to come out?

Her vision, though poor at close range, was fair enough at a distance.

Embers glowed eerily below. She scanned the ruined shelters, the blackened shell of the synagogue, the kitchen and the meeting tent. All was desolation. There was no sign of life.

"It is finished," she wheezed. "All dead. All gone."

Still, she knew there might be some watcher hidden in the wreckage, waiting for a Jewish straggler to return. It would not be safe to descend—not even to examine the bodies for a sign of life.

No. The children of Judah the Galilean were her charge. She had watched over them and would protect them till her dying breath. They called her Grandmother, though she was no blood relation. She had lost her husband and her own son to Roman crosses and so had taken special pleasure in caring for the son and daughter of Judah, the fierce warrior whom some compared to Judah Maccabee.

Pain radiated from the old woman's chest and focused in her lower jaw. Perhaps she would die soon too, but she would lead them out to safety first.

She muttered, "Help me, Adonai. We'll climb out over the ridge. I have that much strength left in me."

She groped back through the opening into the pitch-black den. Listening for the deep breathing of the little ones, she located them, giving the boy a shake.

"Jude!" she whispered. "Wake up!"

The boy groaned in protest.

She nudged him harder. "Jude! We must leave before dawn."

He struggled to sit up. "Grandmother?"

"Yes."

"I dreamed. A terrible dream. Am I dreaming?"

"No, child."

"Is there a lamp?"

"We have no light."

"The Romans. Did they . . . ?"

"Aye."

"And did I hear a soldier? Searching for us? Did he say that to celebrate Purim, the Romans would crucify Papa at the crossroads of Sepphoris?"

She hesitated. "He meant to make you cry out as they searched for you."

"Will they crucify Papa?"

Her tone told him the execution was accomplished. "Jude, we must be gone. Must leave this place."

"But my father! Papa?"

"Hopeless."

The boy's voice trembled in disbelief. "But . . . Grandmother . . . it's Purim. Papa said . . . the rabbi said . . ."

She rasped, "The Purim moon has turned to blood above us. Above your father. Above the patriots who followed him these many months."

"Purim. The old ones say the enemies of Israel fall on Purim! How can it be?"

"Aye. Purim. What better night for Romans to slaughter Jews? The whole camp is betrayed."

"Betrayed?"

"Aye. Get up. No time to lose. Help me rouse your sister. You must help me with her, boy. We'll take the goat track up and out. Don't look down. Don't look back. We must be miles away by morning."

His name was Zachariah, meaning "Yahweh has remembered."

Frail and bony-shouldered and of advanced years, Zachariah was unlike any other of his generation. Some years ago, East of Jordan, he had noticed that old friends and acquaintances began to forget simple things. Yet Zachariah discovered he remembered every detail of every day of his life since the angel Gabriel had appeared to him in the Temple of Jerusalem.

Zachariah not only remembered what day it was, but he vividly recalled everything that had happened to him on this exact date all the way back to the Days of Awe thirteen and a half years before.

He was a walking human archive containing exact recitations of world-shaking events, as well as a repository of insignificant conversations between two people overheard in the marketplace. In any binding legal agreement, Zachariah was called upon by Jew and Gentile alike as witness.

Every jot of Scripture he read, every mark of the pen, every word of commentary was as fresh in his mind as though a scroll lay open before him.

Remembering was not only the core of Zachariah's name, it had been the hub of his life for thirteen years. Something had happened to him on that fateful day in the presence of the archangel.

Zachariah had finally fulfilled the meaning of his great name.

Tonight, his wife, Elisheba, called to him impatiently, "Zachariah! Hurry! You'll miss it!"

"Coming, love! Coming, my dove!" Then he muttered sarcastically, "My dove. Heh. Elisheba. Cooing like a dove. Cackling like a hen. I will get to the roof before morning, be assured."

Though his mind was as fresh as a boy's, his body pained him. He labored to climb the steps to the rooftop of his house east of the Jordan River. Knees creaked like hinges in need of oil. His gnarled fingers groped for a secure handhold.

His son, Yochanan, almost thirteen now and the original reason for the angelic visit, peered down the stairwell. "Papa, the moon is the color of blood. Hurry! A shadow has fallen over the brightness and . . . hurry!"

Zachariah sighed and labored upward. "Tell it to wait for me."

"Husband." Elisheba demanded sharply. She had not aged in face or body since the miraculous child had been born in her old age. Her mind also was sharp and her tongue sharper still.

"As you say." His grizzled head emerged above the roofline. A blast of cool air filled his lungs. Looking above him he spotted the apparition. He had seen such portents in the sky before.

"What is it, Papa?" His son was a strapping lad, nearly six feet tall, with a broad, sunburned face and arms as big around as those of a young man twice his age.

"An eclipse." Zachariah took Yochanan's hand and scuttled to a chair positioned beneath the starry skies of the wilderness.

The trio sat close together, necks craned back as they took in the image.

Elisheba asked, "What does it mean, Husband?"

Zachariah remained silent as recollections of other such celestial events flipped through his mind. Days and dates and times, all tangled up with prophecies and the rising and falling of the great men of the world.

"Remember . . . we saw this very sight before the death of old Herod the Butcher King."

Elisheba nodded and grunted. "And now his evil son—twin soul, they say—Archelaus . . ."

". . . has fallen." Zachariah completed her sentence.

"But, Papa," Yochanan asked, his voice cracking with the change to manhood, "we knew this. What is this sight? And on the night of Purim too?"

Zachariah remembered. "This bloody sign is in the heart of Yerushalayim, where the high priest, Annas, is appointed by a Roman governor and confirmed by the drunkenness of Herod Antipas." Zachariah closed his eyes and the letters and words of the Isaiah scroll flamed before him. *"For your hands are stained with blood, your fingers with guilt. Your lips have spoken lies and your tongue mutters wicked things. No one calls for justice; none pleads his case with integrity. They rely on empty arguments and speak lies."*[9]

Yochanan clasped his father's hand. "But what does it mean for us, Papa?"

Again the letters of Isaiah flamed in Zachariah's memory. *"So justice is far from us. We look for light, but all is darkness; for brightness but we walk in deep shadows."*[10]

Elisheba shuddered and clutched her shawl close around her shoulders. "But surely, Husband, this can't be all!"

Zachariah's eyes snapped open as the penumbra began to slide from the face of the moon. "It means . . . the end of all as we have known it . . . is near, my dear. He who shall oppose them all is among us. It is written, *Arise, shine, for your light has come, and the glory of the Lord rises upon you. See, darkness covers the earth and thick darkness is over the peoples, but the Lord rises upon you and his glory appears over you. Nations will come to your light, and kings to the brightness of your dawn."*[11]

The tint of crimson moved slowly from the face of the moon. At last the bright orb stood directly over the place where the City of David was planted.

Yosef was alone on the rooftop of his house in Nazareth. Intense cold had settled over the Galil during the journey home from the Purim service. The carpenter was cocooned in a blanket, but his head was bare as he examined the sky. It was already at least an hour past midnight. Yosef could not sleep, though Mary and Yeshua were both wrapped in slumber below.

High, icy streaks of cloud flowed across the heavens from the direction of Mount Hermon. The moon, long since out of its eclipse, now bored a yellow-tinged hole through the curtain of vapors overhead. The Lord of the Sabbath kept close company with it. The star of The Virgin's heart, The Star of Atonement, winked fitfully nearby.

With the exception of the carpenter, Nazareth seemed to be asleep. No lights showed in the village. Chimneys displayed only wisps of smoke from the banked fires beneath.

All was as silent as a grave . . . almost. The tormented cries punctuating the Purim gathering had tapered away with the advancing night. Occasionally Yosef heard a moan from the crucified ones, a sound that almost could have been mistaken for a night bird's call.

There was no release except in death for those condemned by Rome. For their sakes, Yosef hoped the bitter cold would speed their departure from this life and their welcome into *olam haba*, the world to come. "Be merciful to them, O Lord," he prayed. "Bring a swift end to their suffering."

And the bloody face of the moon—what had it meant?

The ruddy moon that had appeared just before Herod's death was widely regarded as a portent of his doom. But tonight's apparition? When the boot of Rome was on the throat of Israel, how could it mean anything good for the Jews?

Yosef shifted his weight, struggling to keep the blanket tight since every small gap admitted a knife of freezing air.

There was a rustling on the stairs. Mary emerged on the platform, likewise swaddled in a blanket, with a scarf over her head and bundled around her throat.

"I heard you moving up here. Are you all right?" she asked.

Yosef was remorseful. "I'm sorry I woke you. I'm fine. Just couldn't sleep is all." He pulled her close, cloaking her in an additional fold of his own blanket.

Mary glanced up at the moon, then peered toward the south as if she could see through the hills to the parade of crosses marching into the distance. "So much cruelty in the world," she murmured. "Tonight's moon . . . so dark, so red . . . it means something, doesn't it?"

"Perhaps," Yosef said, noncommittally, hoping to spare her his own anxiety.

"And it is in the sign of The Virgin . . . isn't that right? You taught me so much about the wonders of the sky."

For the first time in his married life Yosef regretted having shared his fascination with the stars with Mary. This remorse was reinforced by the next words she spoke. "I can't help but remember what Old Simeon said to me: 'And a sword will pierce your heart as well.'[12] Is that what we saw tonight, Yosef? Blood on the heart of the virgin?"

Yosef tucked her head beneath his chin. "The Almighty has kept us safe, hasn't he? Twelve years, and he has never failed to keep us sheltered, eh?"

"It's not that," Mary responded, peering up into Yosef's worried frown. "The Lord is faithful and trustworthy at all times. I can't help but think that something's happening . . . or about to. It just seems that something is about to change; some new corner of a plan we don't yet understand is unfolding even now."

"Come," Yosef said. "It's late and it's cold. Let me get you back inside."

As Yosef escorted Mary down the steps, a new constellation rising in the east caught his eye—one he was grateful Mary appeared not to notice.

It was the sign of the swan winging upwards . . . the form of a cross splayed over the darkest part of the sky.

lmond trees in early bloom carpeted the hillside above the verdant Galilean valley in pink. The floor of the swale was splashed with red poppies. A soft, cool breeze rustled the branches of the grove outside the city of Sepphoris, but on it was carried the sweet-sick smell of death.

The old woman did not want to come to the site of the executions, but the boy refused to listen to her voice or follow her until he searched for his father.

"Grandmother, what if Papa escaped?" Jude steeled himself to look up, without flinching, into the face of horror. "What if he's alive? How could we leave without knowing?"

Grandmother croaked in a singsong voice to the boy and his sister, who followed close behind, "I pray he has flown away. Oh, Jude! To come to such a place as this. The breeze, eh? It will not comfort the dying. Only prolong their suffering."

"Papa," whispered the boy, covering his nose and mouth with his tunic's sleeve against the stench of decay.

The old woman tapped her hooked nose with a gnarled finger. "The smell of betrayal and shame. The smell of Beelzebub. Don't forget it when you are tempted."

The boy choked and nodded.

Jude was only nine years old, yet the contrast between the beauty of the Galil and the barbarity of human suffering did not escape him. Jude and his sister, Kerah, walked between the rows of executions flanking the road between Sepphoris and Nazareth. The stand of crosses was a macabre leafless orchard bearing the rotting fruit of Galilee's uprising against Roman taxes and Roman rule.

Brother and sister passed beneath the shadows of the dead and dying. Where was their father? Where was the hero of the Galil who had rallied an army of farmers and fishermen in a futile attempt to fight the trained legions of Rome?

Kerah, at six, was fragile and fair, but she had the intellect of a toddler. Oblivious to the orchard of human agony around them, she smiled into the bunch of wildflowers drooping in her hand.

Jude noticed the poppies' scarlet matched the fresh blood oozing from the wounds of the crucified prisoners. He brushed a tear of fury from his cheek. "My father isn't here," he said to Grandmother.

Jude had lived nine turbulent summers of the nearly eleven years since old Herod the Butcher King had died, his son Archelaus had taken the throne of Judea by the will of the emperor Augustus, and Antipas had been made tetrarch of the Galil. Jude had seen many crucifixions in his short lifetime.

The old woman screwed up her face. "Crucifixion. Aye. They don't look like themselves. I hardly knew my son after the Romans finished with him. If your father had not taken me in to care for you two, where would I be?" She paused and squinted at the distorted features of a criminal tortured in the most prominent position at the junction of two highways. "Oh, where is he? Our champion? Judah of Galilee?"

The dying man's eyelid fluttered. The mouth contorted in a desperate attempt to speak.

Could it be?

Jude's head jerked up. His eyes widened with horror as he spotted an old scar on the victim's shinbone, now outlined with dried blood.

Grandmother cried, "Look, boy! Is that him?"

Jude clasped his sister's hand. Blossoms spilled from her fingers. She dropped to her knees to retrieve them from the dust.

The old woman declared with certainty, "Yes, it's him. Your father. He was the most important of the rebels. So they've executed him here, where everyone will see him."

Jude staggered and wailed. He reached out toward the twisted feet nailed to the post and shook his head violently. "Papa!" He stumbled, fell to his hands and knees, then crawled to the side of the road.

Kerah, oblivious, picked up flowers one by one.

No! Please! Not Papa! Couldn't be! Jude lay facedown beside a white stone mile marker.

Minutes passed.

The crone called to him, "Boy! Still alive, I think. See—his eyes moved. And when you cried out, he tried to speak. He sees Kerah. Poor, dumb creature plucking at the flowers. He is looking at her playing with the poppies in the road. Jude! Your father calls to you. See—he mouths the words . . . your name! Get up! You must speak to him before he flies away. Go on."

Jude struggled to sit up, to look up. His father's eyes, clear for an instant, locked on his. Still here. Somehow aware of his children beyond the agony of the cross.

Yes. Papa.

Papa silently mouthed the words, "You must take . . . Kerah . . . Take . . . her to . . ."

The boy pleaded, "Papa? Where? Where do we go?"

Then an audible word formed—broken but clear. "Ye . . . ru . . . shal . . . ayim . . ."

The effort was too much. The body convulsed. Blood and sweat struck Jude's cheek like warm rain.

Raising his gaze, Jude called, "Papa! Papa!"

The gore of days of suffering congealed on the wooden cross. Vultures circled slowly above them. There was no coming back.

"Oh, Papa! Don't die. Papa!"

Papa struggled to raise himself and draw a final breath to speak one word of comfort to his son. The movement forced blood and water from his lungs. The mixture oozed from his lips onto his beard. He coughed, at last unable to inhale. A single cry of agony escaped his lips.

Kerah leapt to her feet and proudly extended her bouquet to Jude.

The body sagged forward, suspended by the spikes in grotesque surrender.

Yosef heard Rabbi Mazzar's wheezing greeting before the old man came in sight around the corner of the carpenter's shop. There was an urgency in Mazzar's voice not solely due to the climb up the hill to Yosef's home.

Gasping for breath, Mazzar was at first unable to speak.

"Here! Sit down," Yosef urged, sweeping a square, a compass, and the plans for a wedding chest off a block of wood. "Are you ill?"

A violent negative shake of the head and a single palm held aloft instructed Yosef to wait a moment.

"Trouble? More arrests?"

Another shake of the head.

Yosef reached for a bucket hanging from a beam and drew out a ladle of water, which he passed to the rabbi.

"Better," Mazzar managed after a swallow of water and a half score of deep breaths. "It'll be Sabbath in a few hours."

"Yes? And . . . ?"

"The Roman centurion . . . he just now gave permission for the crucified Zealots to be removed from the crosses. The young, sneering officer . . ."

"The decurion?"

"That's the one. He said no, but the centurion will permit it, you see. But we have to hurry to finish before sundown. We need your tools: ladder, pry bar, pincers . . ."

"I'll round everything up at once," Yosef agreed grimly.

"And . . . we need your help as well," Mazzar added.

Yosef nodded, then turned at the creak of the gate between the house and workshop opening.

Yeshua entered and stood before Yosef and the rabbi. "I heard," the boy said. "I want to help as well."

Yosef frowned and shook his head. "It's no place for children."

Yeshua raised His chin and saw the determination in Yosef's wide-set brown eyes. "You and Rabbi taught me it is a mitzvah to respect the dead. This is my thirteenth year. I am old enough."

Yosef caught Rabbi Mazzar's blinking approval. "Very well, then," he said. "Load a work bucket with tongs and pry bars. I'll carry the ladders."

The old woman had only two denarii in the leather pouch tied around her waist. She seemed very weary, Jude thought as he held her hand. "You would like to rest, Grandmother? Before we go on?"

"It is a distant place your father sends us to." She touched the money pouch. "Many days. The Roman legionaries patrol the highways. But if we are careful, we can sleep in the orchards. Buy bread as we go. Perhaps . . ."

"Yerushalayim," Jude said glumly as the trio of fugitives walked south, avoiding the small villages that dotted the landscape of the Galil. "So far, Grandmother?"

"None in the Galil would dare take us in. Maybe there is a reward. Even for an old woman."

Jude envisioned torture to extract the names of men who had been part of the rebellion. "We can't stay. But Yerushalayim. What waits for us there? The new Roman governor . . ."

She shrugged. "I had a cousin lived there long ago. My mother's uncle's son. He had a shop on the Street of the Tinsmiths. . . . God will provide. . . ."

A mother's uncle's son seemed to Jude a distant hope. But at least it was something.

Sunlight broke through the clouds, illuminating the whitewashed stone houses of Nazareth on the hillside. From this distance the buildings had the look of a flock of sheep dotting the terraced ridge.

"We'll find today's bread there," Grandmother wheezed as she fished out a coin and clasped Jude's fingers around it. "Go quickly."

"What if someone asks who I am? Or where I am going?"

She jerked her thumb at Kerah. "Be as silent as your sister. Speak to no one except to buy our provisions."

Jude studied the coin in his palm. His stomach growled. How could he think of food while Papa's body still hung on the cross?

The old woman seemed to hear his thoughts. "You must eat. And Kerah must be fed. And I . . . I can't go on unless . . ." Her breathing was labored.

"Sure." Jude patted her on the shoulder. "I'll come back for you. But where . . . ?"

"I'll not take another step. Kerah and I will shelter here in the almond grove. Look. Poor creature." The old woman stared at Kerah as the girl gathered a handful of fallen pink blooms from the dust beneath the trees. "How she loves the blossoms. Look at her. As if the almond branches are clouds at sunset and she is a bird flying through the sky. She must eat. And rest."

Jude kissed the old woman on her cheek. "I won't be long."

"Go then. Hurry! Run ahead and buy unleavened bread and cheese before the souk closes. Apples too. And a skin of apple juice."

4

CHAPTER

Jude, all spindly arms and legs and wild, uncombed hair, trudged up the rutted road into Nazareth. He saw a woman watch his slow progress as she churned butter beneath the sukomore fig tree in front of the house.

Unwashed, ragged, and alone, he knew he had the look of grief and hunger and poverty about him. But Jude kept his jaw set and his eyes defiant as he neared the stone fence. He felt himself anger personified—the hatred of a Zealot living inside the body of a little boy.

The woman smiled at him and nodded. He glowered back at her as though she were an enemy.

His heart whispered, *Do not speak kindly to me or I will crumble. Show me no kindness or my heart will break.*

Would she know somehow that he was connected to the men on the crosses?

She left her churn to gather in the washing that lay across the fence. Clasping the clean, dry, boy-sized tunic, she folded it over her arm and approached the gate as he drew near. "Shalom!" she greeted him.

Her voice startled him. He heard her clearly but did not respond.

His pace faltered and slowed. Then, as if she were a menacing dog, he moved to the center of the road.

She tried again. "Are you hungry?"

He stopped and stared down at his feet. Both hands went to his belly. *Hungry. Yes.* That was a question the woman did not need to repeat.

She stepped aside, opening the path to the house for him. "Come on, then. And welcome. There's plenty for you to eat."

He hesitated, then nodded. Placing two fingers over his lips, he gave the beggar's sign that he was mute, then showed her a coin to prove he could pay for food.

"A coin. You're not a beggar."

He shook his head emphatically from side to side. Not a beggar! He could and would pay.

"Where is your family?"

Jude shrugged. His eyes brimmed.

"Your mother?"

He shrugged.

"Your father?"

He could feel his lower lip trembling as the facade of toughness dissolved. Involuntarily he looked away across the pink cloud of almond orchards, beyond which Roman crosses bloomed.

So, his secret was known in an instant. He was the proud child of a fallen Zealot. Yes. But he still could not speak out in the open. Someone might hear him. Someone might see them talking together and ask what was said. The woman seemed to comprehend this unspoken need for caution.

She led the way to the house. Removing her shoes beside the door, the woman offered him water and the two washed their feet. He imitated her actions, leaving the basin black with mud.

Touching the mezuzah on the doorpost as she entered, she blessed her guest: "May Adonai bless your going out and your coming in . . ."[13]

A cauldron of lentil soup simmered over the fire. Lavender dried in the rafters, filling the tidy space with a clean, welcoming aroma. Loaves of bread cooled on the window ledge. At the sight of such wholesome ordinariness, Jude's hard edge softened into wild desperation and longing.

The woman put her hand on Jude's head. "What is your name?"

He blurted, "Jude. But I'm not supposed to tell!" Then he began to cry. "Not . . . supposed to speak."

"I won't tell." She folded him into her arms. Like a mother, she held him close until his sobs subsided. "Jude. A good strong name."

"I wasn't supposed to . . . speak. It was the plan. Just buy bread and get back."

"You're not traveling alone?"

"Yes. I mean . . . no! I mean . . . please . . . I'm not supposed to . . ."

"I see. Then no more questions, Jude. So sit. Eat." She poured a bowl of soup and made him sit in front of the fire. Tearing a loaf in half, she put a dollop of fresh butter on it and slid it across to the boy.

As he slurped down his meal, she packed a leather satchel with bread and cheese and dried figs. Enough provisions to last one person a few days but not so much that he would have difficulty carrying it back.

Watching her every move, Jude saw her frown at his filthy, ragged tunic, then fetch clean clothes from a chest. Scraping the bowl with a crust of bread to get every last drop, Jude finished the soup and held out his bowl for more. The woman filled it twice more before sending him to change into the boy's clothes.

She stood watch in the doorway as if half afraid a troop of Romans would ride up the highway in search of fugitives.

Jude knew that same fear and shivered. Had he stayed too long already?

But no one came.

The boy expected the woman to ask how many of their band had survived the attack. And how many were in hiding? Where would they go now?

But she asked nothing. Jude was grateful, because he knew he would have told her . . . everything.

"It will be dark soon," Jude said, looking round the room. He wanted nothing more than to stay with her.

"Soon."

He ran his hand across the fine woolen tunic. "You have a boy."

"Yes."

"He is lucky. . . . A mother . . . this house . . ."

"I am blessed."

He held out his coin.

She refused it with a single shake of her head. "Almost dark. It will be cold tonight in the Galil."

"No one will see me."

"I have something for you." She returned to the trunk and took out a fleece-lined coat made of lambskin. "My son wore this when he was your age. He has outgrown it. I'm sure he would want you to have it."

Jude had never seen such a fine coat. The leather was tanned to withstand moisture. The inside fleece was golden and soft. "You have no other son to wear it?" he blurted.

"It was a gift to my son sent to us in Egypt when he was small. The coat of a Passover lamb. Sent to him by a Temple shepherd who tends the flocks in Beth-lehem. My son asked me yesterday where it was and said he would like to give it to a boy who would wear it."

Jude embraced the coat, burying his face in the wool. It smelled of lavender, like the house. "I . . . will. I mean . . . thank you. And your son. A thousand times."

"I know we will meet again."

He felt foolish and ungrateful. He had taken everything and had never even asked her name. "What are you called?" He wavered in the doorway, leaning against one doorpost as he donned his shoes.

"Mary."

"Shalom, Mary. Maybe . . . someday I'll come back."

"You will be most welcome. Shalom. Adonai go with you." She embraced him and caressed his cheek. He pulled himself from her embrace, grabbed the satchel, dashed out the door, and sprinted down the road. The rhythmic flap of his sandals drummed a retreat into the growing darkness.

Flights of evil-looking black birds spiraled overhead. A single file of men trudged from Nazareth out to the main highway, where the executions had taken place. The word had also gone round to every nearby village and hamlet. Each turning produced another column of grim-faced workers.

There was very little conversation. Everyone knew the horrors that lay just ahead; everyone knew his duty.

Another squad of men was already at work digging graves on the hillside above the town. Unused tombs would also be pressed into service as temporary resting places until the end of Sabbath.

The first sight of the Roman orchard of execution caused each man a gut-wrenching moment. Even Yosef, sturdy and unafraid, who had viewed similar scenes before, trembled with the horror of it.

He put his hand on Yeshua's shoulder, found the boy steady but tense, as one who kept Himself tightly controlled.

At the meeting of two roads hung the Zealot chief, Judah the Galilean. Just as the Romans displayed his torment as an example, so the men of the Galil wanted to remove his body first.

Above him in the air and perching on boulders beside the cross were the ravens . . . like eager demons.

Yeshua struck the air with the back of His hand in a gesture of command. *Be gone from here!*

The scavenging flock took flight, winging off toward the south.

Yosef volunteered that he and Yeshua would retrieve Judah's body. Planting the feet of the ladder firmly in the dusty soil, he was ready to ascend before Yeshua spoke.

"Let me go. I'll go. I knew this man, Papa. I met him once in Sepphoris before the revolt. He was always sad, I think. Now his children are alone. Let me do this for him and for them."

Yosef studied the boy. The carpenter read firm resolve in Yeshua's gold-flecked eyes, saw determination in the set of the jaw and the muscular shoulders. The boy's calloused hands confirmed Yeshua's experience with tools.

Yosef nodded. "Take the pincers and the pry bar."

Tucking the tools into the belt securing His tunic, the boy climbed without hesitating. Yosef steadied the ladder. A coil of rope over His shoulder, Yeshua of Nazareth rose past the pierced feet, the tortured limbs, and the slumping chest till he drew near the agonized features.

"Slip the rope around the chest, under each arm, and then over the crosspiece," Yosef instructed. "That way we can lower him after he's free from the nails."

A single bird, a sparrow, remained on the beam beside Judah's outstretched, clawlike right hand. It spoke softly as Yeshua arranged the rope.

With Yosef and another man grasping the ends of the rope, Yeshua worked at freeing the right hand from the piercing nail.

When it was clear He could not loosen the clinched nail that went all the way through flesh and wood, He used the pincers to clip off the head of the spike protruding from Judah's crushed palm.

It took all the boy's strength, working from what was an awkward position, but the iron parted finally with a snap. Yeshua gently touched the dead man's hand, palm to palm, as if apologizing for causing him pain.

To Yosef, gazing up from below, it seemed the boy measured His own hand against the crucified fingers. The image made him shudder and caused the world to spin.

With a yank on the wrist, Judah's right arm sprang free of the nail. Even though Yosef and the other helper were ready for the weight, the sudden movement allowed the arm to drop, falling across Yeshua's shoulder in an embrace.

And the bird spoke softly to Yeshua alone.

The sun dipped below the horizon as Jude reached the verge of the almond orchard.

Shaqed, whispered the wind passing through the blossoms, "God is watching."

Jude felt safe and warm inside the coat.

It was dark beneath the trees. "Grandmother?"

Jude paused to listen for Grandmother's voice. Silence.

Shaqed . . .

The fabric of his new tunic felt clean against his skin. He felt washed, as though he had bathed in a fresh stream. He wondered about the boy who had worn it before him. What must it be like to live in a house like that in Nazareth? to have a mother and a father and a room of his own?

"Grandmother?"

Jude could not remember the time when his father had owned an almond grove of his own. He only vaguely recalled his father's fight with the Roman mercenary in the street of Sepphoris.

The knife.

The blood.

The man dead on the pavement.

Jude only vaguely remembered them all running away. . . .

Mama refusing to leave Papa, even though she was pregnant.

Hiding in caves in the mountains overlooking the Jordan.

The night Kerah was born.

And the day Mama died by the sword of a Herodian soldier. . . . Kerah had not spoken a word since then. Before all that, what had their farm been like? Jude wished he could remember. Had there been lavender drying in the rafters? A stone wall around the garden? Washing drying in the sun while Mama sang and planted vegetables?

What would their lives have been like if only Papa had accepted the insults from the soldier? If he had not fought the man and won? Would they still own the almond grove outside of Sepphoris? Would Mama and Papa still be alive?

With a sigh, Jude sat down beneath the shadows of a tree and waited. Perhaps Grandmother was sleeping. Kerah could not answer, so it would do no good to call her.

Minutes passed. The shadows pooled into blackness. Where in the tangle of trunks and branches and pink petals were the old woman and Kerah?

Jude looked up and saw the stars winking on like candle flames. Were his mother and father now among the lights? In the southern sky the stars seemed to form the image of a cross rising on the horizon.

The image of Papa on the cross reared up in his mind. He closed his eyes tight and groaned. He tried not to think of it. Burying his face in the sleeve of the tunic, he pretended for a moment that Mary was his mother and that he lived in the white stone house in Nazareth. She set a place for him at the table and called him "My son. . . ."

What was that blessed family doing now as the darkness thickened? What would it be like to be always safe and warm and loved? to never wonder if a Roman gladius was drawn and poised to take your life? to never live in the shadow of a cross?

Jude's shoulders shook as he silently wept for the home of his imagination. "Mama, I can't remember now what your voice sounded like. Papa, I see you with blood spilling from your lips!" He threw his head back and shouted, "Grandmother! Please! Where are you?"

A hacking sound replied to him. "Jude? Boy? Is that you?"

"I'm back! Bread. Cheese. And figs too. Where are you? Talk to me! It's so dark. Speak and I'll find you."

The old woman called his name. "Here. We are here."

He leapt to his feet and groped from tree trunk to tree trunk, at last coming to the fireless encampment where Grandmother and Kerah waited.

"Food! Here. I brought our supper. And enough to last a day or two if we're careful. Maybe most of the way to Yerushalayim. A very kind woman gave it to me. *Gave it*. Wouldn't let me pay her. Look . . . here's a skin of apple juice too."

The old woman chuckled with delight, then burst into another fit of coughing. She broke the bread and gave a piece to each child.

Kerah ate her portion like a bird pecking at the crust. She sniffed it, then pecked at it, one morsel at a time until it was all gone. She snuggled against Jude, clasping the hide of the Passover lamb and inhaling the lavender scent.

At last Jude fell asleep beside her and dreamed of Mama and Papa inside the little house in Nazareth.

n the Sabbath morning after the mass burial of the crucified, Nazareth was sunk in gloom and tinged with fear. Roman pursuit of the insurrection had moved away to the east and south. The Galil seemed peaceful for the moment, but apprehension reigned supreme. A careless word in the ear of a paid informer might bring the wrath of Rome, however wrongly delivered, down on the little west Galilee village. Roman legionaries on the track of rebels tended to execute without regard to guilt or innocence. Roman discipline encouraged the use of horrifying examples as a deterrent to others.

Besides, the recent executions had already struck too close to home. Those who did not have a cousin among the executed men at least had a friend or, in two cases, a brother.

Rabbi Mazzar searched the day's Torah portion to see if there was any comfort to be found there. *Parashah Tetzaveh* began with the admonition in the book of the Exodus to keep a lamp burning continuously before the Ark of the Covenant, just outside the Holy of Holies.

The lamp, both in the wilderness tabernacle as well as now in the Temple in Jerusalem, symbolized HaShem's abiding presence within the veil. *The Almighty is here, though you may not see him. Though you may not enter the innermost chamber, he is there, and his promises are forever. His promises are true and righteous altogether,* Mazzar thought. *But how very hard it is to see past the suffering sometimes.*

Rabbi Mazzar cast a satisfied eye toward his Yeshiva students. Perhaps it was time to speak again to them of not confusing facts with Truth. The book of the Exodus taught as fact that the Israelites fleeing from Pharaoh were trapped between the pursuing Egyptian army and an uncrossable sea. The fact was, their situation was hopeless.

The Greater Truth was that the Almighty was perfectly capable not only of opening a way through the waters but of closing them over the heads of the enemies.

The fact was that the men hung on the crosses were dead, dead, dead.

The Greater Truth was that He Who Is Faithful was capable of raising them back to life again.

The fact was that the crucified had suffered horribly.

The Greater Truth was that HaShem committed Himself to keep account of suffering. Better to suffer a little while in this life than to fall into the hands of angry Elohim!

Mazzar glanced over the scroll of the *Haftarah* for the day. The reading was from the book of the prophet Ezekiel. It spoke of how angry HaShem was at the sinfulness of Israel. The prophet went on delivering HaShem's message as follows: *For seven days they shall purify the altar, and they shall cleanse it and inaugurate it.*[14] The passage ended with this promise from the Almighty: *"And I will accept you with favor." The word of the Lord!*[15]

Thanks be to HaShem, Mazzar breathed.

But when would The One come who could ascend the Mountain of the Lord in Jerusalem and cleanse the Temple once and for all? When? It seemed impossible against the entrenched power of Rome.

But the Almighty does not count time as men count time, Mazzar reminded himself. *Never confuse facts with Truth! Regardless of a myriad of things that cannot be comprehended, trust in He Who Knows the End from before the Beginning. Look beyond the facts of this world by trusting in The One who held the universe in the palm of his hand.*

"But a little help with our trusting," Mazzar muttered aloud, "a little reminder you are paying attention would also help, eh?"

Hours later, his face nestled in his knotted and trembling hands, Rabbi Mazzar closed his eyes but continued to study the Torah page in his mind. Even as his fingertips gently massaged his tired eyes he viewed the lines of Hebrew as clearly as they appeared on the scroll spread before him.

The rabbi of Nazareth lifted his chin, stretching aching neck and shoulder muscles. Seven decades of studying Scripture had left the upper part of his spine permanently bowed in humble adoration of the Word of God. The same seventy-plus years had robbed him of most of his teeth, but praise the Eternal, not his intellect, his strength, his vision, nor his love for the Word.

Opening his eyes he studied the shadows creeping up the wall of the chamber. The village housewives would be impatient for firewood to be split and water drawn and animals fed before suppers could be prepared. These, his Yeshiva students, were needed at their homes . . . all three of them.

He never grew tired of that bit of humor. *His Yeshiva.* A slight wheezing chuckle emerged from his lips at the grandiose-sounding phrase. Nazareth was not a large, and certainly not a prosperous, village. A hundred people at synagogue service was a great crowd; two circumcisions in the same month a population explosion!

Yet the aged scholar was as proud of these three advanced students as if they were his own sons, which in a way, they were. All were of an age—past their twelfth birthdays and into their thirteenth years. In the months ahead all three would be called to the bema to read, to take their places as *b'nei mitzvah,* Sons of the Commandment.

And they would be leaving the school.

Cautious, round-faced Beriah would join his father's olive business. Instead of plucking nuances of learning he would learn to pluck the ripened fruit. Instead of pressing the 613 holy obligations into his mind, he would be pressing out the pale green, fragrant oil for which his family's small grove was known.

The second student, smoothing out an error on the wax tablet on which he meticulously copied Scripture, was Nicolas, the stoneworker's boy. Where Beriah was stout, Nicolas was tall and lean. No matter how much he ate, Nicolas always remained hungry. Rabbi Mazzar hoped his hunger for study would continue but knew this outcome was unlikely. Soon enough Nicolas' appetite would be for punches, chisels, and mallets, limestone and granite. There had already been occasions to scold Nicolas for drawing balustrades and mosaic-tiled floors on the margins of his slate.

And then there was the final student—in between the other two in height and weight, but excelling both in His scholarship and His dedication to study.

Yes, Mazzar had high hopes for Yeshua, the carpenter's son.

Like the others, Yeshua would also be officially apprenticed this year. His days would no longer belong to the parchment and wax aromas of the Yeshiva but to a workshop filled with the tang of cedar and the penetrating turpentine reek of pine. Instead of holding a scroll or stylus, His fingers would grip saw and hammer and plane.

Yet Mazzar saw in Yeshua one who would continue to immerse Himself in Scripture all His days. Already the boy was the first to ask, "Why does it say that? Why does Torah include that story, that phrase, that particular word?"

The scholar had hopes that this boy would be his crowning achievement as a teacher . . . that perhaps the boy would even become a rabbi someday. No rabbi out of Nazareth had ever achieved great fame in the rest of the Jewish world. Galilean rabbis were not reputed to be pious like those educated in Jerusalem or brilliant like those from Babylon or creative thinkers like those from Alexandria.

But Yeshua . . . here was a penetrating, insightful mind to be reckoned with. Good-natured, not aloof or arrogant, Yeshua seemed to study people as well as Torah.

Such a one could make a great rabbi . . . perhaps even the founder of an enduring school like Shammai or Hillel.

The shadow of the western hills reached halfway up the eastern wall. "Boys," Rabbi Mazzar summoned with a clap of his hands, "put your things away. We are finished for today."

᚛

"So . . . this year in Yerushalayim, little ones," Grandmother wheezed. "Your papa . . ."

Kerah grasped the old woman's hand and gazed pensively into her face.

Jude fingered their coin. How much could a night's lodging in an inn cost? He was the man among them now. He would have to make a decision. "We should rest."

"Aye. A night." Grandmother's breath was labored as they traveled. "Caravansary. Nain."

Jude noted her skin was ashen. She rubbed her right shoulder as they moved slowly up the incline of the road. Nain was a mile ahead. No more than an hour away if they could walk at normal speed. He could have jogged to it in half that time. But Kerah and the old woman slowed him down. At this rate it would be almost nightfall before they reached the shelter.

The old woman staggered and leaned upon Jude's arm. "A moment. Rest, eh? Eh?"

He spotted a stump-sized stone and led her to it. "Sure."

Above their heads a raven cawed in fear and flew away, pursued by a brave sparrow.

Grandmother caught Jude's gaze and somehow read his mind. "A brave little fellow . . . that sparrow is."

From the knoll, Jude observed the ensuing battle. The tiny bird protected its nest, diving on the black-winged menace again and again. "The raven is afraid."

"Remember him." Grandmother gasped the admonition. "Courage . . . little sparrow."

Jude nodded as the small warrior chased his enemy out of sight over the hill.

Kerah sat serenely plucking blades of new grass. She knew so little of the world around her. Jude was convinced she did not know the rebellion had been crushed and their father executed.

Hunger chewed at his belly. How could his body demand food at such a time?

"Grandmother," he said, "you are hungry. That's what. When we get to Nain, you can eat. You need hot food and shelter. Then you'll feel better."

"Aye. Of course. Why didn't I think of it?" She reached for him and he helped her stand. Now he was the caretaker of the trio. She swayed a bit.

"Lean on me." Jude draped her arm across his shoulders and nudged Kerah as a signal that they must move on.

"She looks sick." The innkeeper of Nain spat and wiped his mouth with the back of his hand as he eyed Grandmother. "Gray as that stone wall she be. Ain't goin' to die, are ye, old woman?"

The hostel smelled of sour sweat, donkey dung, old wine, and vomit.

So did the innkeeper.

Grandmother pulled herself erect and managed a scowl, though she did look terribly ill to Jude. "I'll be here long after ye're gone!"

The innkeeper looked doubtful. "Aye. If y' die, ye'll be here 'til Judgment Day. Someone dies here, it'll be bad for business."

Jude stepped between the greasy landlord and the old woman. "She'll be fine. A good night's sleep. We come a long way is all. Don't mean she'll die here."

"Well then." The innkeeper relented and held out a grimy palm. "I suppose ye'll be wantin' supper."

"We brought our own," Jude proclaimed. "We need a place for Grandmother and my sister to sleep out of the cold."

"Ye can pay?"

"I can."

"Y' have the coat of a rich man's brat. Did y' steal it?"

Jude snarled, "It is mine. . . . My mother . . . gave it to me. It was my brother's coat. A shepherd's coat."

"I can see that. Oh well, then. No need for offense. Lemme see your money first."

Jude produced a denarius. The landlord's eyes brightened. He plucked the coin from Jude's fingers.

"I got a room." The landlord jerked his thumb toward the opening of a tiny cubicle at the end of a shabby portico. Shrieks of laughter and a coarse oath came from one of the nearby alcoves. "It'll suit an old woman and two kids. One denarius tonight. Water there in the well for washin'. Bread in the mornin'."

uirinius, the Roman governor of Syria, of which Judea was now a province, was on an inspection tour of Herod's Jerusalem palace. With Quirinius was Aeneas Coponius, the new prefect of Judea, Idumea, and Samaria.

Coponius was a short, slightly built man. The top of his closely cropped dark head reached only to the governor's shoulder. Austere by nature and Spartan by Roman military training, Coponius looked around at the ornate Oriental furnishings with evident distaste. The walls were hung with heavy folds of scarlet and gold cloth, imprisoning a twenty-year-long reek of perfume and incense. The aroma seemed forever destined to mimic the funeral rites of King Herod.

"I'll have this cleared away at once," Coponius said. "Replace these couches and divans with good, sturdy, sensible furniture. And air this place out!"

"You needn't stay here much," Quirinius reminded him. "Your official residence in Caesarea is quite comfortable. Jerusalem will only require your presence during the Jews' holy days . . . like the one coming up—their 'Passover'—and for special audiences. More important than clearing away furniture is clearing away the debris of Archelaus' mismanagement."

There now. The challenge had been laid down. Coponius was on probation until he proved his ability to govern. He was not a noble, not related to Augustus. Coponius was of the equestrian class—a manager of things and men—a senior civil servant of the Empire.

"The tax rolls will be restored to order," he promised.

"See that they are," Quirinius warned. "A dozen years ago Herod called for a census and a loyalty oath, but he made a hash of it. Since then his unlamented son seemed to think Judea existed solely to line his own pockets . . . not that he'll find many luxuries to buy in Gaul!"

Both Romans chuckled at the image of an Eastern potentate accustomed to palm trees and sumptuous living shivering among mud huts and bare stone walls beside the Rhone River.

"I have invited the new high priest to join us here so I can introduce you," Quirinius noted. "In fact, here he comes now."

The trial had begun, Coponius knew. This high priest was a replacement for one who had been sympathetic to the rebels. Although no high priest for the past forty years could have survived without Rome's approval, this man was the first directly nominated by Imperial authority.

Bearded but boyish, ingratiating but with a calculating expression, eager to prove his love of all things Roman, the highest religious figure of the Jews bobbed his head in acquiescence to every demand.

At only one requirement did he hesitate.

Coponius finalized his expectations by saying, "Your ceremonial vestments. I want them delivered to the Antonia before sunset today. When they are required, you may request them from the centurion in charge but will return them immediately after each use."

"But they are the emblem of my position," the high priest sputtered.

"Exactly," Coponius agreed. "And as a powerful symbol, they must be guarded against misuse by rebels and traitors. . . . Wouldn't you agree?"

There was really no choice.

And so the last vestige of Jewish autonomy was swallowed up by Rome.

The high priest departed, still bowing and smiling.

"You did well with him," Quirinius praised the prefect. "But you'll do even better to watch him closely. That Annas ben Seth is an ambitious man, and he has a brace of sons for whom he's ambitious as well. He is consumed with envy . . . and his envy can only be soothed with gold."

Rabbi Mazzar sat on the windowsill of his home behind the synagogue. Though not yet spring, the air was mild and filled with the sweet, nutty scent of almond blossoms. The ground beneath the tree at the rear of the rabbi's home was carpeted with rosy-white, waxy blooms gleaming in the light of the full moon, though the tree was still innocent of leaves.

One month from now it would be Passover.

"A time to be watchful," Mazzar murmured to himself. "*Shaqed* . . . almond. *Shaqad* . . . watchful."

"Did you say something?" his wife of fifty-five years inquired.

"Nothing," Mazzar responded. "Just thinking aloud."

Glimpsed through the almond's boughs was the pale yellow wandering star known to the Gentiles as Saturn and to Hebrew speakers as Shabbatai, The Lord of the Sabbath. The moon's glare made it impossible to see details this night, but for several previous months Shabbatai had been rising away from the constellation of The Virgin, emerging from her nurturing grasp. In the months ahead it appeared that The Lord of the Sabbath would join Ma'Adim, The Adam, reddish-hued Mars, within the figure of The Lion of Judah.

A time to be watchful indeed!

Mazzar turned from the window. He studied his wife as she combed and braided her once-auburn, long-since-silver hair. What a beauty she was! What a treasure! She was several years his junior. It seemed to the rabbi that he could not recall when she had not been part of his life.

Which made what he was about to say all the more difficult.

"Zibbiah," he ventured. "Zibbiah, I want to go to Yerushalayim for Passover this year."

Zibbiah did not remark on the foolish whims of age. Instead she carefully suggested, "A week's journey at least. The new Roman governor not yet settled in Judea. The census riots barely past. Bands of Zealots still roaming the canyons and Roman soldiers harrying the roads. Do you think it's wise?"

"No," he replied, grasping a double handful of his white beard. "Neither wise nor prudent. But perhaps . . . necessary?"

Zibbiah waited for him to explain.

"This is my last bar mitzvah class, I think. My three boys—Beriah, Nicolas, and Yeshua—must make pilgrimage to the Holy City this year as part of their coming of age. They will reach thirteen, even as I attain sixty years past my first bar mitzvah. . . . I should go, don't you think?"

There was a touchingly wistful note to his words.

"Of course you must go," Zibbiah countered at once. "You, their mentor, and your Yeshiva, all together? This year in Yerushalayim? And your very last class? It must not be missed!"

The night sounds of the caravansary died away. Jude sat awake in the dark and fingered their last remaining silver denarius as though it were a talisman for luck.

Grandmother whispered, breaking his gloomy reverie. "Jude?"

He inhaled deeply. "I'm here."

"I didn't hear you . . . say your prayers tonight."

"I . . . said them to myself," he lied.

"You will need to pray, boy." She coughed, a hollow rattle from deep in her lungs.

"Sure."

"I am . . . sick."

"When you rest a bit . . ."

"No. Hear me. You must . . . leave with Kerah."

"Tomorrow we will go together, Grandmother."

"I . . . cannot."

"Then we'll stay with you until you're better."

"He'll take your money . . . and throw you out anyway. You must take Kerah and go."

"But . . . how can we go on without you?"

"I am dying, boy," she rasped.

He dug his fingers into the straw as the image of his dying father leapt vividly to his mind. "Don't . . ."

"Can't help it. Can't . . . You must go . . . take Kerah . . . to the tinsmith . . . my kinsman."

"Grandmother? Please . . ."

"Listen, Jude . . ."

"Please, Grandmother!"

"Jude . . . don't forget. . . . Be a good boy. . . . Remember to . . . say your prayers."

She fell silent. No matter how he begged, she would not answer him.

Hours passed. He dozed and awakened with a start. Soon it would be finished, Jude thought. Grandmother's breathing became more labored. Jude clung to Kerah, who was oblivious to it all.

The old woman . . . dying? How could Jude ever pray again if she died?

He stared into the darkness where Grandmother lay and wondered what he should do after the old woman breathed her last. What would the innkeeper say in the morning when he peered into the dingy cubicle and found a body lying on his dirty straw?

"Bad for business! Bad for the inn! Give me your money!"

Who would bury the old woman? The landlord would demand Jude hand over the last coin. Jude had counted on the money to feed Kerah and help him get her to Jerusalem. It was the sum of everything—every hope of reaching their destination.

Grandmother gasped as if a pain had shot through her heart. Jude's head jerked up. He held his breath until she breathed again. Shallow. Irregular.

Jude buried his face in the sleeve of his new tunic and counted the final ragged breaths of the old woman.

One . . . two . . . three, four . . .

"How will I take care of Kerah without you to help?"

Fifteen . . . sixteen . . .

"Please don't leave us now. We've hardly started. The soldiers will be looking for us."

Thirty-one, thirty-two . . .

"Grandmother! How will I find your cousin? Supposing we get to Yerushalayim? How will I know which tin shop is his?"

Fifty-one . . .

"If we turn back . . . or if we go home to Sepphoris, surely we'll be killed. And probably tortured. Tortured to make us name names. Kerah . . . they would hurt her, but she couldn't understand or answer. . . . Oh, Grandmother! Don't! Don't leave us!"

A horse nickered softly. Kerah sighed and turned over.

Silence.

And so the old woman flew away.

The landlord locked Jude and Kerah in the room with the body lest the lodgers see them cry and know the old woman had died.

Unclean was a word religious Jews proclaimed loud enough when someone died inside a house.

Grinning, pale, and blinking rapidly, the innkeeper sought to conceal the death of the aged lodger from his other guests. He wrung his hands, willing the crowd of pilgrims to depart so he could deal with the human refuse and change the straw.

It was midmorning before he unbolted the door and let them out.

The half-wit girl smiled at the sky. The boy, ashen and shaking, looked dully ahead.

"What am I supposed to do now?" The landlord grasped the neck of Jude's tunic and gave him a shake. "I told you! I said she was too sick to stay. She swore she wouldn't die. Now this!"

Jude could not reply. Words fled his brain. He could only partially comprehend what the man was shouting at him.

"Money. It takes money to dispose of a corpse. Give me what you've got!"

Jude produced their last denarius. So Grandmother had been right.

They should have escaped when they had the chance. Jude sank to the ground and sat cross-legged near a heap of dung. Flies buzzed around his face. He could not raise his arms to brush them away. Could not.

"Now what am I to do? Eh? Call the rabbi? Say *kaddish*? He hates me enough as it is. He'll put me out of business over this. Unclean, he'll say. Some'll blame it on the plague and my reputation will be ruined!"

Grandmother's last words to Jude had been that he must say his prayers. But he did not know how to pray. How could he say *kaddish* over Grandmother if she was not there to help him say the words?

The tyrant nudged Jude hard with the toe of his shoe. "Get up! This is your doin'. I'll fetch a spade and you'll dig a grave down in the gully there. There!" He jabbed a greasy thumb eastward. "In the gully where we dump the rubbish! You're big enough to dig a grave, I say."

Kerah wandered to where a donkey was tied to a post. She stroked the beast's velvet nose. For Kerah, it was a pleasant morning.

The landlord fetched a spade for Jude. Then he ordered his Nubian slave to wrap the body in a blanket and dump it on the back of the donkey.

"Go with the brat, Pergamon. Make sure he digs the hole deep enough. And covers it well. No arms or spindly legs poking out for someone to stumble across."

Zachariah remembered, "It is thirteen years since the day Mary came to us in Beth Karem. Your mother saw her and you danced within her womb at the sound of Mary's voice."

Yochanan smiled through his youthful beard. "And now I am almost a man. So must my cousin be . . . almost a man."

"And I am seventy-three years old." Zachariah tapped his fingers on the study desk. "I had lived threescore the year you were born. And now I have lived thirteen more . . . a second childhood. I am due for a second bar mitzvah."

"Papa—" Yochanan looked toward the mountains in the west, where he knew Jerusalem was—"where was your first bar mitzvah?"

Zachariah's ancient face crinkled with pleasure. "My first bar mitzvah was in Yerushalayim. At the Temple. Passover, it was. Your grandparents were there." He raised a finger. "I see them now. Ah! There is my mother weeping because I am no longer a boy. My father and uncles, celebrating because I am a man of Israel . . . like them."

Yochanan sighed. "I have never seen Yerushalayim, Papa. Archelaus is gone now."

"Aye. Shivering in some hut among the Roman peasants of Gaul." He smiled. "But those who remain behind are still sons of Herod the Butcher King. Herod Antipas. A drunkard. Wishes to style himself Israel's king."

"Will they keep us from our heart forever? I am almost thirteen. I study for my bar mitzvah, yet you have not told me where it will be. Passover will be here soon."

"Yes. We must go to Yerushalayim for Passover this year. Where else could you meet this great obligation? We will travel to the Temple, where the angel told me of your birth. There you and I will celebrate our bar mitzvahs together. You for the first time at thirteen and me for the second time at seventy-three."

"And my cousin? Yeshua, son of Mary? I would like very much to be with him there. Perhaps he is also studying for bar mitzvah, Papa?"

"It makes sense. Like you, he is in his thirteenth year. We will send a message to Nazareth."

"Come on, boy!" Pergamon the slave glowered and snapped at Jude. "Hurry, before I beat you!" He led the burdened donkey toward the back gate—the rubbish gate—lest anyone see.

The servant's show of anger satisfied the landlord, who stalked off to drown this unpleasantness in a pitcher of wine.

Jude, shovel over his shoulder, clasped Kerah's hand and followed after the ebony giant. He could not bear to look up. Grandmother, folded over the donkey's back, jostled as they walked down the path toward the garbage heap.

Pergamon, out of earshot from the caravansary, turned and called to Jude. "Boy, you got a name?"

"Jude."

"And your sister?"

"Kerah."

"A slow wit, eh? And what about this old woman?"

Jude frowned and answered sullenly, "Her name was Grand-mother."

"Ah, well. You know how to say *kaddish*, boy? You're a Jew, eh? My master don't know how to treat the dead with respect. Nor the living neither. But she, this old lady . . . you live so long and die going on a journey . . . maybe you deserve to have words spoke over you. Maybe your family like to say *kaddish*. Family maybe pays if we dig a grave in a nicer place than the rubbish heap, eh?"

"I suppose so. She had a cousin in Yerushalayim. . . . She was a good woman. Said *kaddish* for my father herself. But I don't know how. I don't remember."

Pergamon's eyebrows shot up. "Your father—he dead too? How did he die?"

"Quit breathing."

"It happens that way. So. Now they cross the river. Mother and son, together, eh?"

There was too much to explain and danger in saying more. Jude felt threatened. Had he said too much already? "Yes."

The slave eyed him sideways and whined the next question in a singsong voice. "You got no mother?"

"She crossed the river too. I don't remember when."

"So you and this girl child . . . slow wit . . . you two got no family? Two children. No family at all? No one knowing you gone?"

A glint shone in the man's eye, warning Jude of danger. The slave of a caravansary would know well enough the price of slaves. What were two children worth to the passing Arab drover? How easy it would be to sell two orphaned children into servitude!

"We've got plenty of family. We were on the way . . . when Grand-mother took sick. . . ." Jude stooped and snapped up a fist-sized rock.

Pergamon halted and turned, leaning on Grandmother's body as he studied the two children. "I am thinking you are lying, boy. I am thinking you got no one to ask questions."

Jude fingered the rock behind his back and grasped Kerah hard by the arm. "I tell you, we've got . . . lots of family . . . a tinsmith in Yerushalayim . . . and . . ."

"Nobody, I'm thinking . . . and Yerushalayim is a long way for two kids to go." The man took a step toward Jude. "Did you steal that coat? Huh? Fine coat for an orphan boy. Worth something, I bet."

Jude uncoiled his arm and let the stone fly, hitting the giant hard on the forehead, knocking him backwards onto the ground.

With a whoop, Jude slapped the donkey on the rump, sending it careening over the fallen slave, then galloping up the road toward town.

"Stop! Donkey!" The slave tried to rise in pursuit, but blood from his wounds blinded him.

Dragging his sister behind, Jude sprinted in the opposite direction. "Kerah, run!"

No doubt the people of Nain would recognize the innkeeper's beast of burden. And there would be questions about the dead body of an old woman strapped to its back.

CHAPTER 8

The sun was setting. There were few Jewish travelers continuing on the highway at this late hour. Jude and Kerah stood at the junction of four roads.

"Which way do we go?" Jude asked no one.

A cold blast blew down from the heights of Mount Hermon on the border of Lebanon. Jude turned his face northward toward the snow-capped peak of the mighty mountain and hoped Jerusalem was not in that direction.

Two travelers camped just off the highway.

The thin fabric of Kerah's coat clung to her skeletal frame. She shivered and pulled away, running toward the camp where rough-hewn drovers stared into the flames.

Were they escaped rebels on the run?

"Kerah!" Jude shouted after her, even though he knew she would not heed him.

The faces of the men glanced up furtively at the children and then down again.

"Get off with y'!" A bearded, greasy fellow flung dust at Kerah, warning her. "Go away! It's no good for you here!"

Yes, Jude decided, he knew them. He recognized the men from

his father's band. To stay with them so soon after the crushing of the rebellion would be dangerous.

Kerah covered her face and ran toward a heap of boulders. Jude stared openly at the man for a moment. Recognition and an unspoken warning were plain in the fellow's eyes.

"*So. These are the two brats of Judah the Galilean. They're as dead as their father if the Romans catch them.*"

Jude nodded once and backed up a step.

His stomach rumbled with hunger.

Now he had no money. No food. A little sister deaf and simple-minded. How far was Jerusalem? The obstacles to their survival seemed insurmountable.

Jude slapped down waist-high weeds as he marched toward Kerah's stone shelter. "Stupid! Stupid girl! How am I supposed to feed you? How can I keep you warm?"

He found her tucked like a frightened rabbit beneath a low over-hang of limestone.

He crept in after her. She crouched with her hands outstretched beside a scorched circle of cold stones where a fire had once warmed a traveler. At least they were out of the blast of the north wind.

"Stupid girl. There's no fire. You warm your hands on nothing. No fire. No wood."

Yet Kerah smiled. She seemed comforted by the memory of warmth evoked by the stones and charred brands.

Jude was not so lucky. His bare, dirt-blackened feet ached with cold. He peered out of the mouth of the shelter.

The sun melted on the horizon like oozing wax. As dark gloom settled over the land, images of the crosses in Galilee rose in Jude's imagination with the fury of the wind.

The tap on the door was hesitant, seemingly fearful.

In the carpenter's household only Yosef was awake. By the cupful of light spilling from a single oil lamp Yosef read from the scroll of Isaiah, borrowed from Rabbi Mazzar.

It was late, well past midnight from Yosef's glance at the sky through the small window beside the fireplace.

Not an hour for anyone to come calling.

Yosef half turned toward the back room where Mary rested, then faced the door as the rapping sounded again.

It could not be soldiers. They would hammer on the door without regard to the time . . . or simply break it down.

Such a late caller could be someone on the run from the Romans, seeking shelter. Or it could be a Roman informant, pretending to be such a refugee in order to denounce rebel sympathizers for the reward Rome offered.

As Yosef approached the entry he instinctively grasped the wooden staff given to him by Zadok the Shepherd a dozen years before. "Who's there?" he demanded.

Rabbi Mazzar's quavering voice answered. "Yosef? I know it's late, but I saw your light and I . . . I was too excited to sleep. May I come in for a moment?"

Thrusting the cudgel back against the wall, Yosef raised the beam that barred the door. He invited the rabbi into the house and seated him near the hearth.

Keeping his voice low, Yosef inquired, "Is someone ill? Is there trouble?"

"Nothing like that," Mazzar assured him. The rabbi was trembling.

"Then what is it? The weather's turned chilly again, and you have no cloak. Aren't you cold?"

"Cold?" Mazzar repeated as if the idea had not occurred to him. "Yes, I suppose I am. Never noticed, you see."

"Rabbi," Yosef asked with concern, "are you ill? Sit here while I get Zibbiah."

Rabbi Mazzar waved his hands dismissively. "She's been asleep for hours. Besides, she already knows what I've come about."

"She knows? Then . . . what is it?"

"Yerushalayim is what," the rabbi replied with assurance. "A Passover pilgrimage. All three of my bar mitzvah–age students. And their families, of course. Zibbiah too . . . she insisted."

"Rabbi," Yosef said doubtfully, "I know Herod's son no longer rules in Judea, but the riots . . . the crucifixions. Why this year?"

And Rabbi Mazzar explained his plan to make the Passover pilgrimage a graduation of sorts for his last and best Torah school class.

"This is the year to introduce them to the responsibilities of the annual pilgrimages . . . while all their studies are fresh in their minds."

"Aren't you a bit . . . what I mean is, are you sure you should . . . at your age?"

"Nonsense." Mazzar bristled. "I feel as good as I did a dozen years ago . . . better even! Why, I don't think I've aged at all since the summer of your wedding. What do you think of that? And besides, Yosef, don't you have to return to Beth-lehem for the census this new governor has ordered?"

Yosef chewed his mustache before replying. "That's true. But I expected to go alone and come right back. . . ." His eyes stared past the corner of the ceiling into the memory of another year, another census.

"Well, there you are, then," Mazzar said conclusively. "We'll all go. You'll see. It'll be perfect. And if you support the notion, the other families will agree."

"I promise to pray about it . . . but that's the best I can offer now."

In the darkness of their shelter, the two children huddled together, sharing the fleece coat, borrowing one another's warmth as the temperature continued to plummet.

Jude's back was pressed against the stone wall of their burrow. His arms encircled Kerah. Her teeth chattered in her sleep.

Jude could see, beyond the shelter, the glow where the fugitives slept. Sparks flew up and scattered with each gust. *Wasted light. Wasted warmth.*

What would be the harm if Jude snuck into their camp and warmed himself for a few minutes? They would welcome him, would they not? He was the son of the rebel leader, after all. They had followed his father in war against the Roman garrison in the Galil and fought beside him when the rebel outpost was discovered and attacked. Would they not honor Jude, son of Judah the Galilean Zealot?

Gruff voices interrupted his reverie. Fluttering light and footsteps approached the shelter in the mound of boulders.

Two men. Breaking Shabbat, they carried forbidden torches high as they scoured the ground for tracks. Jude peered over Kerah's shoulder. What were they looking for?

"They're round here somewhere."

"What was their names? We could call 'em."

"Don't remember."

"The boy and his sister. Simpleminded girl."

"Recognized 'em right off as belongin' to Judah. In spite of the layer of dirt. I says to myself when I sees 'em . . . them two are Judah's brats, all right."

"Why'd you send them away?"

"Didn't think of it. Not until later. Then the idea come to me sudden-like."

"Hostages."

Jude stiffened with fear as their plot unfolded.

"Aye. Roman garrison might take the brats of Judah of Galilee in exchange for . . . somethin'."

"Money."

"We got plenty for pointin' out where the Zealots was hidin' out."

"Always use more."

"Hostages. Now that's worth a few denarii."

"It's done among the highborn all the time."

"But the Romans might just as well kill 'em. They're just kids. Ain't highborn."

"Even so. We hand 'em over. A gesture of goodwill to the new governor, y' might say. Demonstration of our loyalty."

Jude tasted bile in his throat. *Loyalty?* These men had betrayed his father and hundreds of others hiding in the hill country. Jude's father hung rotting on a cross because of these men!

If I only had a sword!

Kerah stirred, seeming to sense the nearness of evil even in her sleep. Jude held her tighter and buried his face in her back. *Traitors! What would Papa do? What?* Jude's heart pounded in his ears as they closed in. *Papa had a sword. He would have fought them! He would have marked them as traitors and cut off their heads!*

Jude closed his eyes as the firebrand moved nearer their hiding place. *If only I had a sword!*

Kerah squirmed in his grip.

Oh, don't wake up, Kerah! Don't make a noise!

9 CHAPTER

Y osef's head nodded over the Isaiah scroll as he pondered the rabbi's request. Take Yeshua back to Jerusalem, that hotbed of political turmoil and religious intrigue? The last twelve years had all been about living quietly . . . protecting Mary and Yeshua . . . establishing a normal life in Nazareth . . . avoiding the attention of all forms of authority, civil or religious.

Casting his thoughts back across the intervening time, Yosef shivered. Only a divine warning had set the family on the road out of Beth-lehem, mere steps ahead of Herod's murderers. Nor had that angelic alert prevented the massacre of all the other boy babies in Beth-lehem.

That horrifying event, along with Herod's other atrocities, was still whispered throughout Jewish lands. The tragedy fulfilled ancient prophecy: *A voice was heard in Ramah . . . Rachel weeping for her children.*[16] It was said the anguished cries of the mothers of Beth-lehem that fearful night had indeed been heard in Ramah, some ten miles away.

Nor had the angelic warnings ceased then. When news reached the Jewish colony in Alexandria that Herod the Butcher King had died, there were spontaneous celebrations in the streets. Yet Yosef was still directed to avoid Judea and go instead back to Nazareth.

Once again events proved the timeliness of the counsel: Herod's son Archelaus ruled Judea in his father's place. As ruthless as his father but even less subtle, Archelaus had quickly proven himself a tyrant . . . and every bit as likely to assassinate anyone proclaimed as "the true King of the Jews."

While Yosef had been apprehensive about how his family would be treated in Nazareth, given the way they had been shunned by gossipy villagers, none of his fears were realized. The months of their absence in Beth-lehem and Egypt had allowed scandal-serving neighbors to move on to other topics, other victims. By the time of their return to the Galil, the area was fully embroiled in the behavior of Archelaus. There was little time for barely remembered rumors.

Arrests, torture, and executions mounted each upon the other throughout the nine-year span of Archelaus' reign. Revolts real and imaginary plagued the last decade. Archelaus' oppressive cruelty ended only when delegations of Jews and Samaritans, agreeing on something for almost the first time ever, protested his brutality to the aging emperor Augustus.

And just like that, Archelaus was gone.

In his place the Romans brought in their new governor with his new census to impose a new round of taxes. The Romans had quickly and ruthlessly suppressed one more rebellion . . . and now an uneasy peace lay across Judea and the Galil.

True, Antipas, another of Herod's sons, ruled in Galilee, but so far he had shown himself more interested in pleasure-seeking than in spies and secret tribunals. Still, he had responded with inherited ferocity to the rebel attack on his pleasure city of Sepphoris, concurring with the Romans that rebels should be crucified and many innocent inhabitants sold into slavery.

Perhaps this was a good time to get out of the Galil after all.

Live quietly and unobtrusively.

Go or stay? Which was the safer course?

The lone flame gnawing at the twisted wick slurped up a final drop of oil and began to sputter.

Yosef's forehead bounced gently against the words of Isaiah 9: *The people who walked in darkness have seen a great light. . . .*[17]

Then he slept.

The moment Yosef's head touched the sacred page it bounded upward again, or so it seemed to him. There, just below his nose, was a familiar passage of Scripture about *Galilee of the Gentiles*,[18] while just a few lines further down the parchment was a verse he had pondered many times: *For to us a son is born, to us a son is given, and the government shall be upon His shoulder, and His name shall be called Wonderful, Counselor, Mighty God, Everlasting Father, Prince of Peace.*[19]

Nor did the prophet's utterance about the coming Messiah stop there. Though the scroll required turning to reveal the next lines, Yosef heard an almost audible voice continue: *Of the increase of His government and of peace there will be no end, on the throne of David and over his kingdom. . . .*[20]

The throne of David was in Jerusalem. David's birthplace was Bethlehem, but his kingdom was centered in the Holy City.

The parchment seemed to glow; the black ink of the words was as distinct on the page as if silhouetted against the sun.

Yosef glanced at the oil lamp. No such energetic flame emerged from it; not even a wisp of smoke remained. The carpenter recognized musical notes, as if chimes were being stirred by the wind . . . but there was no wind. He inhaled the fragrance of lavender, though none existed in the room.

"Welcome," he said without fear to the gleaming figure who appeared in the corner of the room, surrounded by—no, giving issue to—the radiance now suffusing the chamber.

Shalom, Yosef, son of Jacob, son of David.

"I'm dreaming?"

Of course. Shall I tell you why I was sent?

"Please."

What says Isaiah about the character of Messiah in chapter 11?

The scroll, which a moment before had been open to Isaiah 9, now unaccountably displayed a later passage that read:

> *There shall come forth a shoot from the stump of Jesse, and a Branch from his roots shall bear fruit. And the Spirit of the Lord shall rest upon Him, the Spirit of wisdom and understanding, the Spirit of counsel and might, the Spirit of knowledge and fear of the Lord. And His delight shall be in the fear of the Lord.*[21]

Reverence for the work of HaShem will consume Him, the angel interpreted. *A shoot from the stump of Jesse. A Netzer . . . a fresh, green Branch among King David's descendants . . . will be eager to be in the House of HaShem.*

"And none too soon, either!" Yosef agreed. "Even here in little Nazareth, friends and neighbors, who by Judeans are derided as 'ignorant Nazareans,' know the need for a new David. And Yeshua will be he?"

The angel bowed his head at the utterance of the name *Yeshua* . . . *Salvation.*

"But he's still so young. Only twelve. Must he go to David's capital already?"

From Nazareth . . . the Nazarean . . . He who is the Netzer . . . must already be about His Father's business. But have no fear, Yosef of Nazareth. . . . Have no fear. Remember: He will be full of wisdom and understanding, counsel and might, knowledge and the fear of the Lord. You yourself will bear witness. Sleep now, Yosef. But when you awaken . . . remember!

The plodding of horses' hooves startled Jude out of a doze. Too fearful to sleep but overcome with weariness, he had kept watch as best he was able. Now, in an instant, he tried to still the pounding of his heart and also listen for the rustling rush betraying an attacker.

Muffled voices echoed hollowly inside the rocky den. Jude shrank back into the depths, willing himself to be as quiet and solid as the stones. The movement of his eyes alone took in Kerah. Gesturing, he urged her to remain silent, afraid that the slightest peep or moan would give away their presence.

Who were these newcomers? More brigands, no doubt, here to join their traitorous friends.

This thought added another layer of worry: Come daylight, a renewed search by many men would certainly reveal the children's hiding place.

The leaping flames of the campfire had died to an orange glow. No sounds came from that direction, as if the first two thieves were sound asleep.

A horse whinny, quickly stilled, indicated the location of a second set of newcomers.

Why did they not ride directly up to the camp? The wind was still bitingly cold. If they had traveled far by night, surely they must be anxious to stoke the fire and get into snug bedrolls beside their comrades.

What was going on here?

The clink of armor and a gruff command froze Jude even more firmly in place.

Roman soldiers!

The shadowy forms of a half dozen troopers floated across the boulders outside the den . . . like wraiths in search of victims.

The hobnailed boots of the cavalrymen screeched on the bare rock. Despite the sighing wind, within a few more paces the grating cry drawn from iron on shale woke the sleeping pair.

Jude heard shouts of alarm and the scrape of swords being drawn. The same gruff voice overheard issuing orders gave another command now: "Drop those weapons!"

A blade's hasty plunge produced a ringing clang, followed by another. A man's voice Jude recognized as belonging to the bearded, oily ruffian cried out with relief, "It's you, is it, Decurion? Gave us a right start, you did! Thought you might be Zealots come to slit our throats in the dark."

One of the troopers must have tossed an armload of wood on the fire. It crackled with renewed vigor and blazed upward.

Almost against his will, Jude was drawn forward to see and hear what was happening. He expected the traitors to denounce him at once, and then the search would begin again.

Jude made up his mind to run. He had little hope of escape, even in the dark—not from eight armed men. Perhaps he could remain free long enough to lead them away from Kerah's hiding place. After that . . . well, after that, she would be on her own.

I'm failing you, Father, he thought. *But I'll still be trying to obey you when they kill me.*

"So what have you done with all the money you got for betraying better men than yourselves?" Jude heard the Roman officer demand. "Come on, hand it over."

"What?" the second traitor whined. "But we spent some on food. And anyway, it wasn't much. Barely twenty denarii and a handful of coppers. Have a heart, Decurion."

A money pouch clinked at being tossed over.

Jude's anger boiled. *Father sold and his life crushed out for less than a month's wages?* The boy raised his head above the boulder to see down into the camp.

The Roman officer poured the coins into his palm and scowled at them. "Six denarii left? Pity. What with Zealots now bringing thirty silver pieces a head. Supply's drying up, you see."

Jude caught the slightest flick of the officer's wrist—so trivial as to be easily missed, were it not for the terrible result: a trio of pila arched through the night air.

The first weighted spear impaled the greasy brigand in the throat, pinning him, shrieking, to the ground. The sudden violence drew a cry from Jude, but his stifled gasp was covered by other louder screams.

The second traitor rolled to his right, causing the second javelin to miss its mark.

But the third pilum caught him between the shoulder blades.

In moments the betrayers were silenced forever . . . without revealing the presence of Jude or his sister.

"See if they have any valuables or hidden money," the decurion ordered. Then he observed, "Dead traitor's worth just as much as dead Zealot. Cut off their ears as a token for the centurion and leave the rest for the crows."

Only once did one of the troopers speak. "Shall we strip their clothes?"

"You want to wear them flea-ridden things, then go ahead. Otherwise, let's get moving. Be spending tonight's work in a tavern by daybreak if we get to it."

Jude slunk back into the shelter. He held his breath until long after the last hoofbeat had faded into the distance.

With the final howls of the victims, the wind died. Kerah, mercifully, slept through the slaughter of the traitors and the gleeful departure of the attackers.

Jude considered the many ways it had been a good thing the children had not been welcomed into the warmth of the camp. And how fortuitous it was that their hiding place had not been found.

So, Jude thought, he had not needed a sword to avenge his father after all. Those who had betrayed Jude's father were dead now. Their blood money had been taken and their bodies left to rot in the open just like those of the men they had helped destroy. Corpses lay askew on the ground like dolls stuffed with straw. Mouths wide and eyes frozen in horror, their expressions told Jude that in dying they had seen the demons rush in to take their souls.

Jude was glad for their terror.

Now he emerged from the shelter and shuddered as he eyed the dying embers of the fire and the ransacked belongings. Was there anything left behind that he and Kerah might use?

A thick wool blanket lay near one of the dead men.

Jude approached cautiously. What if they were not truly dead? What if they were only pretending?

Jude sniffed the air, rank with unwashed death.

Had any attacker remained behind? Was there a demon lurking nearby to snatch him from life?

Jude hesitated, listening. At last, the pop and cracks of burning wood drew him in. The only thing still living in this camp was the fire.

Staring fiercely at the wide, gaping eyes of a traitor, Jude murmured, "So, the Evil One lured you into his snare. In the end, you die too. You will not meet my father or your comrades in hell."

Jude plucked up the blanket, shook off the dust, and threw it over his shoulders like a cape. Gathering an armload of branches as fuel, he carried a burning brand to build a small fire where he and Kerah slept.

Within minutes the burrow filled with warmth.

Waving off the smoke, Jude spoke aloud as if his father were in the burrow with them. "Papa, your true enemies are dead. Your true enemies who called you brother. It is a small thing, this stolen fire, but what warmed them now warms us. Providence and justice have saved our lives tonight. You must be watching over us." He stretched his hands to the warmth. "So, Papa. Yerushalayim, you said. Go there. Take Kerah there. I promise I will watch over her. We will find our way to Yerushalayim."

Exhausted, Jude lay down beside his sister and covered her with the blanket. A moment later he fell into a deep sleep.

10

CHAPTER

Jude left Kerah snuggled beneath the Nazarene's fleece before emerging into the blue gloom of predawn.

Kerah would need to eat something this morning before they resumed their journey. Perhaps the Roman murderers had left food in the sacks of the traitors.

Jude drew himself up and walked forward as if the death scene were a market stall and he was shopping for bread.

The dead men were rigid. Their skin was the color of gray stones. Spilled blood was the consistency of drying mud.

A tin plate of fish and a half-drunk cup of wine sat on a flat rock.

Jude retrieved the dead man's supper and brought it to Kerah, placing it just under her nose. Her eyelids fluttered awake at the aroma.

"Sure. Breakfast. Fish. It's cold, but eat it. Go on. That's it."

Not daring to climb out from the warmth of the blanket, Kerah picked at the feast and drew a meager portion to her mouth.

Jude watched her chew and swallow and reach for a second bite. "Good." He left her and resumed scavenging.

Nudging a half-empty rucksack with his toe, he spilled out its remaining contents. A single, shiny silver denarius bearing the image of Augustus Caesar gleamed in the dirt.

Jude whooped and snapped it up. "They left one behind! One is enough!" It lay in his palm. The rising sun glinted on Caesar's face. "Enough. Enough to get us to Yerushalayim if . . ."

Then his words faded at the realization that this single coin was all that remained of the blood money received for his father's life.

A wave of rage swept over him. His fist clamped down hard around the coin. With a shout he threw it away. Wavering a moment, he marked the place where the hated thing fell, then charged after it. Throwing himself to the ground, he clawed the dust until he found the coin.

"They killed Papa for this! For this!" Clutching it to his heart, he howled like a wounded dog and beat the ground.

He lay there sobbing for a long time until Kerah's finger poked him hard in the neck.

He rounded on her. "What do you want? Stupid girl! Don't you know what has happened?"

Wrapped in the blanket, her too-broad cheeks and slanted eyes peered out at him like a distorted reflection of a human face in water.

Kerah did not notice the dead men a few paces from them. She smiled and held out the plate. Half the fish remained. She offered it to Jude.

"Oh!" he cried, shaking his head. "Don't you know? Don't you know anything?"

Again she urged her brother to eat what remained.

It was pointless to try to explain. She could not hear him. Would not understand him. The dead men were no more to her than the scattered stones beside the road.

Jude devoured the last meal of the dead man.

Wiping his mouth with the back of his hand, Jude led Kerah to a stump and sat her down facing away from the carnage. With a raised finger he warned her not to move.

For twenty minutes he rifled through the remaining belongings of the dead men. Yelping with joy, he found a block of cheese and a packet of unleavened bread wrapped in a napkin. The greatest prize was a long, dull iron knife. Jude decided it would become his sword. He held up the rusty blade and imagined running it through the heart of the Roman who had crucified his father.

"Someday, Papa, I'll show them I'm your son. Someday they'll regret it!"

Lastly, in a discarded money pouch, he found iron and flint. He struck the two together and grinned as a spark leapt out.

It was enough. "Our own fire."

Perhaps now they would survive the journey.

He looked toward the highway. "Which way is Yerushalayim, Papa? Where do we go?"

Jude supposed the route to Jerusalem must be where the light of morning shone first.

After packing their meager belongings in the leather satchel he got from the woman in Nazareth, he clasped Kerah by the hand and led her east and south toward the Mountains of Moab and the rising sun.

Coponius, Roman prefect of Judea, scratched the bald spot on the crown of his head. What a backwater province to have as an assignment! The only comforting thought was that this region was so troublesome a man could truly earn promotion here. "Do well in Judea," Governor Quirinius had said, "and you will get a plum for your next duty. Of course, if you fail . . ."

Coponius had no intention of failing. That was why he had summoned his senior tribunes to join him there in Jerusalem.

"Is it true that a million pilgrims will converge on this city?" he demanded.

He was assured this was an exaggeration . . . but not by much.

"Then summon all the garrisons from Idumea to the Galil and bring them here," he ordered. "There will be no rebellion this holiday. Not here, not now. Clamp down and clamp down hard! Anyone speaking treason will be condemned to the galleys. And I want a curfew. No one is to be on the streets after midnight without written authorization from the Jerusalem commander. Violators to be arrested on suspicion of treason. Repeat violators to be crucified. Clear?"

Wind whistled in the olive trees at the edge of the village. The breeze, combined with the bustle of market day activities, prevented anyone in Nazareth from hearing the approach of the mounted men. Yosef, shepherding Mary and Yeshua from booth to booth in their shopping, was the first to get warning of the threat. The sight of a head scarf fluttering atop a nearby knoll caught his eye. A herdsman among the boulders there with his goats frantically signaled to those below, but no one else noticed.

The carpenter's family was outside the door of the potter's shop. Hastily Yosef drew Mary and Yeshua away from a table displaying bolts of blue cloth. One hand on each of their shoulders, Yosef thrust mother and son into the doorway.

"Yosef? What?"

"Stay inside," Yosef ordered.

Back out on the street Yosef had no time to warn more than the linen merchant and his wife before the clatter of hooves announced arriving soldiers.

A pair of troopers came from each end of the town's dusty main street, sealing off the market square. The shoppers, anxiously drawing away from the sudden menace, backed into each other in a huddled mass.

His snorting animal clearing a path, a scowling man wearing a short, bronze-handled *puglio* dagger to signify his decurion rank, drew rein beside the village well. "Stay where you are," he ordered gruffly. "No one move. I have more men in the side streets. Anyone caught sneaking away will be treated as a rebel."

Everyone knew what that threat meant, Yosef thought. He hoped no one would panic and run . . . or do something foolhardy. The carpenter scanned his neighbors. Most were wide-eyed, practically holding their breath with fear. They looked like a flock of sheep brought to bay by a pack of wolves. Glancing quickly back toward the shop displaying a shelf of clay lamps in the window, Yosef saw Mary and Yeshua and the sweating face of the potter peering out.

The decurion stepped off his mount onto the stone rim of the well. Sneering at those around him, he pointed at a boy in the crowd and ordered, "You! Hold the reins" and tossed the knotted leather straps to the child. "What's your name, boy?" the legionary demanded.

"Th-Thad, sir," the boy stuttered.

"How old are you?"

Thad stared dumbly.

"Are you too stupid to answer? I said, how old?"

"Eight, sir."

"Eight? Who's your father? Where is he?"

Thad raised a trembling hand to gesture toward the shop behind Yosef. "There," he said, voice squeaking. "Lamech the Potter, sir."

The decurion removed his close-fitting helmet by the cheekpieces and ran a hand through his cropped sandy hair. "Who else knows this child? Does he belong to the potter?"

Enough! Yosef thought, abandoning his own sense of caution. "I vouch for Thad . . . and his father," he said, stepping out from the crowd and advancing toward the Roman. "What's this about, anyway?"

The cruelly spiked spurs on the heels of the officer's boots glinted dully in the sun. Together with his chain mail armor and angular features, he resembled a demon risen out of the pit.

"Who are you?" the decurion said, scowling.

"Yosef the Carpenter," Yosef replied, trading an even look with the other man. "Everyone here belongs to our village. What is it you want?"

"All villagers, eh? Not a rebel in the bunch either," the decurion scoffed. "We'll sort that out presently; don't think we won't. For the moment we're looking for a pair of runaways . . . a boy about eight and a girl a little younger. They say she's mute . . . or touched. They may be with an old crone. Who's seen them? Speak up? Who's seen them here?"

No one spoke.

From a leather pouch at his waist the decurion withdrew a pair of silver coins. Rubbing them together, he remarked, "Information is worth money. Keeping it from me earns a different kind of repayment."

There was still no response from the crowd.

"Brainless sheep," the Roman muttered. Replacing the coins, he donned his helmet but left the leather strap unbuckled and dangling. Hopping down from the ledge, he grabbed the reins from Thad and shoved the child roughly away.

Remounted, he shouted, "Anyone hiding these fugitives will suffer for it. And hear me: I will find out about it."

With a jerk of his head in dismissal of the other troopers and a savage tug at the reins, the decurion spurred out of Nazareth, giving the silent onlookers barely enough time to leap out of the way.

The project under way in the carpenter's shop was a chest called a *genizah* for the synagogue. It would be used for storing damaged Torah scrolls. Only once every seven years were the discarded rolls of the Law removed and carried out in formal procession to the cemetery, there to be buried with great solemnity.

The Nazareth synagogue already possessed a genizah, but it was little more than a utilitarian box. What Yosef planned was a piece of furniture to grace the interior of the chamber. He and Yeshua had constructed the container itself of cedar for its fragrance, beauty, and durability. The carpenter had selected the planks with care, alternating pale red with pale yellow to form the panels of the chest.

What added an extra measure of beauty to the otherwise unornamented genizah was the framing that outlined each panel. For this purpose Yeshua had chosen the still harder and tighter-grained acacia—all the pieces in a matching dark brown shade.

The work was almost complete. Joints and hinges were masterpieces of close-fitting perfection. The interior was lined with linen. The exterior, which had been left unvarnished, nevertheless glowed with a fine patina, as if already of great age.

Yosef and Yeshua had spent a week polishing the finely sanded chest with layers of beeswax. The final coat was being applied and buffed, leaving the chest with a silky finish.

Yosef and his twelve-year-old apprentice were so absorbed in their work they did not notice the newcomer's arrival until he cleared his throat.

The Passover lamb, tethered outside, bleated.

"I seek Yosef the Carpenter," the man framed in the doorway said. "The smell of sawdust told me I'd located the right shop even before I entered. Now, are you the right man?"

"I am," Yosef agreed, straightening up and stretching as he faced the short, bald-headed stranger. "And you are?"

"Merari of Medeba, merchant in fine oils and lotions." The man's stooped shoulders bobbed agreeably.

Medeba was a village far to the south and east of the Jordan, in the land of balsam trees. It was on the trade route linking the perfumed East to the consumers of the West.

Yosef spread his hands and smiled. "Beeswax is what carpenters use for lotion. Or did you need some woodwork done yourself?"

"Didn't I say? No, I suppose not. I have a message for you. I am traveling through here to Sepphoris and was asked to carry a message to Yosef of Nazareth."

Yosef was instantly cautious. He could not recall any acquaintances in Medeba. "But I don't . . ."

Merari waved off the objection. "My route took me through Heshbon. The message is from kin to your wife: Zachariah the Levite." Drawing a leather string around his neck, the perfume merchant extracted a leather pouch from the folds of his tunic. From it he produced a folded parchment tied with a pale blue ribbon.

Zachariah! Had something happened to Elisheba or Yochanan?

Merari extended the letter, taking a step nearer to place it in Yosef's hand. "I don't know what it contains," he explained. "Like you, I'm troubled by unexpected news."

"Please. Sit," Yosef stammered. "I have no manners today. Yeshua, water for the merchant. Will you stay to supper? Do you need a place to stay?"

Waving aside all offers, Merari replied, "Nothing, thank you. I need to push on to reach Sepphoris by nightfall. If it helps, Zachariah, though old and feeble, did not seem distressed when he spoke to me."

With that observation Merari made a cheerful gesture of farewell and strode away.

Yosef untied the ribbon and unfolded the note, then moved to the doorway for better light.

A moment later he bounded toward the house. "Mary!" he called. "Mary! They're going to Yerushalayim. Zachariah and Elisheba and Yochanan are going up to Passover. They'll meet us in Jericho!"

Elisheba, her round face red with indignation, shook her finger in Zachariah's face. "You send a letter to my family . . . to Mary . . . two weeks ago that we are coming to Yerushalayim, but you do not tell me? Your wife?"

"It was meant to be a surprise." Zachariah spread his hands in innocence.

"This is like what Avraham told Sarai as he took Yitz'chak away to sacrifice him on the holy mountain. 'It was meant to be a surprise.'"

"It is Yochanan's bar mitzvah, not his sacrifice."

"You take our boy up to Yerushalayim now and it will be a sacrifice, not a bar mitzvah. He will be discovered, and I tell you . . ." She clutched at her heart. "Those Herodian sons of the Butcher King will have his head on a platter!"

"Archelaus is deposed."

"And his evil brothers set up in authority in his place. They have been waiting for Yochanan's bar mitzvah for thirteen years."

"They no longer remember me. . . . Where is the story of the old priest in the Temple who was visited by an angel?"

"No longer remember? You may have forgotten, but they have not! Who in all of Eretz-Israel has forgotten the night Herod sent his soldiers to butcher the babes of Beth-lehem? And all those babes would be the age of our son now. Thirteen years old, thereabouts!"

"The sons of Herod are not thinking of our son. Their father believed he killed every threat to Herodian rule on that night."

Elisheba leaned against the study table. "Zachariah, I tell you the truth. My heart is sure they will be looking closely at every boy who comes to the Temple for bar mitzvah this year. They will be asking themselves, 'Is this the one about whom the angel prophesied to old Zachariah?'"

Zachariah glowered at her now. "And since Yochanan is the prophet the angel told me about, where else can he go but to Yerushalayim this Passover? And who else would he meet there but a cousin of his own family . . . his cousin Yeshua, whose name means 'Salvation'! The two will climb the road together into the City of David!"

She sank down on a low stool and moaned. "I should stay here and sit shiva all the while you're gone. As Sarai would have done if she had known what a fool Avraham was to take their boy up to Zion!"

"Don't you remember what Avraham said to the servants he left behind?" Zachariah asked.

"You are the only one who remembers everything—everything—but you forget about me. You forget my heart!"

"Avraham said to his servants, 'Wait here while the boy and I go up to the mountain to worship. And when we have made our sacrifice, we will return to you.'"[22] Zachariah thumped his hand on the table. "You see . . . he believed Adonai. He was certain even if Yitz'chak died as a sacrifice that the Lord would raise him up again and they would return. They would come back down alive from that place of danger because the Lord himself had made a promise."

Elisheba wailed, "This is meant to comfort me? Men of the Galil hanging on crosses in Sepphoris! Rebellion and murder everywhere, and you speak to me of Avraham?"

He studied her a long moment. Was she listening? "Our son and the son of sweet Mary—they are the fulfillment of the covenant Adonai made with Avraham. We must take Yochanan up the mountain and he must confirm his covenant with the God of his fathers this Passover."

"You remember everything," she accused, "and so have an answer for everything."

"Elisheba, you must remember what the angel said to me. Yochanan is a miracle. He will be called a prophet of the Most High. He will make the road straight for the one to come after him. For the Son of Mary . . . the Son of the Almighty![23] If these things are true and we believe them, then I tell you, like Avraham, we will take our son up and offer him to the Most High where Avraham offered Yitz'chak. And remember, Elisheba! We will come down again alive from Mount Zion!"

It was early morning, one Sabbath before Passover—the last Sabbath to be celebrated in Nazareth before the Passover journey began. The Parashah for the date was Vayikra, taken from the first five chapters of the book of Leviticus.

Yosef, as one of those who would be called to the bema to read this Sabbath, studied the Scriptures ahead of time, under the tutelage of Rabbi Mazzar. Outside the Nazareth synagogue a misting rain swirled. The single heap of glowing embers on the charcoal brazier in the corner of the chamber produced barely enough warmth to keep the men's breath from showing as they read.

The title of the passage meant "He called" and referred to the opening words: *He called to Mosheh and spoke to him from the Tent of Meeting, saying, "Speak to the people of Israel and say to them . . ."*[24]

What followed was a list of the instructions for properly presenting sacrifices to the Lord: sheep and goats, birds, grain and oil and frankincense. But Rabbi Mazzar proceeded no further than the opening sentence before calling the group's attention to something.

"It says the Lord called to Mosheh from the Tent of Meeting and told Mosheh to give these instructions to the people. Why didn't HaShem just give the instructions himself?"

Abiram the Goatherd suggested, "Because being the one chosen to relay the message increased Mosheh's authority?"

Mazzar stroked his beard thoughtfully. "This is a good answer. Anything else?"

No others seemed inclined to speak, so Yosef noted, "Because no one else could hear HaShem's voice?"

"Ah!" Mazzar concurred, smiling. "So say some of the sages. Not that HaShem whispered or spoke in an unknown language, but perhaps only Mosheh heard because . . . only Mosheh was listening. See what the psalmist says: *For He is our God, and we are the people of His pasture, and the sheep of His hand. Today, if you hear His voice, do not harden your hearts. . . .*[25] So we *can* hear his voice, but we do not always chose to do so."

"And how do we hear the voice of the Almighty?" demanded Abiram, perhaps emboldened by the shepherd imagery of the psalm.

"It is said the Almighty has written his word in Torah, in the wonders of nature, and on the hearts of those who seek him."

"Yes, Rabbi," Abiram persisted, "but what about really hearing him . . . with my own ears, I mean. I'm no scholar, heaven knows. Why can't he speak with a human voice?"

Yosef considered the many times the Lord had spoken to him in dreams and visions, but of this he said nothing.

Mazzar considered the query. "When the prophets say, 'Thus says the Lord,' did they not speak with the voice of the Lord?"

Yosef thought about the row upon row of now-empty crosses that remained as the silent but powerful voice of Rome.

"And someday," Mazzar continued, "HaShem will speak with the voice of the Messiah. Pray that it may be soon."

"Omaine," the minyan agreed. "Omaine."

PART II

Every year His parents went to Jerusalem for the Feast of Passover.

LUKE 2.41

12

CHAPTER

The morning of the departure for Jerusalem everyone in Nazareth was up before dawn to make an early start. Not everyone in the village was going, but all wanted to offer *Derek tov!*—"Safe travel! Good journey!"—to those who were.

Yosef reflected on the morning bustle as he readied his family's own provisions for the pilgrimage. An air of excitement pervaded the hillside town, a sense of relief that they could set aside the crushing weight of the crucifixions and again find joy in their lives.

The first day's journey would not be difficult . . . down out of the hills into the Valley of Jezreel by way of the village of Nain. It was a comfortable way to begin a weeklong trek. Nain was not only close enough to be familiar to the Nazareans but at just nine miles away to the southeast could actually be seen from the knob above Yosef's home.

Once beyond Nain, the way would be less recognizable. From Nain to Beth Shan—the goal of the first day's travel—many from Nazareth would be in unknown territory. Yosef was not worried about the trip. He and Mary had made the Passover pilgrimage to Jerusalem every year, even while Archelaus ruled Judea.

_ 77 _

Some went every few years; some once in a lifetime.

For Yeshua this was a first. Because of Yosef's concern for His safety, the boy had been left with Mary's parents each spring. This year, for the first time since His appearance at the Temple when He was an infant, Yeshua would once again be in the Holy City.

It was cold this morning. Even the donkey's breath steamed in the frigid air as Yosef saddled him. Yosef, Mary, and Yeshua would all be walking; the donkey was furnished for Rabbi Mazzar to ride.

Calling Yeshua to him, Yosef placed a pack on the boy's back, then gripped His shoulders with approval. Yeshua was growing to be a fine, sturdy young man. It was good His friends from the village, Nicolas and Beriah, would share this experience with Him. It was even more satisfying to know that Yeshua's cousin Yochanan would take part in it with Him as well.

That notion brought to mind a flood of recollections of the miraculous events of a dozen years before.

"We're ready, Papa," Yeshua confirmed, interrupting Yosef's reverie. "I double-checked the sack of feed grain and our own bread and cheese supply." Achi, the Passover lamb whose name meant "brother," danced at the end of the cord Yeshua held.

Because it was the wet season, water was easily available all along the way. Most nights would find the pilgrim band near a city and able to buy food and even obtain shelter. Their packs carried extra clothing, blankets, and dried provisions for the times with no village nearby.

"We're ready, Mary," Yosef said, putting his head in at the door. He touched his fingers to the mezuzah and then to his lips.

"And I am ready as well," she returned, smiling.

This morning Nazareth's market square was filled, but not with shoppers. The stalls and stables were empty, but a crowd was present even so.

"Shalom! Safe travel," the villagers called to the pilgrims.

"May the Almighty keep you," the travelers replied.

"Bow your heads and pray for blessing," Rabbi Mazzar invited. *"The Lord bless you and keep you; the Lord make His face to shine upon you and be gracious to you; the Lord lift up His countenance upon you and give you Shalom! Amen!"*[26]

And the Passover pilgrimage was begun.

The first leg of the Passover journey ended some eighteen miles from Nazareth, about four miles west of the Jordan River. To generations of Jews making *hag ha'aviv*, and others wearied by commercial journeys, it was known as Beth Shan or "House of Rest." Located at the juncture of major trade routes, its soil was rich and watered by countless bubbling springs.

Beth Shan was famous for its olive orchards and other tree crops. The Jewish inhabitants were proud of living in a place called by some "the gate of paradise."

But Jews were not the only citizens of Beth Shan; in fact, they were in the minority. Beth Shan was the only city of the Decapolis—the ten independent, culturally Greek cities—located west of the Jordan. By Gentiles the city was called Scythopolis, and it had both a checkered past and a dubious present.

Lying as it did in the land ascribed to the tribe of Manasseh, Scythopolis should have been thoroughly Jewish, but the Israelites of Joshua's day had failed to drive out the pagan inhabitants. It had not been added to Israel until Solomon ruled, four hundred years after Joshua.

Yosef, walking half a dozen paces behind the trio of boys, could overhear Yeshua's conversation with His friends, Beriah and Nicolas.

"This is where the Philistines hung King Saul's body on the city wall," Nicolas asserted, pointing at the ruins of an ancient stone wall protruding from the rubble of a hilltop fort.

Beriah shuddered and looked over his shoulder as if expecting Philistines to charge out of a nearby canyon. "My father told me they used to worship Dagon here and other wicked things. It's scary here."

Nicolas shrugged, worldly wise at age twelve. "They're still pagans . . . worshipping Isis and Apollo and . . ."

The stonecutter's son lowered his voice but Yosef read his lips. "Caesar," Nicolas hissed.

Nicolas' father Kepha observed to Yosef, "Romans are building a theater by the creek. I hear it'll hold six, maybe seven thousand. Lot of work for a stonecutter. May have to relocate here."

Yosef shook his head. "*Rest* and *paradise* it may be, but not very Jewish if you ask me."

"They pay well." Kepha shrugged. "Need carpenters too."

Yosef said nothing but resumed listening to the boys.

"What do you say, Yeshua?" Nicolas asked. "Do you think it's scary?"

Yeshua frowned. "I think it's sad."

"Sad? Why? What are you talking about?" Nicolas demanded.

Yeshua pointed to a marble monument beside the road. *Live well while you can*, the carving read. *All roads end in the grave.*

"Gentiles believe in everything . . . and nothing," Yeshua observed. "It's sad."

Nicolas snorted. "Who cares? They're only Gentiles anyway."

Jude was certain Kerah was dying. Whatever disease had carried off Grandmother had remained behind to fill Kerah's lungs. She coughed, a rumbling cough, like water boiling in her lungs. Breathing was shallow and labored. She was burning hot to the touch. Her usually wide, cheerful eyes were filled with misery. She did not understand her pain.

Jude understood it well enough. Twice in their years with the bandits and rebels, sickness had swept like a flood through the camp, taking with it one-third of everyone who breathed the contagion.

So many had died and so many had been weakened that the renegade rabbis had questioned if the God of Israel had turned against them. Jude had fallen ill but had survived. Papa had sent the old woman and Kerah away to the Jordan Valley and the Dead Sea for safety.

But now the illness had found little Kerah. Her eyes were glazed as Jude led her to an outcropping of rock that opened to the east. Jude propped Kerah against the wall and hurried out to gather dry brush to make a fire. Soon the stone of their shelter resonated with a pleasant heat, but still Kerah shivered.

She slept and moaned in her sleep. Jude watched her from the opposite side of the cave, certain she would fly away before sunrise.

13

Jude sat a distance from Kerah beneath the outcropping of rock. She was wrapped snuggly in the blanket. He studied her shallow breathing and wondered if she would die soon. Had he wrapped her too warm? She was burning up with fever. Beads of sweat formed on her broad brow. Lice climbed through her matted hair.

"Oh, Kerah! Don't . . ." He did not finish the thought. He wanted to ask her not to leave him alone, but he had no right to keep her alive any longer.

Jude closed his eyes, not wanting to see her suffering.

Rain fell, filling the air with a clean scent. He hugged himself and flapped his arms against the cold. When Kerah died, he would bury her in the blanket. It was all he had for a shroud.

If only Kerah would open her eyes and look at him. If only he could have some hope that she would live. His empty stomach felt as if it would claw a hole in his backbone. He needed food, but he dared not leave her to forage. What if she awakened and he was not there? What if he came back and found she had tried to find him and collapsed in the rain?

"Papa," Jude said quietly, "I failed. She's dying, Papa. Soon enough she'll fly away to be with you."

Kerah's fragile ribs heaved, laboring over every breath.

Jude clutched his knees to his chest in an effort to stay warm. He closed his eyes and thought of the day Mama had died. Papa told the rabbi there was nothing left for him to live for. Nothing at all.

Jude wondered what he had to live for. First Mama. Then Papa. Now Kerah.

Jude would be alone.

"Oh, you! God . . . God of Israel. Take me instead. She is so innocent. She don't know anything. She don't even really understand she's not supposed to suffer. Please, God, take me!"

Jude knew this was a selfish prayer. The God would never answer such a prayer. Better Kerah fly away and leave Jude down here to suffer. She could not take care of herself. She could not so much as find her next meal.

He sighed and tucked his head against his knees. "All right, then. Take her. But don't leave me long behind."

Touching his sword, Jude pictured himself making a desperate last stand against the Roman garrison in Jerusalem. He would not die like a criminal on a cross. He would not die like his sister on the damp earth in a rainstorm. He would die fighting a Goliath. He would fall like a man of Israel, battling against the Romans in Jerusalem.

The barn in which Nicolas, Beriah, and Yeshua bedded down for the night was old. The roofline sagged like a swaybacked donkey and about half the slats had ripped free. Dark blue sky showed through holes overhead. Pigeons, eager to roost in the rafters, flew in with clattering wings.

Beth Shan's Jewish homes provided shelter for the women and small children of the pilgrimage. The menfolk talked politics on the rooftops of the houses until the cold forced them into the synagogue for the night.

The boys enjoyed their status as almost grown-ups. Not quite old enough to remain with the men, Nicolas was proud to be trusted away from his mother's gaze. "Away from squalling babies," he said. "Sniffles and whines. My sister's the worst."

"Won't we get cold?" Beriah worried.

"Two blankets and your cloak and this heap of nice clean straw to burrow into? Not a chance," Nicolas said.

"My feet hurt," Beriah complained.

"So do mine," Nicolas agreed. "Father says everyone aches after the first day's travel. That's why this place is called House of Rest, eh? By noon tomorrow our legs'll be in shape and then we'll be real pilgrims."

Nicolas turned his attention to the silent Yeshua, who lay on His back facing the darkening sky. "You asleep?"

"Not yet," Yeshua said. "Just watching the stars come out." He pointed out the west-facing door, to where Jupiter and Venus pursued the fading sunlight. "Righteousness and Splendor." Then lifting His arm to gesture straight up to an overhead gap, He added, "And there's Ma'Adim . . . The Adam."

"Do you know the names of every one?" Beriah challenged.

Yeshua's reply had a smile. "It's fun."

"Torah is enough for me," Beriah retorted.

"Too much for you, you mean. . . . Ouch!" Nicolas jerked as Beriah kicked him for the insult. Then he said to Yeshua, "Did you mean what you said today . . . about it being sad because Gentiles don't believe in HaShem . . . or *olam haba*? I mean, mother has a cousin who's a Sadducee. She says they don't believe in *olam haba* either. Not angels or demons or anything. He says dead is dead."

There was a pause before Yeshua responded. "Do you remember when Rabbi Mazzar taught us about Mosheh and the burning bush?"

"Sure." Nicolas scoffed at the simplicity of the query. "*Take your sandals off your feet, for the place on which you are standing is holy ground.*"[7]

"And how did the Almighty introduce himself to Mosheh?"

This was a little harder, but Beriah ventured, "He said, *I am the God of your father, the God of Avraham, the God of Isaac, and the God of Ya'acov.*"[28]

Yeshua agreed. "He did not say, 'I was the God of your father' . . . like they were dead and gone. Adonai Elohim said, 'I am their God . . . they are still alive and I am still their God.'"

Even Nicolas was impressed. "You reason like a rabbi."

"Look there." Yeshua waved His hand toward a gap in the roof that showed the east.

"Ugh! A bat!" Beriah observed.

"Further up than the bat," Yeshua corrected. "The golden glowing spot. The Lord of the Sabbath is moving from The Virgin toward The Lion."

How long had Jude and Kerah huddled in the cave? Jude had lost count of the hours . . . or was it days? Still, Kerah clung to life.

Would Kerah die before morning?

Jude, wrapped snuggly in his new coat, observed her from the opposite side of the fire pit, afraid to go closer, afraid to share his warmth with her.

She shuddered and sighed in misery. Not even the warmth of the blaze seemed to help. Her clothes were damp and caked with filth.

How to help? If Grandmother were here, she would know what to do. Jude tucked his chin deeper into the collar of the shepherd's coat and inhaled the clean fragrance. Visions of dried bundles of lavender in the rafters of the Nazarene house came to his mind. The gentle face of the woman there seemed to smile back at him, urging him to do something for Kerah. He fingered the cuffs and remembered how much it had meant to him to receive such a gift. It had given him a will to live. Would such a gift give Kerah hope as well? If he put his new coat on Kerah, perhaps she could get warm.

In an impulse of pity he wrapped her in the fleece covering of the boy from Nazareth. The size of it swallowed her up, covering her chin to the sole of her foot.

"Kerah! Live!" Jude towered over her, expecting some miracle in that instant. But nothing changed.

He plunked down to watch and wait. Her frail form heaved, shuddering with each exhale.

Soon it would be over. Such suffering must end! And then what would he do? Here in the wilderness without a spade to dig a hole, how would he bury her?

Now he regretted giving her his coat. He had nothing to keep himself warm. Surely his beautiful new coat would be Kerah's shroud.

How to pray? What to say as Kerah lay dying?

Jude whispered, "Kerah. I've not been a very good brother to you. Oh . . . Kerah. If you will only live!"

But this was not a prayer. He was begging her, begging her to get well so he would not be alone. She could not understand his entreaty.

He tried again. "Adonai . . . if only . . . sir, if you will let my sister live. Let her get well . . ."

If only what? What use was it to bargain? Jude had nothing of value to offer to the great Eternal One God of Israel in exchange for his sister's life.

"Sir . . . I will . . . do whatever you ask of me . . . if only you would let my little sister live. . . ."

Gnawing hunger awakened Jude from his sleep. How long had it been since he had eaten? It seemed like a very long time indeed.

Where were they? The rebel camp? A quick succession of images shattered his drowsiness. *Papa. Dead! The caravansary of Nain. Grandmother's death and their escape from the Nubian slave. And Kerah! Sick and dying* . . .

Outside the mouth of the cave a thrush sang cheerfully. Daylight crept in, shining pink through Jude's closed eyelids.

And Kerah . . . what of her? The memory of the long night returned. Her struggle to breathe. The raging fever. The fragile body that could not stop shaking.

This morning all was silent. The rasping of Kerah's breathing had stopped.

"Oh! Then she has flown away!" Jude squeezed his eyes tighter, not wanting to open them, not wanting to see her pale and stiff with the coldness of death.

The thrush sang louder, chirping as he hopped into the mouth of the cave. A shadow fell over Jude, blocking the light.

Jude's eyes snapped open. He gasped.

Kerah stood, smiling, above him. Morning light framed her like a halo. The sleeves of the Nazarene's coat hung below her hands. Was she an angel?

"Kerah?" he asked. "Are you dead?"

She put a hand to her rumbling stomach.

No. Jude was fairly certain the stomachs of angelic beings did not growl.

Kerah was not dead. She was alive. She was awake.

And she was hungry.

14

CHAPTER

From Beth Shan, the pilgrim road dropped steadily into the Jordan Valley. Once across the ford—no easy undertaking at this high-water time of year—the trail from the west that had descended the Valley of Jezreel met up with another road coming south.

At the crossroads the travelers from Nazareth encountered another pilgrim band. These had come down the east side of the Sea of Galilee.

Long before Yosef could distinguish individuals from the mass of moving homespun fabric and donkeys, the arrival of the second group made itself known in song.

Drifting down on the breeze from the north came the opening words of "The Traveler's Psalm."

"Anasha ayeenah al harim; I lift up my eyes to the hills," they sang, one bass voice in particular booming the melody. *"From where does my help come?"*[29] The familiar accents of northern Galilee betrayed the origin of the choir.

Since the pilgrims were deep in the gorge of the Jordan, surrounded by hills on every side except for the way south, the hymn seemed a particularly appropriate choice. At the end of verse one, the newcomers stopped singing.

"A challenge, children," Rabbi Mazzar instructed. "Nazareth may be poor, Lord help us, but we can sing with the best of the Galil. So? Together now."

And the pilgrims from Nazareth replied with: *"My help comes from the Lord, who made heaven and earth."*[30] Nearby cliff faces multiplied the words so that it seemed many hundreds were in the choirs.

"He will not let your foot be moved; He who keeps you will not slumber,"[31] intoned the others.

The Nazarenes replied with *"Behold, He who keeps Israel will neither slumber nor sleep."*[32]

Yosef had a pleasant baritone, Rabbi Mazzar a quaking tenor. Beriah's piping tended to lag a beat behind the others, while Nicolas had a true, high, sweet pitch.

"Yeshua," Beriah said at the end of verse four, "your voice is cracking."

"So it is," the carpenter's son agreed with a smile.

At the moment the two bands of sojourners coalesced, they chorused the last lines together: *"The Lord will keep your going out and your coming in from this time forth and forevermore!"*[33]

"Well done," Yosef praised the man with the booming voice.

"And your group as well" was the reply.

"Who are you and where are you from?" Yosef inquired of the stout, jovial-appearing man with the ginger-colored beard.

"Asa of Capernaum" came the reply.

"Capernaum? Wouldn't you have saved several miles by coming down west of the lake?"

"No doubt, no doubt! But Romans are hunting rebels around Magdala, or so we heard. Why put our necks in a noose, eh? Eh? Besides, we met some cousins in Bethsaida and traveled together. Better that way. Here they are now . . . my cousin Jonah and his son Shim'on. Fisherfolk they are, but the smell wears off after twenty miles or so."

Jerusalem! Jude and Kerah entered with a band of pilgrims, then turned aside. The Street of the Tinsmiths was crowded with shoppers. Openfront shops displayed their specialty wares. In one were rows of cups and containers of various sizes. In another were bowls and kettles; in yet another, shining tin plates.

"Grandmother's cousin," Jude mused as he studied the abundance of shops. "What sort of things would he sell?"

Kerah raised her hand to point above their heads. A tin lantern hung above the entrance.

"Yes. Grandmother loved a good lantern." He pursed his mouth in contemplation. "Do you remember the tin lantern belonging to Eusebius?"

Kerah shook her head in the negative.

"No. I don't suppose you would. But before you were remembering things like this and that, old Eusebius from Tyre had a tin lantern all pierced so the light of a candle would shine out on the walls like little stars."

Kerah smiled and nodded. She pointed up again at the sign of the lantern.

As they entered, a broad-faced man of about fifty turned around from the workbench. "So. We have pilgrims, eh? In search of a lamp?"

Jude bowed stiffly. Kerah mimicked him. "Sir, we have come all this far way in search of Grandmother's cousin."

The smith studied them with hammer poised. "First things first. From where? No, don't say it. The accent tells me Galilee."

"How can you tell such a thing as that?" Jude marveled.

"The pilgrims of Galilee never use five words in a sentence if they are allowed the time to use twenty."

This made perfect sense to Jude. He had often heard that the men of Jerusalem were curt and short of speech. But this fellow seemed as long-winded as anyone in Galilee.

"That is true," Jude concurred. "We love a good story."

"And I am asking: What is your story? The girl is wearing a fine fleece coat. Of the sort made from the hides of Temple lambs and sold for a high price. How did you come by such a garment? You being from the Galil."

Jude considered his explanation carefully, lest he give away his true identity to someone who might sympathize with the Herodian dynasty or the Romans.

"It belonged to our mother's firstborn son. She kept it for us.

And we came here because Father, in his last breath, spoke the word *Yerushalayim*."

"Then he did not see a vision of heaven," the tinsmith muttered. "And? So? You came here to my shop why?"

"Our grandmother told us to find you."

"Me?"

"Well, I mean . . . someone like you. A tinsmith by trade. A cousin she knew as a girl."

"And how old might this cousin be?"

"I can't say."

"How old is your grandmother?"

"Very old. Very, very old indeed."

"Where is she now?"

"Dead."

"I am not so old as all that. What makes you think I am the man?"

"Kerah . . . my sister? . . . she recalled how much Grandmother admired lanterns. She pointed to the one over your door."

He smiled and resumed punching holes in the tin. "So, your grandmother admired lanterns, did she? And so I must be the cousin?"

"Unless you are not the one."

"And then what will you do?"

"It is a long street, but we will not give up."

"A good-hearted boy. And what might your grandmother's name have been?"

"Grandmother," Jude explained. "I never knew her as anything but Grandmother."

Kerah concurred with a nod.

The smith inquired further. "And where was her home in Galilee?"

"Sepphoris."

The smith's eyebrows rose slightly. His interest was raised. "And what of her other family? I mean . . . besides you two? You say you had a brother? He who wore the coat of the lamb before?"

Jude blurted, "Crucified."

"Your father?"

"Crucified."

Genuine surprise and admiration crossed the face of the craftsman. "A good man, then."

"I don't know exactly why he was killed. But then, *why* don't exactly matter to the Romans. And so my father took her in. And when my father died, she took us in. . . . Or rather, none of us had any place to go, so we came here. . . . Perhaps you know how it seems to go with such things."

The smith seemed impressed. "Spoken very . . . roundabout. Like a true Galilean. Who am I to doubt your word?" Then the smith turned and shouted up the stairs. "Ezer! Old man! You and the wife! Get out of bed and come down here! Your rustic relatives from Sepphoris in Galilee have arrived on a pilgrimage."

Shim'on bar Jonah joined up with the three friends from Nazareth. Slightly older than they, Shim'on had a scraggly beard. His shoulders were broad, his hair curly. He talked with the hard accent of the north country, leaning on the distinctive syllables as if proud of his Galilean heritage and determined everyone should know it.

By contrast the Nazareans were aware of their humble, often despised origin and generally quieter when with strangers. *Quiet* was not a word anyone would apply to Shim'on. A head taller and twenty pounds heavier than the other boys, he introduced himself as "Shim'on, fisherman of Bethsaida."

Beriah was awestruck with hero worship and took to Shim'on instantly.

Just as immediately Nicolas looked askance at Shim'on and drew the opposite conclusion. His suspicious glare made it clear he regarded the newcomer as puffed-up and a potential bully. "You mean, apprentice fisherman?"

"Not on your life," Shim'on responded scornfully. "Apprenticed at age five. I can haul nets as well as any man. Know how to sail, too, and all the best spots for catching. Was made bar mitzvah two years ago . . . not still a child like you."

Yeshua thrust out His hand and gripped Shim'on by the forearm. "Welcome, Shim'on bar Jonah," He offered. "Do you sing? The Psalms of Ascent, I mean."

"Know them all by heart!"

"Well then. Shall we challenge the grown-ups?"

"In a heartbeat!"

"Which one?" Nicolas put in. "Let's be certain we all know all the words."

"How about *O Lord, my heart is not lifted up?*"[34] Beriah suggested. "It's short and easy to sing."

"Too slow! No punch," Shim'on objected. "Besides . . . *my soul is like a weaned child*!" He shook his head vigorously. "Not my kind of song."

"What do you suggest?" Yeshua inquired.

"*Greatly have they afflicted me*," Shim'on replied without hesitation. "Let the Romans in Yerushalayim know we're coming!"

The quartet, soon expanded to a chorus of a dozen boys and teens, burst into song: "*Greatly have they afflicted me from my youth. Let Israel now say, 'Greatly have they afflicted me from my youth, yet they have not prevailed against me.'*"[35]

Shim'on bellowed out the psalm, especially the line about "them not prevailing." He gave the impression he would not be prevailed against by anyone. He was a half-step flat, and it could not be said he knew all the proper notes, but there was no mistaking the words or the sentiment.

"*The plowers plowed upon my back; they made long their furrows. The Lord is righteous; He has cut the cords of the wicked.*"[36]

The adult pilgrims listened to the youthful effort. Some smiled indulgently; some appeared to wish Shim'on's group was singing from farther away . . . like Egypt, perhaps.

"*May all who hate Zion be put to shame. . . .*"[37]

By the time the boys came to the last verse, Shim'on had shifted the key so that the tone now matched his voice. With even greater vigor he pronounced: "*Nor do those who pass by say, 'The blessing of the Lord be upon you! We bless you in the name of the Lord!'*"[38]

"That's the stuff," Shim'on concluded with evident self-satisfaction. "Zion-haters withered like grass, eh? That's what we'll all sing under the governor's balcony when Messiah comes, eh?"

ld Ezer and his wife, Bethalia, considered the children of Ezer's
cousin as they wolfed down a supper of stew and bread.

Ezer rubbed his greasy beard. "Jude and Kerah is the whelps'
names. Didn't know we had a Jude or a Kerah in the family line. Must
be named for the mother's side of the family."

"Always wanted a girl child," said the old woman. "But a boy too?"
She looked sideways at Jude. "Never favored the boys."

"Aye. But a boy child would be useful in the shop. Cleaning up. An
apprentice, if you like."

Bethalia sniffed indignantly. "Never had much luck with the boy
apprentices. Run off within a fortnight or two after their first beating."

"But this one is kin." Old Ezer shrugged. "Or at least he might be
kin . . . or some sort of relation if he is sent from my cousin Tabi, may
she rest in peace."

"Ezer, are y' blind? Ye can see the boy eats like a centurion's war-
horse. Look here. He has not even sat down to eat. Just inhaling his
food like it's air . . . like he ain't et in days."

"Perhaps he ain't et in days, Wife."

"It's not a good sign. He'd eat up all the profit we might take from his work. But the little girl . . . perhaps she is simpleminded. Oh, well, take a bit of cleanin' up, but she would make a fine servant for the shop, eh?"

Ezer lowered his voice and whispered into her ear, "What'll we do with the lad?"

She squinted as the plan sprang to life. "Why, Ezer! Sell him off as a house servant for the new Roman governor. Exchange him for taxes."

"Well, now . . . Fortune has come knockin'. Indeed, Fortune has come to sup at our table."

Herod Antipas peered out the window of his tower bedroom. The courtyard of the Hasmonean Palace was shrouded in gloom, like the entire city of Jerusalem.

The same description applied to Antipas as well.

It was so late there were no lights in any of the windows, no sparks of Sparrows' torches lighting revelers to their homes. Part of the curse of Antipas' addiction to drink was it made him fall asleep in the middle of an evening's entertainment. The other half of the curse was it just as powerfully awakened him with gummy eyes and a raging thirst in the middle of the night. Nor could he, once awake, easily return to sleep until dawn crept onto the stage of this farce.

Just now the moon blazed in at the window. Its cheerful brilliance only served to emphasize the shadows on the Holy City and its would-be king. Antipas had heard excited reports about an eclipse of the moon during the Purim festivities, but he had not seen it himself. He told himself he had no interest in omens and such. Old Herod, his father, had spent way too much time and energy worrying about such things. Everything in life had a practical—usually political—explanation. Once understood, the only questions remaining were what outcome was most desirable, what action was more expedient, and by what means was the result most to Antipas' advantage.

Take the numerous slaughters committed by Papa Herod. In the end he was still dead, most of his sons were dead, and his dream of a dynasty was practically dead. And Augustus, who had once called Herod "friend," so distrusted all things Jewish that independence was more a remote dream than ever.

So much for Herod the Butcher's attempt to eliminate all rivals, real and imaginary. The midnight massacre of babies in Beth-lehem had accomplished no more than to make Herod the most reviled ruler since Pharaoh treated Jewish babies the same way more than a thousand years earlier.

Had it been a night like this? Antipas could not recall. There was something about a sign in the sky . . . a mystic star . . . foreign sooth-sayers talking nonsense about a newborn Jewish king.

Antipas considered that thought for a moment. There had never been any proof that the murdered children had been special. Once dead, all babies were much the same.

But what if the Butcher's extreme strategy had failed? What if there *was* such a child . . . a rallying point for fanatical Jews to gather around? What if he had survived?

Antipas squinted at where Mars, the Roman god of war, hovered just outside the moon's glare, beneath the outline of The Lion. His pudgy lips moved in and out with calculations. How old would such a phantom men-ace be? About thirteen, if Antipas' headache-plagued memory served.

A man, or almost one.

Perhaps ripe to be proclaimed, announced to the nation as the rightful heir to the throne of David.

Antipas snorted and a fit of wheezing seized him.

There was a Roman in David's capital at the moment, and David's throne was held hostage to the servility of the Jews.

Antipas formed a new resolve. If Rome could ever be dislodged from Judea—and the vision, while remote, was never far from Antipas' thinking—no one except the rightful heir, Antipas himself, would ever occupy David's throne. There would be only one king of the Jews, no matter what the cost, and it would never be some religious madman born to *am ha aretz* in a smelly village like Beth-lehem.

The tinsmith and his wife locked Jude and Kerah into a shed behind the shop that was filled with sheets of tin and tools of their trade. The accommodation was, the couple explained, for their own good—to keep them safe in such a wicked city as Jerusalem.

Jude slouched against the wall and considered their prison cell. A pail of water for drinking sat beside a toilet bucket. The single blanket, threadbare and moth-eaten, was tossed in for them to share. The light of the moon streamed through the high window.

"So much for Grandmother's lantern." Jude sighed.

Kerah nodded. The look of contentment that had followed their meal faded moment by moment, as if she was finally understanding that they could not come and go as they pleased. "Grandmother," she said sorrowfully.

"Kerah?" Jude noticed at last Kerah had spoken.

Expectantly, she turned her round face to Jude. She replied with one syllable. "Go."

Strange how, with Kerah's spoken words, Jude suddenly no longer felt alone. He gazed into her face. "What happened to you, Kerah? You understand . . . things."

She nodded, absorbing language as though she were a plowed and planted field and his words watered the furrows of her mind.

On impulse Jude reached out to touch the coat that still warmed her. He wondered about its former owner—the Nazarene boy whom he had never met.

"These people are not Grandmother's people," Jude asserted. "Just because they're tinsmiths and a lamp is over their door doesn't mean they help people see in the dark."

Kerah shook her head emphatically. "No."

"Well then, look up. There's the moon shining through the window. . . ." He leapt to his feet and attempted to jump up and reach the ledge. Too high. His fingers brushed the sill and he fell back with a clatter on the tin.

Kerah puckered her face in deep contemplation as she stood slowly. Her gaze fixed on the moon.

"What is it? I see you have a plan," Jude coaxed her.

She smiled, took off the shepherd's coat, and motioned for him to let her stand upon his shoulders. "I can reach the moon."

"All right. Sure. You can reach the window if you're on my shoulders!"

They wobbled as she gained her perch, and then, stretching upwards, she clasped the bottom of the narrow windowsill. Jude grabbed her feet and pushed her up the rest of the way.

"Well done!" he chirped as she grinned down at him like a cat on the ledge.

But now what? How would he get up?

Kerah peered at the free earth behind her. Clapping her hands, she motioned for Jude to toss the coat. She caught it, then dangled it from one arm, urging Jude to take hold.

"I'll hold tight! Yes! I understand," he said as she grasped the other half of the coat and slipped out of sight. Her descending weight on the other side of the window helped Jude as he jumped up, pulling him the extra inches as he grasped the windowsill. Kerah dropped to freedom beneath him. Jude climbed onto the narrow ledge and let the night air fill his lungs.

A moment later he jumped down, and the two of them crept from the alleyway at the side of the tinsmith's shop.

16 CHAPTER

Jerusalem was cold. Jude shivered and huddled close to Kerah as two boys with torches aloft led a family and their donkey through the dark street. They turned a corner, and Jude pulled Kerah from the alleyway to follow outside the circle of light.

One of the torchbearers proclaimed, "The inn is just ahead. There's a stable behind for your beast. Clean straw. Best place for the money."

The head of the family seemed grateful. "You're worth your penny," said the man as they arrived outside the structure.

The link boy pounded on the gate. "Sparrows here with a link! Open the gate! A donkey for the stable."

Jude and Kerah crept nearer as the hinges groaned and the party entered the compound.

There was a moment of pleasant conversation between the gate-keeper and the pilgrims. Another few seconds as the traveler paid the link boys. A stray cat dashed in.

Jude and Kerah slipped in through the gate behind it.

"What was that?"

"A cat, I think," said the link boy.

"Yerushalayim cats." The gatekeeper scowled. "A plague of cats instead of locusts. Ah, well. No rodents in our inn. You'll find fodder for your animal round back."

Jude and Kerah cowered in the shadows as the torchbearers took their leave and the gates swung shut, leaving the enclosure in darkness.

Stars gleamed brightly overhead as the Southern Cross rose slowly above the horizon.

Jude and Kerah spent the night in the straw of an empty sheep pen behind the inn. The two shared the coat of the Nazarene as a blanket. The straw was indeed clean and fresh as the torchbearer had promised.

The unexpected crisis came just after midnight. The pilgrim camp had enjoyed a rousing time of singing, ending with the 134th psalm: *"Come, bless the Lord, all you servants of the Lord."*[39] They sang it over and over again, each village represented in the throng picking up the refrain in turn until the hills echoed with the joy of it.

After the mournful entreaty of *"Out of the depths I cry to you, O Lord,"*[40] and the ominous warning of *"Unless the Lord builds the house, those who build it labor in vain,"*[41] it was good to conclude the evening on a quiet, peaceful, and uplifting note. *"Lift up your hands to the holy place and bless the Lord! May the Lord bless you from Zion, He who made heaven and earth."*[42]

It would not be long before this entire company, and thousands more of their fellow worshippers, stood together before the great Temple of the One God. They would, indeed, lift their hands and bless the Lord; they counted on His blessing in return as they completed their pilgrimage to Zion.

Had the Lord not sevened Himself? Had He not made this vow about the house built for Him in the Holy City: *My eyes and My heart will be there for all time?*[43]

To stand where prophets stood. To be where David ruled, where Solomon the Wise built, where Abraham in obedience offered up Isaac. To see what Moses the Lawgiver longed to see but was denied. To be where King Messiah would, some Passover, arrive to claim His rightful throne!

It raised Jewish pride in the hearts of everyone present. It kindled pity for those too ill, too old, too worldly, or too afraid to make the journey. These sentiments filled the minds of the pilgrims as they drifted off to sleep.

The shouting, the jangling armor, and the pounding of hooves out of the midnight watch destroyed both pride and pity and replaced them with terror.

The first shouts of alarm erupted from the throats of those bedded down farthest north. A lone rider galloped into the camp from that direction crying, "Help me! Hide me, brothers!"

His horse, lathered and blown, could not go much farther. The mounted man, one arm dangling uselessly, looked nearly as spent.

Before anyone could respond to his entreaty, a wave of Roman legionaries burst out of the darkness into the waning campfires' glow. They rode heedless of sleeping families. Their charging horses knocked drowsy pilgrims out of the way and trampled others with indifferent cruelty.

Yosef shielded Mary and Rabbi Mazzar behind him, urging them to the shelter of the boulder. Hurriedly he scanned the grounds for Yeshua and was relieved to spot the boy nearby with His friends.

Though the fugitive jumped to the ground to try to hide himself in the crowd, it was already too late. A dozen troopers, lances leveled, surrounded him.

Their officer, a decurion, rode into the circle and confronted the man. Loudly he announced, "No one move! This man is a criminal, sought for crimes against the government. Anyone who interferes will be judged a rebel like him and treated to the same punishment!"

It was the same decurion who had appeared in Nazareth seeking a pair of children. Now here he was again, halfway to Jerusalem, but still harrying and threatening.

Yosef gasped as he saw Shim'on bar Jonah reach for a knife in his unsuspecting uncle's belt. As Shim'on was in the act of drawing it, Yeshua's hand closed around His companion's wrist. Carpenter's grip vied with fisherman's for a moment.

Yosef heard Yeshua say urgently, "Now is not the time!" Reluctantly, it seemed to Yosef, Shim'on agreed.

In any case, the drama was over. His hands wrenched around and tied behind his back, a noose looped around his throat, the captive was led away. The man stumbled in a shambling attempt to keep up, lest he fall and be dragged to his death.

The decurion departed last. He gave no sign of recognizing anyone in the wide-eyed crowd. "You know what his end will be," he reminded them with a sneer. "So shall all traitors be repaid. Remember this lesson when you go to serve your God: He cannot protect you from the justice of Rome."

No one slept the rest of the night.

It was daybreak. The sharp staccato notes of the shofar awakened Jude and Kerah as it announced the first Temple sacrifice of the day.

Jude tucked his head beneath the fleece. His breath warmed his face and blocked the light. His left shoulder ached with cold. "Kerah, you robbed me of the blanket too last night!"

Kerah lay warm and comfortable, wrapped in the coat of the Nazarene boy and the woolen blanket. She opened her eyes and smiled back at Jude's indignation. "I am hungry."

He was unable to remain angry. The sound of her voice reminded him of Mama. What had happened to make Kerah speak again? She had only been managing to utter single words. His name. *Yes. No. Go. Hurry.*

Now here she was, actually speaking complete sentences and thinking clever thoughts like how to escape the tinsmith's prison! Perhaps the pilgrimage to Jerusalem had brought on this miraculous change in Jude's sister. He could not say what had caused this wondrous change to erupt from her mouth.

"Who taught you to tell me you are hungry?"

"My stomach. It is growling at you, Brother," she replied, suddenly precocious.

"Kerah . . . how . . . why have you not spoken to me before now?"

She sat up and brushed straw from the Nazarene's coat, returning it to Jude, who slipped it on. "I was never so hungry before." She rose and pointed to the open gate, where travelers came and went freely. "Come on."

Raising her nose to the breeze, Kerah seemed to sort through the smells of the city. She caught the scent of something cooking. "Can't you smell it, Brother? Meat. Like when Papa cooked a calf in the camp for a feast of his men."

Jude placed his hand over her mouth and looked around the empty sheep pen. "Shhhh! Someone might hear you."

She pried his fingers loose. "I smell meat cooking."

"It's the sacrifice. Yerushalayim always smells like this, they say. Sacrifices. All the time. Every day. Cooking there behind those great walls."

"Let's go get some."

Jude rolled his eyes. "It's food for the priests and Levites. The rich people. Not for us poor ones."

"Why don't they share with us?"

"The God has given them everything."

"It seems unkind of him when we are so hungry."

"This is why the priests are so fat. They eat all the time while the beggars go hungry."

Kerah stood and smoothed her clothing. "We'll need to find something to eat."

"We have no money. And I will not beg."

"Then you'll die. And so will I. Just like Grandmother. We must find a priest to share his breakfast with us."

17 | CHAPTER

Between Zarethan and the fords of the Jordan there were no towns along the river. Pilgrims who pressed ahead could reach Bethabara and sleep there, but not without walking until very late at night.

Out of consideration for Rabbi Mazzar, among the oldest of the pilgrims, and those traveling with small children, the group from Nazareth elected to camp out for the night. There had been no rain since leaving the Galil. The frigid wind that often rushed down from Mount Hermon to seize the Jordan Valley in icy talons was mercifully absent.

"Not like when we passed this way twelve years ago," Yosef recalled to Mary as the two sat beside the fire within the folds of a blanket pulled close around their shoulders. "The wind knocking us about with every step." He shivered at the memory.

"And there was so much of me then for the wind to target." Mary laughed. "I think about my father's poor donkey and what he went through on that journey."

Mary studied her son at a neighboring campfire where Yeshua and His friends joked and talked together. The boys toasted bits of bread on forked sticks. A frown crossed her face, and Yosef suspected she remembered the terrors of giving birth and the flight from murderous Herod that came after.

"Yosef," she said, confirming his concern, "were we right to bring him on this trip? Is it safe? I know Archelaus is gone and we're away from where the Romans . . ." She shuddered.

Mary had seen the forest of crosses. The same horrifying image was emblazoned in Yosef's mind.

"So this is a good time to go to Yerushalayim," he maintained stoutly. "To see Zachariah and Elisheba and cousin Yochanan. He was such a big, lusty baby. Must be a strapping big youth by now."

"And that bloodred moon?" Mary wondered. "Who was it for? What did it mean?"

Yosef scanned the sky. A half-moon was sinking in the west, followed by Mars, The Adam. The Lord of the Sabbath was nearly directly overhead, between the constellations of The Virgin and The Lion. "Remember that the angel told me to not be afraid," he reminded Mary. "This is right for us to do. Yeshua may be from Nazareth, but his future lies in Yerushalayim."

Mary nodded. "I know, but I can't stop thinking about how pleasant the last years have been. I trust Adonai and . . . I trust you, Yosef. But there's so much I don't understand. I heard Rabbi Mazzar speaking about the Anointed One liberating the captives, and it sounds so good and so right. Then I think about what the prophet also says of him: *Surely He has borne our griefs and carried our sorrows; yet we esteemed Him stricken, smitten by God, and afflicted.*[44] I don't understand!"

Leaning toward her, Yosef kissed her forehead and tucked her close beneath his chin. "Nor do I," he admitted. "But I remember a young girl who trusted Adonai for something very great she had no way to understand. If everything made sense and we understood every reason, what place would there be for trust?"

"You're so strong," Mary murmured. "So good and so strong."

"And so needy to hear the same words spoken to me! But there is the sign of The Virgin and The Lord of the Sabbath." He pointed upward. *"The heavens declare the glory of the Almighty,"*[45] he quoted. "And there—" he angled his chin toward the circle of laughing boys and indicated Yeshua—"there is the proof of his faithfulness. It is enough for right now; we will go on trusting."

As the pilgrim band approached the fords of the Jordan the next day, their numbers swelled as more travelers from settlements to the south and east converged on the route. Yeshua, walking as part of the now-inseparable quartet, looked around curiously at the other arrivals.

"Expecting someone?" Shim'on inquired.

"Yes," Yeshua replied. "My mother's aunt and her uncle and my cousin from Heshbon. We are to meet them in Jericho, but I thought we might encounter them here before we cross the river."

"How can you expect to spot them amid all this?" Shim'on gestured with his muscled, calloused hand at the thousands of worshippers.

"Zachariah is a Levite. He and Aunt Elisheba are very old, but Yochanan is about our age. When I see a group like that, I'll know them at once."

"A Levite, eh? Praying for Messiah to come, no doubt."

"Yes," Yeshua agreed. "I'm sure he is praying that all the time."

"What do you think, Yeshua?" Nicolas piped up. "Will it be this year? Will Messiah appear in Yerushalayim this year?"

"That would be amazing," Beriah commented. "To be in Zion when Messiah arrives. To watch him destroy the enemies of Israel. To have a king again on David's throne."

"But you didn't answer the question, Yeshua," Nicolas persisted. "You're the best student of all of us. Even Shim'on admits that."

"Fishermen have no time for nonsense about books," Shim'on blustered. "I know how to cipher and I can read . . . mostly."

"Not the point," Nicolas honed in. "However much we may want him to come, he can't come until all the signs are right. What do you say, Rabbi? This year?"

Yeshua measured His words carefully. "The prophet Dani'el gives signals that bring us very near this year. His message also agrees with the number of years calculated from the Redemption of the Firstborn of the Levites that started during the Exodus. But I don't think he will be revealed this year."

"Not this year? So you do think he's alive, then?" Shim'on challenged.

"Oh yes," Yeshua agreed. "I'm very certain he's alive."

A lamb bleated in the distance.

It was the low point of the trip . . . in a geographic sense. The lower ford of the Jordan was a handful of miles from Jericho, and beyond that it was but a single day to the Holy City. The crossing was also mere miles from where the Jordan emptied into the Dead Sea. From a point nearly eight hundred feet below the level of the Great Sea the pilgrims would climb out of the canyon and hike upwards over three thousand feet in just thirteen miles.

It was glorious to be nearing the end of the journey. It was comforting to think of resting in Jericho for the night before continuing the ascent.

The place where the route from the east went over Jordan was near a village named Bethabara—not surprisingly, "the House of the Ford." It was also known as Bethany over Jordan, to distinguish it from the village of Bethany near Jerusalem.

"So do you think Messiah will come to Yerushalayim this year?" Shim'on bar Jonah persisted. "Every time I ask my father about it he shushes me, says we're too close to the ears of the Roman governor to mention such a thing. But is that a yes or a no?"

Yeshua stopped to pluck a rock from His sandal. "It would not surprise me to find that Messiah came to Yerushalayim this year. But as I said before, will anyone recognize him?"

"Big sword . . . golden crown . . . white horse . . . sure, he'll be difficult to know. What d' you mean, recognize him?"

Yeshua put his hand on Shim'on's shoulder. "Fishing is important and honorable, but study doesn't hurt either. Haven't you heard what the prophet Zechariah wrote? *Behold, your king is coming to you . . . humble, and mounted on a donkey.*"[46]

"A donkey?" Shim'on repeated scornfully. "You must be joking! Who would recognize King Messiah if he rode into Yerushalayim mounted on a donkey?"

"Exactly," Yeshua concluded. "Let's go down to the river and help with the crossing. Even with the cables strung across, it can still be treacherous this time of year."

18 CHAPTER

West of the Jordan again for the first time after over sixty miles of travel, the pilgrims from Galilee were excited. Jericho was just up the way and Jerusalem not far beyond. There was much hurried wringing out of clothing. Provisions carried over the flood atop heads and shoulders were hastily repacked. Everyone was anxious to continue the journey.

Except Yeshua, Yosef noted. The twelve-year-old stood looking back across the river in the direction of Bethabara. Yosef saw Nicolas urge his friend to "hurry up; get moving," but Yeshua shook off the urgency and gestured across the swiftly flowing current.

Was there danger coming so close behind them? Did Yeshua expect soldiers? Yosef had received no warning like the night of their departure for Egypt, yet his senses tingled as he watched the boy. "What is it?" he asked softly, not wanting to alarm Mary.

"There's someone coming," Yeshua replied. "Look there."

Across the ford, difficult to see against the canyon walls, was a pair of travelers on donkeys. The mounts were being led by a single groom, who plunged into the water with no sign of fear.

"It's Yochanan," Yeshua said eagerly. "Please, let me go help him. Aunt Elisheba and Uncle Zachariah." He passed the lead rope holding Achi to Nicolas.

How did Yeshua recognize them? Yosef wondered. Yeshua had heard the story of the miraculous birth of His cousin a hundred times, but the two had never met . . . until now.

"I'll go with you," Yosef volunteered. "Mary, it's Zachariah and his family. We'll be back soon."

Forging ahead of Yosef, Yeshua moved with purposeful strides against the surge. Yosef saw Him raise one hand in salute, saw the responsive jerk of Yochanan's head.

It was clear the cousin from Heshbon also recognized his counterpart from Nazareth.

Both boys grinned from ear to ear as they met in the center of the stream. Waist deep in the Jordan the two greeted each other like long-lost friends.

"Zachariah! Elisheba!" Yosef saluted the elderly parents. "It's Yosef. And this . . . this is Yeshua. And you must be Yochanan. Let us help you across."

Each boy grasped a lead rope while Yosef walked between the two mounts, steadying their riders. Despite the effort of fighting the current, the cousins were already immersed in conversation about their excitement at seeing Jerusalem, about their upcoming bar mitzvahs.

It was not that they were built alike, Yosef thought as he studied the pair. Yochanan was taller, darker, broader-shouldered. Zachariah's son had coal black hair and dark eyes where Yeshua's hair was dark brown and His eyes brown with golden flecks, like His mother's. Yochanan had coarser features than his relation—like a desert nomad out of Sinai.

Yet there was a resemblance that made the two seem more like brothers than distant cousins. Something about the lean lines of their faces, perhaps—a look of confident determination for tasks not yet fully understood by either, for which they were already preparing.

A double file of pilgrims ascended the hill leading out of the Jordan River canyon, en route to Jericho. A mood of increased anticipation coursed through the throng as they sensed the nearness of their goal.

As they marched, thousands strong, the southern column led off with *"Those who trust in the Lord are like Mount Zion, which cannot be moved, but abides forever."*[47]

And the northern column replied, *"As the mountains surround Yerushalayim, so the Lord surrounds His people, from this time forth and forevermore."*[48]

Just ahead of where Yosef and Mary led Rabbi Mazzar's donkey were the cousins Yochanan and Yeshua. Each boy also held the lead rope of a donkey—Yochanan his mother's mount and Yeshua his uncle Zachariah's. Their heads leaned together as they toiled upward, laughing, sharing confidences as if they had been together for all their dozen years on earth instead of having been raised apart.

Yochanan gestured at the clouds—fleecy, streaming banners against a pale blue backdrop. The vapors looked more like an artist's rendering of how clouds should appear: perfectly formed lily-colored streaks on cerulean parchment.

But the discussion Yosef overheard was not about artistry.

Yochanan maintained that Hebrew words were written in the clouds. "There." The lean arm lifted heavenward and the index finger jabbed the air. "It says *Sheen yod khet* . . . *Shiach*. A shoot. A green branch."

Yeshua nodded. "And so also: *Shiach*, meaning 'an original thought that is newly uttered.' A new idea bursting forth from the mind of the Almighty."

"Like *Mah-shiach* . . . the Messiah . . . the perfectly formed Thought of the Almighty, ready to burst forth and take the world by surprise."

"In the Father's own time," Yeshua noted. "And even then people will say, *Mah?* What is this? Who is this? How can it be?"

How do they know such things, these boys? Yosef's own musings were far from ready to be spoken aloud. The commonly accepted origin of the word *Messiah*, the Anointed One, was that it came from *mashach*, a word meaning "to rub with oil."

Yet the reasoning the cousins shared was clear and compelling, except . . . they found it written in the clouds?

"Do good, O Lord to those who are good, and to those who are upright in their hearts!"[49]

The outcasts of Jerusalem found shelter beneath the viaduct connecting the city to the Temple. They lived in huts and tents erected from branches and scraps of animal hides or fabric. The great stone archways protected the blind and the homeless cripples from the rain. Prostitutes, young women owned by a slaver in the employ of Herod Antipas, inhabited tents in a special section of the compound between the bridge supports. They sold themselves cheaply to soldiers and poor servants from the great houses. The profit was collected by Herodian soldiers.

Beggars gathered around firepots fueled by sheep dung, which was cleaned daily from the pens of sacrificial animals. The source of heat was considered a charity to the poor and provided by the Temple authorities. Likewise, the garbage of Jerusalem and the remains of sacrifices were free for gleaning.

As pilgrims passed over the bridge onto the Temple Mount, tendrils of smoke from the beggars' fires rose as a reminder that hell existed in this life as well as in *olam haba.*

It began to rain. Jude and Kerah used the lambskin coat as a shelter. Spotting the smoke, Jude navigated the alleyways of the poorer residential quarter until he found the pathway leading to the colony of homeless.

Jude held tightly to Kerah's hand as they descended. Men and women, whole families, populated this dark refuge of misery. The place was teeming with people. Hovels leaned against one another, giving the impression that if one fell, all would collapse.

Clearly there was some sort of order in the community. Citizens knew one another. Women gossiped outside the entrances of their huts as though this were a village in the Galil.

Jude and Kerah were the outcasts in this underground assembly. A few beggars glanced up suspiciously as they passed. *The coat . . . the covering of a rich man's child . . .*

None welcomed them to share the warmth of their circle. Their looks said, *Keep moving! Don't stop here. This is the last place on earth. No room. Not one more fraction of earth to spare here! No warmth to spare. Not one more crust of stale bread.*

Kerah put her hand on her stomach. "Not here, Jude."

He jerked her arm hard, warning her not to be so choosy. "If not here, where?"

She could not answer. But was this what Papa meant when he told them to go to Jerusalem?

Jude froze as they neared an open ditch that served as a latrine.

"Anyplace but here. Not here," he blurted, echoing Kerah's sentiments.

Turning round, he discovered he could not see the way out from the labyrinth. A sense of panic nearly overwhelmed him. The two stumbled forward a few dozen steps, only to find they had come to a dead end. A row of dark holes identified the homes of Gehenna's residents.

At Jude's feet lay an old man without legs. He peered up at Jude through a tangle of gray hair. "Boy! What is your name?"

Startled by the question, Jude cringed. "Sir, I am Jude. This is my sister, Kerah."

"My name is Sekhel Tov. You understand?"

Jude nodded. "Yes . . . sir." The name meant "Good Understanding." It seemed a strange name for a man who had no legs upon which to stand.

"Sekhel Tov is a beggar here in Yerushalayim. This is where I reside. Do you understand my meaning, boy?"

Jude replied. "Yes . . . yes, I think so."

"Good. Then understanding my question will be easy. Why have you brought her here? Why have you come into this place?" he asked, then glanced toward the camp of the prostitutes. "They keep young girls in that place. Reserved for the servants of the high priest because they are not yet diseased as the older ones."

Jude stammered, "We . . . my sister and I . . . we were looking for . . . something."

"You will not find it here," the creature wheezed. "Take her out."

"Where? How?"

"Look to the light." The old man pointed at a patch of cloudy sky shining through the bridge. "There is an orphanage for girls. It is run by the charity of the school of Hillel. It is in the Street of the Weavers. Take your sister there to stay."

"And where shall I go afterwards? For myself?"

Sekhel Tov lowered his voice to a whisper. "You are no bigger than a Sparrow, boy. That has some meaning if you understand my words."

"Please, sir. No riddles for me now. I am too afraid to understand."

Sekhel Tov smiled. Good Understanding had no teeth. "Leave your sister in the care of the good wives of Rabbi Hillel's talmidim. Then fly quickly to the quarry beneath Solomon's Temple. You must be the link. You must carry the light of the Rabbi among the Sparrows of Yerushalayim."

"I don't understand your meaning."

"You saw the torchbearers last night?"

How did the old man know? Jude wondered. "Yes. They led a family to the inn. And we followed after them."

"Those are the Sparrows of Yerushalayim. You will join them."

"Where shall I go?"

"Ask the good wives of Hillel's shelter where the Jerusalem Sparrows roost. They will tell you the way." He raised a trembling hand to point over Jude's shoulder. "Take her now! Go quickly. Do not speak to anyone until you are out of this place."

The caravansary where the Galilean pilgrims stopped in Jericho was beyond the customs plaza, between New Jericho and Old Jericho. Old Jericho was home to thieves and bandits. The new city, while recently beautified to provide a proper setting for a lavish palace built by Archelaus, did not welcome the *am ha aretz*.

Around three walls of the animal enclosure were primitive shelters. The chambers were open to the wind on the side facing the corral and had only flimsy walls dividing one compartment from another. Nevertheless the pilgrims were grateful to have a roof against the passing rain shower that blew in from the Great Sea.

It was also the one time of year when the area outside the caravansary was actually pretty. The canvas of newly sprouted grass, not yet smeared by passing caravans, sported exclamation points of wildflowers.

It was along the back wall of the caravansary that Yeshua and His companions sat. The hoods of their cloaks were raised against the drizzle, but the five were deep in conversation bordering on argument.

"And I say only Torah tells you what the Almighty wants," Nicolas maintained. "Anything else is man-made and could be false."

"You talk like a Sadducee," Beriah asserted. "Don't you know that

King Jehoshaphat appointed judges in the land to interpret the Law? If it was as easy as you say, what need would there be for interpretation?"

"And prophets down through time," Yochanan added, "to call people back to the true faith."

"Exactly my point," Nicolas said, pouncing on Yochanan's words. "If they had just kept to the Law, there'd be no need of judges or prophets."

Shim'on, who had taken no part in the discussion so far, contributed: "Ezra didn't tell the priests to just read the Law. He told them to explain it."

This comment came from so unexpected a source that the others turned and stared at him.

"Er . . . something I heard," Shim'on muttered.

"Well said, Shim'on," Yeshua praised. "But the issue wasn't, what does the Almighty want from people? It was, what does the Almighty like? What pleases him?"

"How can we know that?" Nicolas challenged.

"How about by looking around," Yeshua returned, gesturing at the field carpeted in greenery and studded with pinks and yellows and blues. "The Almighty values beauty. . . . That seems clear enough. He likes variety. . . . He likes green a lot, but not only green, yes?"

Now Nicolas was nodding and Yochanan humming to himself.

"He likes orderliness, too," Yeshua added.

Shim'on waved his hand over the tangled thicket of grass and wildflowers. "What's orderly about that?" he argued.

Yeshua smiled. "Perhaps it's a matter of how you look at things. Take that purple flower there. How many petals to its blossoms?"

"Three," Beriah answered instantly, sensing this was a game he could win.

"And that yellow one just there?"

"Five!"

"The blue one here? No, Shim'on, you're looking too far out. Right here—beside the fence."

"Eight," Nicolas said hastily before Beriah finished counting.

"And the white ones over there with the yellow centers?"

Shim'on beat Nicolas and Beriah to the nearest clump of daisies while Yochanan contented himself with looking on from a distance.

"Thirteen?" Yeshua said before the others had returned with the same answer. "Knew that one already," He confessed.

"So?" Shim'on retorted. "We were talking about how the Almighty likes order. What's all this counting prove? They're all different numbers."

"Try thinking about them in order, from small to large."

Each face took on a different expression of study, from Yochanan's stare into the distant olive trees to Shim'on's tight-lipped concentration.

In the end it was Nicolas who replied, "I see it! Three and five make eight, and five and eight make thirteen! Each new pattern is the sum of the two that came before."

"Order, even where none seems to appear," Yeshua concluded. "The Almighty cherishes orderliness, even in the midst of variety, but the two ideas are not opposed to each other. Everything in creation sings together—a hymn to the name of The One who created it."

The home for orphan girls in Jerusalem was called Beth Hadassah. It was named for Queen Esther, the Jewish queen of Persia; the heroine of Purim who saved her people from slaughter at the hands of Haman.

Jude knew the story well. He held Kerah's hand and walked her to the imposing front gate of the orphanage. The squeals and laughter of girls drifted over the high wall.

Kerah smiled as though imagining other children and an afternoon of play in such a grand courtyard.

"You'll be safe here." Jude frowned and tried not to show his emotion.

"But you, Jude?"

"You heard the cripple. Only girls here. I am to be a Sparrow in the charity of the School of Rabbi Shammai."

Kerah spotted a flock of sparrows flying above their heads. Two of the little birds lit on the top of the compound wall. She sighed. "You'll fly here to visit me?"

"If they let me."

"Then you'll sit on the wall so I can see you?"

He banged on the wooden gate with his fist. "Yes. I can do that easy enough."

His promise satisfied her.

The portal swung open, and a young woman with thick, brown, plaited hair and smiling brown eyes greeted them. "Shalom!" she said cheerfully.

"Shalom," Jude answered cautiously. The courtyard beyond her was so clean, Jude noted, peering around her in curiosity. Dozens of girls jumped rope and played tag around an enormous oak tree. "Is this the Torah School for Girls . . . ?"

"Beth Hadassah. Yes. Welcome. I am Helena." She did not seem put off by the dirt-caked faces of Jude and Kerah. "This is a school for girls."

"I would like to enroll my sister, Kerah, in your school. She has no schooling. And only recently did she begin to speak again after a long silence. But now she speaks well enough and seems very clever and quick to learn."

The woman stepped aside, inviting them in, then knelt until she was eye level with Kerah. "Smart and pretty both. Just the sort of student who does well here. But what about your parents?"

Kerah answered, "Flown away."

Jude added, "Both of them."

"And your family?"

Jude replied, "All flown away, we think. We were once told we were related to a tinsmith, but that was only through our grandmother, who was not really our grandmother."

"I see."

"Yes. And if the fellow was a relative, I would not want him to be mine."

Helena nodded sagely. "Relatives who are not really family are like that sometimes." She touched Jude's coat. "And yet . . . such a fine coat. You are loved."

"Our mother. Our brother. A shepherd made it, we are told."

"It can be cold here at night," Helena said. "It's important to have a fine coat."

Jude looked around, wishing this was also a Torah school for boys. He envied Kerah her arrival. "I know boys can't board in a Torah school meant for girls, so I will go with the other Sparrows to carry torches . . . if you'll tell me where they perch."

"First . . . children, are you hungry?" asked Helena.

Kerah nodded eagerly. It was clear from her expression that she felt she had come to the right place. Possibly this was the best place she had ever been.

Helena took her hand and instructed Jude to follow her as well.

"Come on, then. We must wash up first. We were just about to sit down for a meal."

Washed and clean, Jude and Kerah ate in a long hall that resounded with the voices of happy children.

Helena gave Jude directions to the stone quarry where the Jerusalem Sparrows lived. He kissed his sister and bade her farewell with some relief. He could take care of himself well enough now that the burden of worry over Kerah was lifted.

As he strode away from the girls' school he turned a moment to see a flock of sparrows rise from the wall of the compound. They swirled in formation and cut through the sky toward the Temple Mount.

PART III

When He was twelve years old, they went up to the Feast, according to the custom.

LUKE 2:42

20

A dozen miles of desert, entirely uphill, resulted in more than half a day's grueling toil for the pilgrims. Most of their strength renewed by the rest in Jericho had worn off. The road was slick and sticky with churned-up mud and rock-strewn besides. It was made more hazardous by camel drovers who whipped their caravans through trudging travelers with scant regard for life or limb.

The pilgrims were relieved when fig orchards replaced barren hillsides, when orderly rows of grapevines took over from haphazard, boulder-choked gulleys. Fields waving a welcome with springing stalks of grain, lushly green from the winter rains, replenished the spirit.

By the time the throng passed through Bethany, anticipation was again running high. The Holy City was only a couple miles away!

Having gained over half a mile of elevation from the river gorge to the Judean plateau, the Mount of Olives loomed as the last obstacle to be conquered. The journey was so nearly complete that everyone's pace increased; the desire to reach the goal was so intense.

No single group felt it more than Yeshua and His companions. Having received permission to do so, the band of five boys ran ahead of the main body of their group, vying with each other to see who would reach the top first.

Yochanan and Shim'on bar Jonah tied for the honor, followed by Nicolas. Yeshua and Beriah came last, but only because Beriah was wheezing and Yeshua slowed His pace to stay alongside.

As each member of the quintet arrived at the summit he joined a speechless, awestruck line of witnesses.

There, immediately before them, was the Holy City . . . Mount Zion . . . the home of the Temple to HaShem . . . the dwelling place on earth of He whose name is too holy to be uttered.

Jerusalem!

The immensity of what lay spread out to view astonished the senses. Jerusalem, home to hundreds of thousands of souls, could have sheltered all the residents of every Galilean village combined . . . with room to spare.

Vast size and a trick of perspective dazzled understanding. Jerusalem appeared to be a model city—a product of an architect's grandiose dream. It seemed to be no real place at all . . . until one noticed that the tiny human figures glimpsed on roads and plaza were moving, living beings. Then the scene leapt into focus.

The deep Kidron Valley and the height of the Temple Mount looming over it transformed Jerusalem into a glistening island amid a sea of verdant hills and rocky peaks. Stair-step terraces of walls and flat-roofed stone houses rose, rank upon rank. Each successive wave of structures crashing against the isle of Zion inevitably drew the eye upwards and upwards until . . .

"Oh!" Shim'on breathed as he took in the glistening gold and gleaming white of the Temple of the Almighty. Jerusalem was the support column on which the entire world was suspended, and the Temple was its capstone.

"Exactly," Nicolas concurred.

The splendor and majesty of the city dedicated to the One God witnessed to the entire world of His faithfulness.

As the rest of the travelers appeared beside the boys, the entire multitude spontaneously burst into song:

"I was glad when they said to me, 'Let us go to the house of the
Lord!' . . . Yerushalayim—built as a city that is bound firmly together,

to which the tribes go up, the tribes of the Lord, as was decreed for
Israel, to give thanks to the name of the Lord."[50]

The huge cavern beneath the Temple Mount was the womb from which
the stones of Solomon's Temple were hewn. Jude was surprised by the
vast chamber. The floor was packed with orphan boys who lived by the
charity of the School of Shammai. A smoke-scarred ceiling stretched
up and up, containing the echoing voices of the occupants.

These were the homeless sons of the covenant. They were called
link boys by the Temple officials, but officially they were called Jerusalem Sparrows. Originally conceived of by Rabbi Shammai as a residence
and a Torah school, the grand design had dissolved when the numbers
of homeless boys had become too many to manage. School came to an
end when someone among the ruling class of Pharisees took issue with
how many were the cast-off, uncircumcised children of the prostitutes
who thrived beneath the viaduct: "Being of mixed race and doubtful
heritage, the wisdom of Torah must not be wasted on such children."

There remained certain rules of order in the quarry. No boy under
five or over thirteen could occupy a place in the Sparrows' quarry. Food
and secondhand clothing were provided by Temple charity funds. The
Sanhedrin also provided torches for the link boys to light the dark
streets of Jerusalem through night passages.

Each evening as the enormous gates of the city swung closed, teams
consisting of two Sparrows each flocked outside the public buildings
and on the Temple viaduct. They waited hopefully with lit torches to
guide travelers in the darkness. Illumination to any quarter of Jerusalem could be purchased, two Sparrows for a penny. The payment was
split, a halfpenny to each link boy. Owing to the fact that there were
travelers in Jerusalem who might somehow hurt one of the orphans, it
was a capital crime for anyone to harm or kill a link boy. The Sparrows
did, however, vanish from time to time, and small broken bodies were
discovered in the garbage heaps of Hinnom.

Jude's arrival was barely acknowledged. There was room for him. In
the winter months hardly a week passed without a death or two. So it was
easy for a newcomer to find a bit of straw and a place beside a fire.

A red-haired boy about Jude's age scowled at him when he

approached. A moment later he must have thought better of it and moved to one side, offering Jude a seat beside the fire and a crust of rock-hard bread.

"I'm Eizel." The boy said this without embarrassment although his name meant "Fool."

Jude stared at him in silence, perhaps too long to be polite. Eizel did, perhaps, look like a fool. Bright red curls were filled with straw. Freckled face and wide-set, reddish-brown eyes. Eizel's teeth were crooked and in need of cleaning.

"I'm Jude. My father's name was Judah."

"Knowing your father's name makes you *Gavra Rabba* around here. A great man." Eizel grinned and tossed some straw onto the fire. "As for me, I can only guess. No one around here, I suppose."

Jude blushed. Eizel had no shame that he was illegitimate, and this embarrassed Jude, who covered it by saying, "Ah, well. I am sure he must have been . . . a great man."

Eizel howled with laughter. "You're new, that's certain."

Jude swallowed hard. "Aye."

Eizel sucked his teeth. "And I can tell. You are a rustic. From the Galil." He snapped his fingers in pleasure at his own cleverness.

Jude was surprised. "How d'you know that?"

"Because you said *aye*. No one raised in Yerushalayim says *aye*."

"Ah. I see."

"Don't worry. I have nothing against Galileans. Tell the truth, we don't get many Sparrows from the Galil down here. You all have giant families from what I'm told. No orphans in the Galil."

"There are some. I am one. My sister is another. She is at the Hadassah."

"Nice place. So, Jude bar Judah, what are you doing here in the quarry, then?"

"I didn't have anywhere else to go."

Eizel's reddish-brown eyes glinted with a clever plan. "So, Jude, you'll need some guidance. I can teach you how to get along . . . for a price."

"Sure. Yes. I will be happy to have the help."

"All right, then. Providence has sent you here. I was in need of a partner to link with me. Mine died last week of . . . something. Not plague, but something carried him off before his time. I woke up and there he was . . . dead. Cold as ice and dead. The Reaper came and buried him out in the Potter's Field. I cried for days, but now I have decided I am alive and that is good. Now here Providence sends me a Sparrow from the Galil who says *aye* and needs my expertise."

Jude clutched his knees and peered around the vast space. "There are lots of you here. . . ."

"First off . . . we are not *you*. Say *us*. Because you are now *us*."

"All right, then. What do we do?"

Eizel picked a flea off his forearm and crushed it between his thumb and forefinger. "We get along. If anyone don't get along . . . they end up like this flea. See? So fighting and arguing ain't permitted."

It seemed a good rule when there was so much potential for chaos. Jude gnawed the crust of bread. "How do we work?"

"Stick with me. I'll show you every trick. For a price."

When everyone's eyes had drunk their fill of Jerusalem from the top of the Mount of Olives, the procession resumed down the slope to the west.

It was a requirement of the Passover holiday that no rent be charged for pilgrims' lodging. Hospitality was a duty imposed on those fortunate enough to live in the Holy City; they were to provide temporary shelter to those who did not have that blessing. The only compensation they were permitted to receive was retaining the hides of the Passover sacrifices.

The ordinance meant that everyone who sought lodging within the city had to be accommodated.

In practical terms, it was not that easy. Since worshippers came from all over the world to join in this memorial celebration, the population of Jerusalem doubled in size.

This made food prices soar, encouraged pickpockets, and generally made the Temple police and the Romans nervous. And when the Romans grew nervous, they were apt to become harsh in their actions.

Those who journeyed from the Galil had already made up their minds to camp on the hillside outside the city walls. The location was less crowded and provided better access to the Temple ceremonies. The weather, while cold, was not rainy.

So in the midst of a pleasant grove of trees, beside an ancient stone ring, the Nazareans pitched their tents and set up housekeeping.

"This is a beautiful place," Shim'on observed. "What's it called?"

"Gath Shemen," Yeshua replied. "The oil press. The Gentiles call it Gethsemane."

In spite of his name, Eizel was no fool. The epitome of chutzpah, he could dart through the souk with the quickness of a fox and, when his circuit was run, empty from his pockets a dozen kinds of bread and varieties of vegetables.

Or he would stroll and collect twice as much. The merchants he stole from were none the wiser. They liked Eizel because of his red hair. Some referred to the fact that legends about King David described him as a ruddy-colored lad. While Jude engaged in pleasant conversation, Eizel's fingers deftly plucked dates from the cart of the toothless date merchant from Jericho. Apples were larger and thus required more skill. Bread was secreted beneath his cloak and held between his knees as he waved good-bye and walked some distance away.

"Never steal a fish," Eizel instructed Jude. "The smell will give you away every time." Then, with a sturdy clap on Jude's back, he declared, *"Neshane et HaOlam!* You and I will change the world!"

The weather turned warmer. The fleece coat of the Nazarene was heavy to carry, but Jude would never leave it behind in the cavern.

"A fine coat." Eizel fingered the soft fleece of the collar and visions of shekels danced in his eyes. "Too fine for a Sparrow."

"It was a gift."

"When we carry the torches, haven't you noticed? No tips."

Jude stroked the sleeve and shook his head, not understanding. "What's that got to do with my coat?"

"It's much too fine for a Yerushalayim Sparrow. Don't you see?"

"No."

"The rich men we lead have no pity for any boy with such a fine warm coat. It's as good a coat as something their own sons might wear."

"It was a gift. . . ."

"No matter. You don't look like a poor boy. And appearance is everything in this profession," Eizel explained.

"It saved my sister's life. I'm sure of it. I don't know how, but I am certain. . . ."

Eizel shrugged. "What's past is over. So she's alive. What use is it now?"

Jude tucked his head into the collar. "It . . . means something. Something . . . important. It's good luck."

Eizel was unimpressed. He no longer believed in luck. "Let's sell it. We could get enough to buy each of us new clothes to last through the summer. And sandals." Eizel held up his foot, revealing that his toes protruded past the sole of his shoe.

"No. I . . . it was a gift. From a very good lady . . . it belonged to her son. It was a gift to him from a shepherd, she said. The fleece of the best lamb . . . and . . . and I told her . . . I would keep it."

"So. You kept it through winter. It'll be hot soon and then no one will want to buy a coat."

"Then I'll wear it next autumn when it's cold again."

"You'll outgrow it by then." Eizel snorted as he plucked at Jude's wrist, already protruding two inches beyond the cuff.

Jude leapt to his feet, suddenly angry. "I never had anything so nice. It was a gift and . . . I tell you, I may keep it until I am grown with sons of my own to wear it."

Eizel backed up a step and took a bite from an apple. "Children he has already. Growing up. Ambitious plans for a Sparrow." He laughed. "All right. Like Moses, may you live to be 120! Just trying to think of what would be best for both of us. We're partners, you know. Share and share alike." He extended the half-eaten apple to Jude. "*Atah mevine? Understand?*"

Jude tossed his head and accepted Eizel's peace offering. "Sure. All right, then. You'll see. This coat will bring us luck."

21 CHAPTER

Jude held his torch high lest the aged rabbi stumble on the uneven stones of the street. The boy did not know Jerusalem well enough to guide anyone. He was strong enough, however, to hold the fire aloft as his partner, Eizel, led the way through the dark quarter.

"My eyes, you know," Rabbi Yismah said to the boys. "The words of Torah. Such glory and brightness. I have studied many days, and now the pages of the Book make the darkness seem ever darker. I will fix my gaze upon the angels who lead us on this dangerous path through Yerushalayim."

Jude resisted a shudder of fear at the words and the touch of the scholar.

"You are out late, sir," Eizel addressed him.

"I have been studying for some days. I am a teacher at the Academy of Joseph. My name is Rabbi Yismah." The old man placed a gnarled hand on Jude's shoulder to steady himself. "A penny more if you can tell me the meaning of my name."

Eizel pounced on it. "YiSMaH! It means 'He will rejoice'!"

"So I shall! Aye! There's a good lad. You should be in Torah school, not guiding old men through the dark streets by torchlight." Yismah chuckled. "And one more penny if you can spell it!"

Again Eizel retrieved the answer to the lesson. "YiSMaH! The letters are *yod, sheen, mem, heh*."

Jude looked at his partner with a sideways glance of resentment. Two extra pennies for a one-word spelling lesson.

Yismah tapped his temple. "Well done! He will rejoice! Well done! The mind is a treasure house if we will but use it."

Eizel joyfully jabbed the sky with his torch. "Two pennies for only one small word."

The old rabbi clucked his tongue. "YiSMaH, you say? Eh? Only one small word? Nay! YiSMaH is much more than that! It is the mystery of all the ages. It is the blessing the Almighty One promised to our Father Avraham! Do you not know what else the four letters of YiSMaH spell?"

Jude cocked his head at the mystery. "Tell us. We don't want another penny. Just the answer!"

The rabbi cast his rheumy eyes heavenward. "Those same letters point to The One who is coming to reign as King in Yerushalayim! Rearrange the letters of Yismah, and you have the reason we will rejoice! *Mem, sheen, yod, heh* . . . can you say the word now, boy? For all the treasure of heaven and earth is yours when you call that name!"

Jude skipped and shouted the meaning. "MaShiYaH! Messiah! The Anointed One!"

The rabbi patted him firmly in congratulation. "Aye. Well spoken. YiSMaH speaks to you of the day when MaShiYaH will come for you! He will search for you like a shepherd. He will be the Elder Brother who will protect you. In the day Messiah finds you, then you will rejoice! And this is your reward!"

This promise found in the four letters of a single word seemed a much greater treasure to Jude tonight than a sack filled with pennies.

"Where can we find him?" Jude asked, gazing at the flickering flame of his torch as they came at last to the rabbi's house.

The old man fished pennies from his money pouch and counted out the treasure into each boy's open palm. "We will not find him, I think . . . but rather, the Son of David will come here to find us. Wait for him! Look for him! For the darkness is so dark now that he must surely come soon! And remember: Everything means something! Oh, and return here tomorrow at midmorn."

"In daylight?" Eizel said doubtfully.

"I'm going to the Temple. I can use sturdy young arms and legs as props on the steps. Tomorrow, then."

The gate closed behind him.

But when will the Son of David come? Jude wondered. *If only he would find me soon!*

Eizel yawned. "You go with the old man if you want. I'll be sleeping."

While many foreign-born Jews gathered in Jerusalem synagogues with their fellow countrymen, like the Synagogue of the Cyrenians and the Synagogue of the Thracians, pilgrims from the Galil had no such structure.

There was an old joke, repeated to exhaustion by the Judeans, suggesting that the *am ha aretz* of the north should indeed have their own building for worship. After all, they were often more foreign than foreigners, and frequently stranger than strangers.

It was partly to refute this wit, and partly out of native stubbornness, that the Galileans refused to do anything of the kind.

On the east side of the Temple Mount, contained within the colonnade known as Solomon's Portico, was a series of chambers. These were used as classrooms and could be pressed into service as synagogues when occasion demanded it.

This was one such occasion.

Rabbi Mazzar intended to conduct morning Sabbath worship for the pilgrims from Nazareth. This was when the boys prepared for their bar mitzvah would make aliyah. They would be counted in the minyan of ten and come to the bema to read Torah portions as they joined the ranks of "sons of duty."

Moreover, today was an especially important Sabbath. As the last Sabbath before Passover, this was *Sabbath HaGadol*, the Great Sabbath.

The Nazarean pilgrims were joined in their hike up from the Kidron Valley by Zachariah, Elisheba, and Yochanan. Yochanan would also make aliyah today, and his aged father, considered to have lived beyond a man's allotted lifetime, would now have his second bar mitzvah.

As they ascended the Temple Mount, they sang:

"When the Lord restored the fortunes of Zion, we were like those who dream.
Then our mouth was filled with laughter, and our tongue with shouts of joy;
Then they said among the nations, 'The Lord has done great things for them.'
The Lord has done great things for us; we are glad."[51]

Once assembled in the chamber—men standing in the front half of the hall and women and children behind a screen at the rear—and after some introductory remarks by the rabbi, the first reader was called to the bema.

In Torah there was no official ceremony attached to a bar mitzvah. Whether a Jewish boy who had reached the age of manhood read or not, he was considered bar mitzvah. But the custom had grown up to make a boy's first public Sabbath reading something of an occasion.

Yochanan, since his father was a Levite, was actually entitled to go first. But Rabbi Mazzar wanted to keep the cousins together, so he had paired them to do the last set of readings.

The chanting of the Parashah for the day commenced, with each reading between ten and twenty verses. It all went well. Nicolas read with great precision, in a high, nasal voice many attributed to his youth . . . except Yosef recalled that Nicolas' father still sounded like that at forty years of age.

Beriah stumbled over the word *korban-shalom*—peace offering—lost his place, and had to begin again. It caused only a minor delay.

Then Zachariah read . . . that is to say, he glanced at the open scroll and remembered all the words, reciting the passage with perfect precision. He read a passage involving the priest's change of clothing before performing sacred duties . . . even when going from one sacred duty to the next.

This, Rabbi Mazzar explained, was the same as a child going from carefree youth to apprenticeship in the house of his father. It was also akin to the change from boy to manhood just as bar mitzvah symbolized.

A relay of grown men succeeded Zachariah, forging ahead until it was time for Yeshua to be called up. Rabbi Mazzar, naming Yeshua as he did so, requested that He do the *Maftir*, the second Torah reading, which the special Sabbath required.

Looking about the room, Yeshua made eye contact with Yochanan, Zachariah, Elisheba, Yosef, and His mother before commencing:

> *"Now the Lord spoke to Mosheh and Aaron, saying, 'This is the statute of the law that the Lord has commanded: Tell the people of Israel to bring you a red heifer without defect, in which there is no blemish, and on which a yoke has never come.'"*[52]

Yosef heard Yeshua read the ordinance that produced the waters of purification from the ashes of the red heifer. Yeshua flawlessly recited the requirements that the animal be perfect in every way. That it be killed. That its blood be sprinkled seven times to signify the complete forgiveness of the believer before the Lord. That the animal be reduced to ashes and the ashes preserved as a memorial of the sacrifice. Finally, Yeshua intoned that sprinkling with ash-infused water cleansed from impurity. It was used to ritually cleanse those who had touched death.

Yeshua's reading was flawless, His pronunciation and inflection perfect. He read with calm assurance, as if providing silent commentary adding: *What is done by the Almighty is always rightly done. The will of HaShem is more important than anything.*

Why then, Yosef wondered, did a shiver run down his backbone at the moment Yeshua concluded?

Rabbi Mazzar explained how the "water of impurity" was an example of how the *Ruach HaKodesh*, the Holy Spirit, works. Like the touch of the water and ashes on the skin, the Spirit-inspired Word convicts a sinner of the presence of evil in his life. Yet, once aware of his guilt, at that same moment he may recall that a sacrifice has already been made—the red heifer. And if he repents, turns from his sin and confesses his guilt, then he is, at that moment, cleansed and restored to fellowship with the Almighty. Water and ashes can't really take away sin, Mazzar said, but repentance, confession, and renewed obedience will.

"But it is all by the *Chesed*, the Mercy of the Almighty," he said. "Not because of good works, for no one is righteous enough for that."[53]

Then Mazzar summoned Yochanan to read the day's *Haftarah*, the concluding portion.

Yosef heard something in Yochanan's voice he'd never heard in one so young before: grim determination and fiery devotion to the Almighty.

"Behold, I send my messenger and he will prepare the way before me. And the Lord whom you seek will suddenly come to His temple . . . ,"[54] Yochanan read.

Yosef shivered all the way to the end of the reading from the prophet Malachi.

Jude hung back awkwardly, studying Rabbi Yismah from the edge of the bar mitzvah ceremony. The old man was smiling—smiling as if he remembered his own bar mitzvah and the reading that had, no doubt, directed the steps of his life.

Jude replayed in his mind what he had just witnessed. He envied the boys who had a teacher and a rabbi and a father to stand beside them.

Jude's father was dead, and now he had only the memory of Grandmother telling him that he should not forget to pray.

How do I pray? Jude longed to find the answer. He had clambered onto the base of the pillar to watch the bar mitzvah ceremony. What did it mean? These words? The flowing prayer shawls . . . the phylacteries tied onto the arms of the boys who now were declared men and Sons of Obligation as they proclaimed the Torah portions.

"Baruch attah Adonai Eloheinu, melekh ha-olam."

This was a good prayer to remember, even if one forgot every other prayer, Jude decided. He would say it as the rabbi had spoken it and all the other boys as well.

Had the day's Parashah also foretold something about their lives?

The officiating rabbi again placed his hands on the shoulders of the aged priest and his son.

Behind him Jude heard a whisper. "Zachariah . . . his name means 'Yahweh has remembered.' He's the priest the archangel appeared to and foretold the birth of his son. Now there is the son. Yochanan. Aye . . . a true miracle it is!"

The elder Zachariah had made his second bar mitzvah. His young, strong son was just embarking on a long life beneath the watchful eye of the Almighty.

Jude wondered who would stand with him when he came of bar mitzvah age. Anyone? In this moment, the ache of longing for his father became almost unbearable.

When Yeshua of Nazareth had opened the scroll and read the ancient words, the air seemed to grow crystalline. The Word flowed over Jude like warm oil, soothing every ache. He noticed the look on Rabbi Yismah's face. . . . The expression seemed to declare, *"He will rejoice!"*

The spectator at Jude's right had remarked, "Now that boy Yeshua! Such a rabbi he will make, eh?"

Just then Jude recognized the woman from Nazareth. The woman with the kind eyes who had fed him, clothed him, then sent him away with food and the lambskin coat he now wore. The woman whose simple home held the aroma of lavender; the woman whose compassion at his time of great need he would always remember. . . . Mary! Jude breathed in the lingering aroma of the lavender from the collar of the lambskin coat. The scent reminded him of the kindness of her embrace. Could it be that the coat he wore had been worn by the boy now becoming a man in his thirteenth year?

Jude watched Mary, her eyes gleaming with pride . . . and something else. Sorrow? How could that be, at such a moment?

He wondered briefly if she would remember him. Oh, that he could be her son . . . like Yeshua . . . standing for his bar mitzvah! Jude sighed, knowing he would never have such a moment in his future.

He gazed thoughtfully at the young Yeshua—a scholar, yes. A good heart. A dutiful son. All of these qualities were apparent. But Jude recognized something more; he just could not express, even to himself, what he meant.

What Jude knew for certain was that he was destined to now always be simply a witness—on the outside looking in. Never a part of a family or joy such as this. His life was just as it was. Not much of a life, but at least a life. His sister was safe and cared for. He had food and a place with the Jerusalem Sparrows. But he would always remember those moments in Mary's house . . . and wish life could be different.

He wished again that he knew how to pray. What to pray. He wished he believed that Adonai could hear his words and love away the ache in his heart. But if his young life had taught him anything, it was that Adonai did not seem to notice the likes of him.

When the service ended, everyone clustered around to congratulate the young men on the quality of their reading and the rabbi on the excellence of his teaching. It took Yosef several minutes to set aside the notion that he had just stared ahead into a vision . . . layers and layers of visions.

It was then that something startling happened. A small boy emerged from the press of the crowd.

Yosef saw Mary's eyes brighten with recognition. "Jude?" she greeted the lad, wrapping her arms around him.

The child grinned up at her. He was missing a front tooth. He was wearing . . . well, it looked like he was wearing Yeshua's old fleece-lined coat. "I recognized . . . you are his mother. I came to learn to pray." He turned to Yeshua and touched the collar of the coat and then clasped the tassel of Yeshua's prayer shawl, closed his eyes, and repeated the prayer that had opened the service. "*Baruch attah Adonai Eloheinu, melekh ha-olam*. . . . Blessed are you, O Lord, King of the Universe."

Yosef felt his heart jump at the words. Had this little boy spoken the words of the angels on this occasion? Did his heart understand something about Yeshua that the human mind could not comprehend?

Yeshua and Jude exchanged a glance, as though they had always known one another. The small boy's eyes brimmed. He turned away quickly, as though he wanted to hide his emotion. Then Jude vanished as suddenly as he had appeared.

22

CHAPTER

hildren's laughter drifted over the high wall of the orphanage where Kerah was safe and happy.

"*YiSMaH.*" Jude spoke the word aloud as he leaned against the wall opposite the great gate. "He will rejoice."

Clearly there was rejoicing inside Jerusalem's haven for homeless girls. Laughter was a much different sound from the surly complaints Jude heard day and night from the population of the Sparrows' cave.

His eyes brimmed with tears. Who would think that he would miss his pest of a sister? What use had she ever been to him? And yet here he was, hoping the gate would swing wide so he might have even a glimpse of Kerah.

Sighing, he considered the words of Rabbi Yismah. "*Everything means something.*"

But what did Jude's suffering mean to a world waiting to rejoice? What use was his small life? What value did the existence of a Jerusalem Sparrow have to anyone? If he died, there were many more homeless and lost boys to take his place. Too many wandered the world without the light of torches to guide them.

Jude thought of Grandmother's admonishment: *"Remember to say your prayers."*

He had already forgotten the words. How could he know what to say to the Almighty? How could any human know what to say to Him who was so high above the Sparrows that their small voices were lost in the vast gulf of creation?

A burst of joyful squeals from behind the wall made Jude smile in vicarious happiness for Kerah.

"YiSMaH. He will rejoice." Jude spoke the word aloud as he wandered disconsolately back toward the quarry. "MaShiYaH . . . will you ever come to find me?"

Herod Antipas stared morosely out the window. How could he get Caesar to pay more attention to Judea? How could Antipas force Caesar to reconsider his claim to be king of the Jews?

The answer was simple: by doing a better job controlling rebellion than the Romans themselves.

The brutal Roman crushing of the Galilean rebellion had driven the Zealots into the hills or out of the country. But miles of crucified bodies also lit a flame of anger in all but the most traitorous Jews.

The proper way to eliminate rebellion was to make one man suffer for the guilt of many. Crush future rebellions by convincing the Jews there was no future apart from Rome . . . and with Antipas as their protector, of course.

What about that twelve- or thirteen-year-old rumor of a miraculous child . . . or was it two children?

A cross shape of stars stood perfectly upright on the southern horizon. The vertical line of the figure drew Antipas' eyes upward. Directly above the cross, the same vertical line pierced the heart of the figure called The Virgin.

Antipas had heard the prophecy; he knew the rumors. All nonsense, of course. But it was not important whether Antipas believed them. What if the Zealots used the same old Jewish desire for a divine king to fan the flames of rebellion?

A cross loomed large for the mythical child of the virgin, or for any child who pretended to be king without Rome's permission.

The question was, how soon might that child reappear?

It was time to restore his father's network of spies.

Thirteen years? The child, if indeed he still lived, might be in Jerusalem this year. The imposter might even have journeyed to the Holy City to celebrate his coming of age. He might be proclaimed as the true prince at a time when hundreds of thousands of potential supporters were already in Jerusalem.

Antipas would see what more he could learn—and quickly.

It was two days before Passover. Beginning tonight, at sunset, would be the Day of Preparation and the start of *Ta'anis Bechoris*. The next few days would be full of many ceremonies and festivities associated with Pesach.

But today was the first day of the week. Yeshua and His friends were free to explore the wonders of the Temple Mount, to soak up its grandeur and fill their memories with the nearness of the Almighty.

Yeshua, Shim'on, Nicolas, Beriah, and Yochanan had already watched the morning sacrifice . . . Yochanan with particular interest. It was during the morning rekindling of the Altar of Incense within the Temple sanctuary that Yochanan's father had received his angelic vision. It was thirteen and a half years earlier that heaven had announced Yochanan's birth and his mission to be the forerunner of Messiah.

Just now the companions stood atop the Royal Colonnade—the porticoed walkway whose marble columns spanned the south expanse of the Temple Mount. It cost them each a penny to ascend to the top. Rabbi Mazzar had assured them it was not to be missed.

At the southeastern corner of the structure a winglike pinnacle protruded beyond the corner of the building, hanging over a sheer drop.

"Highest point of the Temple," Nicolas reported.

"Where the priest watches for sunrise," Beriah added.

Yochanan stepped to the very edge without hesitation and looked down. To show that he was equally brave, Shim'on joined him, then whistled softly.

Nicolas walked forward also but remained a pace behind the others. It felt like the edge of the world.

Down from here meant more than just down to the stone floor of the portico . . . more than down to the level of the Temple plaza. *Down* meant all the way down, into the deepest part of the Kidron Valley.

Beriah hung back. "It's all right," he said in response to Nicolas' urging. "I can see just fine from here."

"Three hundred feet," Shim'on estimated.

"I make it closer to five hundred," Yochanan offered. "See the whitewashed tombs across the valley? One of those is thirty feet tall. Count how many you'd have to stack up to reach where we are."

"Come on, Beriah," Yeshua offered. "We'll go together."

At the very edge of the abyss was a low stone parapet, no more than six inches tall. On the rock in the very corner of the pinnacle was inscribed *The Place of Trumpeting.*

"So this is where they blow the shofar and the silver trumpet," Nicolas said. "Come on, Beriah. It really is safe, you know."

Beriah and Yeshua stood on the pavement together. Spread before them was the valley, its great chasm emphasized by the looming Mount of Olives beyond. Facing the other direction exposed the entire Temple complex to view, like a set of puzzle boxes nestled one inside the other: Court of the Gentiles, Court of Women, Court of the Israelites, Court of the Priests, magnificent sanctuary trimmed in real gold. Doll-like figures of worshippers and priests and Levites went about their duties, fulfilling vows and offering sacrifices.

"Arise, shine, for your light has come," Yochanan murmured. *"And the glory of the Lord has risen upon you."*[55]

"What's that?" Nicolas demanded.

"It's said Messiah will stand on this very spot," Yochanan instructed. "So says my father, and he has spent his life in study. This is where the trumpet blast announcing the End of the Age will be blown. From here King Messiah will fulfill the prophecy of Isaias."[56]

"Yes, well," Beriah responded, "I'm thinking of Scripture too. The one about angels guarding you: *On their hands they will bear you up, lest you strike your foot against a stone.*"[57] He leaned ever so slightly forward and looked down, almost afraid to breathe. "Foot, nothing! Every bone in your body, most likely!"

Yeshua and Yochanan exchanged a look. "Neither prophecy will be fulfilled today, I think," Yeshua said.

"Come on," Shim'on urged. "Let's go see Beautiful Gate. I hear it's coated with sheets of gold."

"Bronze," Nicolas corrected. "But let's go see it anyway."

On the way back down from the pinnacle of the Temple, the five companions remained divided as to what sight to visit next. Nicolas and Beriah banded together in support of seeing the gate called Beautiful. Yochanan preferred to visit the balcony overlooking the Court of the Priests, from which vantage point visitors were allowed to view the sacrifices.

Shim'on said, "Enough of this! Marble and brass and men strutting around in robes is all well and good, but don't you realize there's an entire city out there?" He swept his hand toward the western hills and the expanse of city just across the viaduct. "They say you can buy things from the four corners of the earth right here in Yerushalayim."

"Buy?" Nicolas scoffed. "And are you so wealthy, O fisherman?"

Shim'on sniffed. "Doesn't cost anything to look," he argued.

The quartet appealed to Yeshua to settle the matter. "I'm going over to Solomon's Portico," He said.

Not "My choice is" or "I vote for" but "I'm going."

The others traipsed along behind.

Solomon's Portico was where the great scholars of the present age and for ages past taught their talmidim. Along its corridors students who had been accepted by teaching rabbis were absorbed in the ebb and flow of dialogues. The followers of Hillel and Shammai, the two most renowned of the pious academics, met at opposite ends of the double-wide colonnade.

As combative students of rival instructors, they also sometimes met in the middle to hold debates and argue differing points of the Law.

Yeshua in the lead, the five friends encountered a group of young men clustered around an as-yet-unseen central figure. The squinted eyes and sagely nodding heads betrayed the onlookers as would-be scribes, experts in the Law, and their master.

As the group shifted and moved, a temporary lane opened, allowing a glimpse of the interior. There, in a sedan chair designed to be carried by four bearers, sat a tiny, wizened figure. He was swathed up to the chin in blankets, and his head rested on his chest as if he were asleep. Another man, about thirty years of age, was closest to the figure in the chair. This attendant periodically leaned closer to either the mouth or the ear of the invalid.

"So." Shim'on shrugged. "Nothing to see here. Let's move on."

Nicolas rebuked him in a hiss. "Keep your voice down. Do you want to be thrown off this mountain for the ignorant *am ha aretz* you are? Don't you know who that is? I recognize him just from the stories I've heard!"

Clearly Shim'on did not.

"It's Hillel . . . Hillel the Elder," Nicolas instructed. "Hillel the Prince," he added when Shim'on still did not give evidence of being impressed. With mounting exasperation Nicolas said, "He's over a hundred years old and the greatest sage since Solomon."

"Closer to one hundred twenty," Beriah corrected. "The man beside him is his *methurgeman*—his spokesman—his grandson, Gamaliel. Hillel can barely hear or be heard, they say, so he whispers to his grandson, who repeats the conversation."

"Let's move up to where we can hear," Yeshua urged.

"Rabbi," the companions heard a clean-shaven, blond-haired man inquire in Greek, "before I decide to become a Jew, I have a question. If I asked you to teach me the whole Law while standing on one foot, could you do it?"

While some talmidim glowered at the impertinent query, Gamaliel dutifully repeated it in his grandfather's ear. A broad smile stretched across Gamaliel's face as he listened for a moment to the reply, then stood erect again. "Grandfather says yes, of course. Here it is: 'What is hateful to you do not do to another. This is the whole Law . . . all the rest is commentary.'"

While Yeshua and the others looked on, the Greek man reacted with a smile of his own. "I asked Reb Shammai the same thing," he admitted. "He called me impudent and drove me away with a stick. I confess I like your answer better!"

Of the two great sages, Shammai was reputed to be a stickler for exact attention to the details of the Law and a harsh disciplinarian. Hillel was more moderate and lenient in both views and manners.

Yeshua waved His hand to catch Gamaliel's attention. "Teacher, I have a question."

Nicolas grabbed his friend's arm. "What are you doing? You'll get us in trouble!"

The condescending, almost angry looks on the faces of the students convinced Beriah that Nicolas was right, but at a whispered command from Hillel, Yeshua was summoned forward.

"Yes, young man," Gamaliel said. "What is your question?"

"When the Lawgiver says *The Lord will raise up a prophet for you like me, from your brothers*, to whom is he referring and how will he be known?"[58]

Among those who studied Torah, this was a much greater question than the usual restrictions requiring interpretation. Often the students debated such rules as whether climbing a flight of steps on the Sabbath required each tread to be counted as one pace or two when determining a proper Sabbath-day's journey. And then how did one allow for slopes with no steps?

To Beriah's surprise and Nicolas' evident relief, Gamaliel did not order all five friends thrown from the Mount. Instead he repeated the inquiry in his grandfather's ear, paused, then listened to the reply.

"Grandfather says Mosheh the Lawgiver is speaking of Messiah. Therefore he will be known because he will fulfill all the other requirements of the Anointed One."

"And will he be greater than Mosheh?" Yeshua persisted.

More angry looks from the talmidim made even Yochanan uncomfortable, but Reb Hillel did not seem irritated. In fact his response, unheard by any except his grandson, was quite lengthy.

"Grandfather says Messiah will be greater than both Mosheh and Elijah," Gamaliel reported. "Mosheh delivered the Law. Elijah restored the Law. But Messiah will complete the Law. Moreover, where Mosheh failed because he grew angry and Elijah failed because he despaired, Messiah will neither grow angry nor despair."

"And why—?"

"Young man," Gamaliel said sternly, "my grandfather is tired and . . ."

Hillel tugged on his spokesman's sleeve. Once more the crowd waited for the reply.

When he stood again, Gamaliel said, "Grandfather says today is too far gone for such a weighty discussion and the holiday is upon us. Come again in two days, when the teaching is open to all. And by the way, Reb Hillel asks who is your instructor?"

"Rabbi Mazzar of Nazareth," Nicolas put in proudly.

The talmidim laughed. "Can any good things come out of . . . Nazareth?" one joked.

"Perhaps . . . one," Hillel wheezed.

The assembly, many of whom had never heard their master's voice, were astonished. Then at a slight gesture of a trembling hand, Hillel's chair was raised, and the party moved off toward the exit from the Temple Mount.

"Well, that was exciting," Shim'on breathed.

"Too bad we can't come back and listen again," Yochanan observed, looking after the departing throng.

"Too much to do," Beriah agreed. "Yerushalayim. Day of Preparation. Passover. But we met the great Hillel! That's enough, surely."

"Enough?" Yeshua repeated.

23

By sunrise Yosef had already been up and working around the camp. The Day of Preparation for Passover would be busy.

Readying for the holiday began the night before in the homes of Jerusalem when fathers gathered leaven into heaps by candlelight. This afternoon would be the sacrificing of the lambs and much scurrying around to get ready. The Passover holiday itself began at sunset tonight with the first seder meal.

Mary gathered the remaining loves of barley bread and put them on the heap accumulated by all the pilgrim families. To this she shook out the crumbs from the pouches in which the provisions had been stored. It was not possible to sweep a campsite, as she would have done in their home in Nazareth, but every bit of leaven would still be removed and burned.

And if that were not already enough to keep track of, this day was also *Ta'anis Bechoris*—the Fast of the Firstborn. Yeshua and Yochanan, also Yosef and Rabbi Mazzar and Uncle Zachariah, were all the firstborn of their families. As such they had been fasting since sundown the night before.

If the Passover holiday recalled the Almighty's providence in freeing the Israelites from bondage in Egypt, Ta'anis Bechoris was a reminder that the historical event was not without cost. The last plague, the one that caused Pharaoh to let the people go, was the death of the firstborn in every household missing the lamb's blood from doorposts and lintels. The Fast of the Firstborn was a particular reminder of the mercy and grace of the Almighty not only in sending the plagues to set Israel free, but also in showing divine mercy and sparing the firstborn of the Hebrews. All the firstborn males observed the requirement until evening, when the obligation to fast was replaced with the Feast of Passover.

At twelve noon Yosef heard the shout go up: "The bread has been removed!" It seemed an odd warning cry, drifting down from the Temple Mount in repeated, echoing waves.

The signal for the burning of the leaven was when the second of two loaves of bread laid in the Temple vestibule was removed by the priest. All across Jerusalem fires of brushwood beneath heaps of bread were ignited and the leaven consumed. From this moment forward and for the next seven days, Jews would observe the Feast of Unleavened Bread.

Yosef saw the flames licking the loaves, scorching them. Soon the whole city smelled like an untended oven—the aroma of sin being put away.

Yosef went looking for Yeshua. It was time for the Paschal sacrifice to take place. The boy had been around all morning, talking with His cousin. Now He seemed to have disappeared.

Yosef scanned the camp. Find one boy, find both, it seemed, but Yochanan was nowhere in sight either.

All the priests gathered in Jerusalem for Passover, regardless of their course of service, were needed to assist at the sacrifice. For that reason Zachariah, old as he was, had already left for the Temple Mount. Yochanan was supposed to go up with Yosef and Yeshua.

The carpenter found the boys within the circle of boulders on the patch of grass behind the camp where the lambs were tethered. Yeshua and Yochanan had already released Achi from the ground stake. The cord looped around Achi's neck trailed on the ground, but the lamb made no move to run away.

Yeshua was seated on the ground next to the lamb. Yochanan towered over them both, his arms folded across his chest.

Yeshua looked up at Yosef's approach. "It's time," the boy said matter-of-factly.

Yochanan's face was grim, Yeshua's set with focused determination. It was the same visage that Yosef had noticed Yeshua used with every difficult emotional situation.

The lamb did not need to be dragged or even led. It trotted ahead of Yeshua as if going eagerly.

Lambs were always chosen at least four days ahead of the feast and kept as pets before being slain, but this time was harder than ever. Grief was important to a full understanding of the holy day. Everyone had to understand that Passover had only been accomplished at a great price.

Only the death of the Egyptian firstborn had set Israel free; only the lamb's blood on the doorposts had kept the firstborn of Israel safe that night. A sacrifice was necessary. The depth of the sacrifice could not be appreciated without a personal sense of the cost.

Now Jews from all over the world were going up to the place where the Almighty had demanded that Abraham sacrifice his only son, then had provided a substitute at the last moment. The concept of a substitute sacrifice was deeply ingrained in all Jewish belief.

Rams . . . bulls . . . doves . . .

Today it would be lambs . . . thousands and thousands of them. The Law required one lamb for every ten members of a household or their guests. Each family dispatched a representative to prepare the sacrifice for them.

Yosef did not know how many people the holiday-swollen lake of Jerusalem contained from the rivers of pilgrims that drained into it. Perhaps tens of thousands of lambs would be needed.

The carpenter thought back a dozen years and more to Zadok the Shepherd and the fields near Beth-lehem. Today's rite would require all the unblemished yearling and younger lambs from all the flocks of Migdal Eder.

The singing of the so-called Egyptian Hallel was already under way. Hidden from view a Levite choir chanted, *"Praise the Lord. Praise, O servants of the Lord."*

And the pilgrims replied by completing the chant: *"Praise the name of the Lord."*[59]

This reverberating chorus continued, verse by verse, through all the first division of sacrifices, as the six hymns of the Hallel were sung.

"When Israel went out from Egypt, the house of Jacob from a people of strange language . . ."

And the first division responded, *"Judah became His sanctuary, Israel His dominion."*[60]

Yosef and the boys arrived in time to join the second division of sacrificers. They entered the court with a great host of others until it was again packed with worshippers; then the gates swung shut behind them.

A double file of priests flanked the incoming crowd of pilgrims.

"There's Father," Yochanan said, pointing.

Halfway to the altar, his hands and the lower half of his robe spattered with blood, was Zachariah. In his hand was a knife; by his side, a golden bowl.

The three joined him there.

"I know you are a man," Yosef said to Yeshua, "but today this is for me to do."

It was required by the Law that each family representative slay the lamb himself. The priest stood by to catch the blood of the sacrifice in the bowl.

Best get this over with quickly, Yosef thought. Accepting the razor-sharp knife from Zachariah, Yosef felt Yeshua's body stiffen beside his, as if all the boy's muscles tensed at once.

Yosef struck the instant the Levite choir began their hymn. Blood spurted into the bowl; Achi collapsed.

Yeshua gave a single, loud groan; then His shoulders slumped. A great sigh came from Him as Yochanan cleared his throat multiple times as if covering the sound of weeping.

Bowls brimming with blood that steamed in the cool air were passed along the line of priests to be thrown at the base of the Altar of Sacrifice; empty bowls were passed back down the row.

Another file of worshippers moved into place.

His voice at first faltering, then with increasing strength, Yeshua sang with the others:

"What shall I render to the Lord for all His benefits to me? I will lift up the cup of salvation and call on the name of the Lord, I will pay my vows to the Lord in the presence of all His people. Precious in the sight of

the Lord is the death of His saints. O Lord, I am your servant, the son of your maidservant."[61]

When Yeshua sang the word *salvation*, He was uttering His name—"I will lift up the cup of *Yeshua*."

Yosef was startled to hear a faint voice whisper, *"Shall I not drink the cup the Father has given me?"*[62]

Those words were not in the psalm. Nor had anyone nearby spoken them.

What did it mean?

Bearing the limp body of the lamb, Yosef thanked Zachariah, then said, "Come on, boys. Let's go back now."

The gates opened and the tide of worshippers ebbed and flowed again.

Jude and Eizel waited eagerly with their torches blazing outside the Eastern Gate of the Temple. Passover was the best time of year for the Jerusalem Sparrows. What made this night different from all other nights?

Eizel answered the question. "So . . . these pilgrims from the sticks? They come to Yerushalayim. They go to the Temple. They come out. They see us standing here. We are a vision. Lights blazing! Sure enough, some religious *meshuggener* will think you . . . or me . . . is Elijah. Or an angel. So we light the way for them back to their tent and they ask us to seder."

Floods of worshippers passed by them, headed for their tents on the Mount of Olives. The brilliant light of the moon cast shadows on the ground.

Who needed a torchbearer with such a moon?

With a broad smile, Eizel approached each ecstatic band of worshippers. "Need a torch?"

"A light to guide you to the Mount of Olives?"

"Through the Valley of Kidron? Dangerous ruts in the road?"

"Help a Sparrow of Yerushalayim tonight!"

There were no takers. The boys sat on the steps. Their torches fluttered in the wind. The broad gates remained wide for the few stragglers who trickled out.

"Need a torch to light your way?"

"Two Sparrows for a penny."

"It's a bargain."

Jude rested his chin in his hand. The air was redolent with the aroma of roasting lamb. "All the food in Yerushalayim tonight. Lamb. Eggs. Fresh matzoh. All of it. Honey cakes. And here we are sitting on the steps . . . waiting. Waiting."

Eizel cleared his throat, commanding Jude to be as silent as an old man—one of the priests—and what appeared to be his son shuffled out of the gate.

Jude recognized them as the priest Zachariah and his son, Yochanan, cousin and close companion of Yeshua of Nazareth. He leapt to his feet, happy to see a familiar face. "Shalom, Yochanan!"

"Shalom!" Yochanan answered, grasping his frail father's arm. "It's a cold night tonight, eh, Jude? Still wearing your fleece."

"Yes." Jude was afraid to ask the question. Eizel nudged him hard in the ribs.

Yochanan laughed. "I thought we were the last to leave the Temple tonight."

Eizel babbled, "If this was Egypt during the first Passover, I suppose we would be in trouble, eh? The Angel of Death spotting us out after dark? No supper, eh?" Eizel shoved his elbow deep into Jude's side.

"Yes . . . uh . . . yes. I suppose we'd miss seder."

The elderly priest cleared his throat. "What are you boys waiting for?"

Jude blurted, "Elijah!"

Eizel laughed. "Or an angel. Or a prophet maybe. You never know who you'll meet up here at the Temple, eh?"

An amused glint appeared in the priest's eyes. "Sometimes an angel. Sometimes Elijah."

Eizel asked the question: "So. You need a torch? We'll guide you, sir. Two Sparrows for a penny."

"A bargain. To light the way for an old man."

Zachariah and his son agreed this was a night when everyone needed a torch to light the way to the Garden of Gethsemane.

Zachariah wheezed, "And you'll come with us. Share our seder, eh?"

"Baruch attah Adonai. Blessed are you, O Lord, King of the Universe, who hast chosen us from among all languages and sanctified us with thy commandments." So spoke Rabbi Mazzar, presiding over the Passover feast in the camp of the Nazareans.

The company reclined on cloths spread upon the ground, the men in an inner circle. The women stood in an outer ring, waiting for the preliminary rites to be concluded. The air was full of the tang of smoke and roasted meat, for each family gathering had at least one lamb broiled on a spit over a wood fire.

Mazzar acted as master for the rite, even though he was not a priest. At this village gathering Zachariah and Elisheba and their son were guests of the pilgrims from the Galil. It was well that Mazzar was in charge, because Zachariah was late returning from the Temple Mount. Yochanan had been sent to seek for his father and to assist him back to the garden.

"And thou hast given us, O Lord Almighty, in love, the solemn days for joy, and the festivals and appointed seasons for gladness; and this is the day of the Feast of Unleavened Bread, the season of our freedom. . . ."

When the invocation was completed, the first cup of wine was drunk. With Yosef carrying the basin and Yeshua the towel, each guest was offered the opportunity to wash his hands.

The meal continued with the presentation of parsley, dipped twice in salt water and eaten; then a second cup of wine was poured but not swallowed, waiting for the significant moment about to take place.

At this moment little Lysias, Nicolas' six-year-old brother, was coached by his father to begin the ritual questioning by standing and reciting, *"Mas nish-ta-nah ha-lui-lah ha-zeh mi-kol ha-ley-lot?* Why is this night different from all other nights?"

Yosef, as the host of the feast, took up the explanation. He recited the history of the first Passover, beginning with how the Hebrews came to be in Egypt because of his namesake, Joseph the Dreamer. The story continued into the giving of the Law at Mount Sinai.

"I'm worried about Zachariah," Yosef heard Elisheba whisper to Mary. "They're very late."

The food having been brought to the center of the gathering, Rabbi Mazzar explained the bitter herbs, the unleavened bread, and the other elements of the meal. All the guests drank the second cup in unison, and the first cake of unleavened bread was broken and blessed.

The festive supper was eaten, accompanied by more singing, more washing, more prayers, and more explanations.

"I'm so worried," Elisheba whispered to Mary. "What if he's fallen? What if he's hurt himself?"

"I'll go," Yosef volunteered, just as Rabbi Mazzar raised his cup and called for the third serving of wine—the blessing cup—to be poured and drunk.

The wind stirred the tent flap, rustling the fabric.

"And we say *Ulu Ush-pi-zin*," Mazzar intoned. "Welcome, Exalted Wanderer, as we invite Elijah to join us at the feast." A sudden gust pounded on the tent. Mazzar continued, "For do we not read in the scroll of Malachi that the Lord says, *Behold, I will send you Elijah the Prophet before the great and awesome day of the Lord comes. And he will turn the hearts of fathers to their children and the hearts of children to their fathers, lest I come and strike the land with a decree of utter destruction.*"[63]

The cry of the wind increased, causing the flames of the candles to flutter. The eyes of every child widened with expectation.

There came the sound of voices outside. And then the tent flap lifted, revealing Yochanan's smiling face.

A groan went up among the children. "Only Yochanan!'

"So! Elijah and his father! Better late than never!"

Elisheba gushed with relief at the sight of Zachariah leaning on his son's shoulder. Two small boys, Jerusalem Sparrows, extinguished their torches and entered with them.

Yosef recognized the smallest as Jude, the child who had greeted Yeshua at the bar mitzvah.

"I worried you." Zachariah kissed Elisheba.

"I am here imagining you have met the Angel of Death, and he was not passing over you, nu?"

Zachariah shrugged. "Sorry. It is memorable to be here this year. This was the greatest number of Paschal lambs ever sacrificed. Two hundred thousand! There was so much to do. I am weary." He smiled. "And happy. Yochanan here to help me. We have brought two sojourners with us. Bearers of the light. Or rather, they have brought us by the light of their torches. Eizel and Jude. Sparrows of Yerushalayim."

Mary's face filled with delight. She opened her arms to the boys and made a place for them beside her.

"Here, Father." Yochanan helped the old man sink to the cushions. He sat at Zachariah's right hand.

The link boys, hungrily eyeing the feast, began to wolf their food without regard to ceremony as Mazzar offered the final prayer:

"The breath of all that lives shall praise thy Name, O Almighty Lord. And the spirit of all flesh shall continually glorify and exalt thy memorial, O our King. For from everlasting to everlasting thou art the Lord, and besides thee we have no King, no Redeemer, no Savior."

Jude, a portion of roasted lamb in his hand, paused and recited quietly, *"Baruch attah Adonai Eloheinu . . . melekh Adonai."* Then he turned to Yeshua, "Did I say it correctly, Rabbi?"

Yeshua nodded. "Aye. Well spoken, brother."

24 CHAPTER

I t had been two nights since Jude and Eizel had earned a penny as link boys. Eizel was cross. No links meant no pennies. There was only so much a boy could steal in order to survive. They needed money.

It was dark. The lambs that remained alive after Passover sacrifice seemed restless in their pens tonight.

Jude and Eizel waited among a dozen other Sparrows, hoping one of the shepherds would require a torch to lead them through the city. Jude spotted the tall, lean man with a scarred, grim face and a patch over one eye.

Eizel whispered, "That one is Zadok the Shepherd of Beth-lehem. Mean 'un. Hates all boys. Never asks anyone for a link. Be careful of him. He'll whack you with his staff if you speak to him."

Suddenly Zadok the Shepherd settled his gaze on Jude. "You! Boy!"

"Yes, sir."

Eizel nudged Jude with happiness at his own escape.

"You're a Sparrow," the looming, grim-visaged herdsman barked.

"Aye. That I am."

"Do y' have a name?"

"I am Jude, sir."

The shepherd scowled. "Jude, is it?"

"Aye. Do you need a link, sir?"

The shepherd stamped his staff on the pavement. He was a fierce fellow who looked as though he would never be in need of anything, let alone a light from here to there. "I can tell from your voice y' are from Galilee."

"I am, sir."

"What are y' doin' here? Yerushalayim?"

"I'm a Sparrow, sir. Among the other Sparrows."

"Where did y' get that coat?"

Jude answered timidly, "In Nazareth, sir."

"Nazareth, y' say?" The shepherd's one eye narrowed. "You're . . . how old?"

"I think nine years, sir."

"Too young. Too young," the man muttered almost in relief. "He'd be . . . near thirteen by now."

"I don't understand." Jude tried to make sense out of the interrogation.

The shepherd grasped the sleeve of the coat between thumb and forefinger. "Nazareth. But where are your parents?"

"Dead, sir."

The face of the angry shepherd clouded. "Eh? Is that so? And were they . . . are y' called Jude bar Yosef? Of the house of Yosef the Carpenter of Nazareth? And do y' have an elder brother? Eh?"

"No, sir." The questioning was so intent that Jude could not lie. "This was given me as a gift. The boy who had it had grown too tall for it. So said his mother. And she took me in and fed me and gave me her son's coat."

The big man relaxed. "Ah! Well then. She would do that. That's like her." Then he stooped to look directly in Jude's face. "Did y' see him?"

"Who, sir?"

"The lad the coat belonged t' before you? Eh? Ye say he's tall now? Outgrown the coat. The age of bar mitzvah, he must be. As my own youngest boy would have been now. This year . . . this year in Yerushalayim. Tell me, lad. Did y' ever see what the boy looked like who wore the coat before you?"

There was the briefest of pauses and then Jude shook his head. "No . . . no, sir. I am sorry. But . . ."

The boy had witnessed too many betrayals, had already seen sorrow on Mary's face. He would do nothing that might bring trouble to the Nazareth family, so he lied.

"No. He was away, I suppose. And his mother took me in and gave me food . . . and kindness. There was lavender hanging in the rafters . . . and . . . she gave me . . . this fine coat."

The shepherd adjusted his eye patch. "Well then . . . she's hung lavender in her rafters, has she? Aye. That would be like her t' do such a thing. T' remember us, like . . ."

Jude asked, "Sir, would you like a torch to guide you somewhere?"

The shepherd replied, "This spot. The Temple sheep pens. You've brought the light of understandin' t' me tonight, lad."

"But where would you like us to take you? What link?"

"A link from thirteen years ago till now. Aye. Thirteen years it'll be this year since he was . . ." He sighed and fished out a silver coin from his leather pouch. "This will see you and your partner through the Passover, eh?" The shepherd flipped the coin and Jude caught it.

Then the big, gruff man turned on his heel and left the boys to marvel at the luck Jude's coat had brought them.

The man who presented himself at the servants' entrance to Coponius' palace was a known informant. He made a living by denouncing rebels to the Roman overlords. He had sold out a Zealot band in Chorazin recently, then relocated to Jerusalem "for his health."

Now he was peddling a new bit of news. "I have important information for the governor," he said to the decurion of the guard detail.

"What sort of information?" the officer demanded.

"I hear that an old priest who claimed to have a vision about a miraculous baby, about the true King of the Jews, is here for Passover."

"True king, eh?" the decurion repeated. "Wait here."

Coponius actually agreed to see the man. "Do you know him by sight, this old priest?"

"No, but I can find him," the traitor agreed, rubbing thumb and forefinger together in a broad hint.

"The cavalry chased a rebel's child all over the Galil," Coponius mused aloud. "Could this be the same 'miracle baby'?" Then he indicated for his secretary to hand over a silver coin. "Let me know when you have something more definite," he ordered.

Eizel extinguished his torch, lest they waste it on the path back to the quarry. He made Jude do the same, then snatched the shepherd's silver coin out of Jude's hand as they walked. He whooped with delight and held the silver disk high as if the coin were his torch. He danced down the dark street ahead of Jude.

"We're rich!" Eizel shouted. "All the money in the world! It's your lucky coat what done it! I told you that coat was worth money!"

Jude hung back, surly that Eizel had claimed ownership of the cash. The shepherd had questioned Jude about the coat, not Eizel. He had paid Jude for the answers, not Eizel. And now Eizel was announcing to all sleeping Jerusalem that he was rich.

"Put it away, Eizel!" Jude warned.

"Put it away? It's as bright as the moon above us! Look at it!"

"You're a fool, Eizel! Put it up before someone . . ." Jude's voice fell away as suddenly a burly figure stepped out of the darkness, blocking their path.

"Yes," growled the man, "you are a fool, Eizel. All the money in the world? Rich, are you? Give it to me."

Eizel shouted, "Run, Jude!" Then he screamed, clearly caught by the assailant.

Jude turned on his heel and scurried down an alleyway as Eizel's bloodcurdling shriek echoed in the Quarter.

The Feast of Unleavened Bread was not over. Many pilgrims would stay to the very end or beyond, taking in the wonders of Jerusalem.

For those who had come from other nations to participate, this might be a once-in-a-lifetime opportunity, and they were in no hurry to leave.

Galileans, whose livelihood was tied closely to the land, had no reason to rush back either. The rain, which had held off so conveniently for the travelers, would soon return in earnest. Grain was sprouting but nowhere near harvest; barley would not be ready for another month, and the wheat not until a month after that. Even the flax stalks from which linen cloth was made, which were ready to harvest now, could not be cut until there was enough sun to dry them properly.

The spring lambs were just beginning to be born. There was never any rest for shepherds and other herdsmen, but the abundant grass simplified things. Flocks could be pastured much closer to the villages than in the dry season; fewer workers were needed. Owners and senior herders could remain at the feast.

For Yosef, as with other tradesmen, the situation was reversed. This was one of the busiest times of year because farmers wanted new implements prepared before the next harvest began. Clothing, out-grown in the last year, was given away as charity and had to be replaced. New furniture was commissioned during the months when everyone remained indoors more. When harvest came again, Yosef and Yeshua would devote their labors almost exclusively to emergency repairs, so now was the time to tackle big, new projects.

To participate properly in a Passover pilgrimage required only attendance the first two days. By the third day of Passover, it was time for Yosef and Mary to go home.

Rain fell as a gentle mist.

"Should we wait and leave tomorrow, Yosef?" Mary questioned.

Yosef considered. "No," he said at last. "The road from here to Jericho is passable. I think this rain will increase; tomorrow the highway will be all mud. Let's get Zachariah and Elisheba out of here today and as far as Jericho."

Mary agreed. "Will you send Yeshua to me to help pack the house-hold things?"

"Of course."

Just outside their tent Yosef met Beriah and the boy's father. "Ah, Yosef," Beriah's father said. "Just the man. Could you spare us some time? A tent too near the stream of the Kidron collapsed in the night, and we need help getting it put right again."

Yosef glanced back toward his own shelter, then nodded. "Mary," he called, "I'm needed down by the brook. Be back soon." Then to Beriah he added, "Yeshua is around somewhere. Please send him to his mother when you find him."

Beriah agreed, then ran to answer his own mother's summons.

Helping out with the collapsed tent took longer than Yosef had expected. Zachariah and Elisheba, mounted on their donkeys led by Yochanan, were already outside Mary's tent.

"Shall we wait for you, dear?" Elisheba inquired.

Mary looked around at the debris of half-packed camping gear, then up at the sky. "No. Get as good a start toward Jericho as you can. We'll meet you there. I'm sure Yosef will be back soon, and we can pack up quickly."

Shim'on's family was also readying to leave. "I can help," he said. "I'll lead one of the animals."

Mary thanked the young fisherman; then to Yochanan she added, "When Yeshua comes back, he can run ahead of us and also help you." Catching sight of Nicolas, she called out, "Nicolas, when you see Yeshua . . . I think he's gone to help with the fallen tent . . . when you see him, please tell him to hurry ahead to help Yochanan and Shim'on with the donkeys."

Then to her aunt and uncle and cousin Mary bid, "Shalom. See you in Jericho."

"So, Eizel the Fool lived up to his name," remarked one of the older boys as the Sparrows filed past the corpse of Jude's only friend. The wicker bier on which the body lay had been donated by the Temple charity established for the burial of the poor and indigent.

Jude, as Eizel's former partner, was considered his only family. He stood beside the flimsy casket as chief mourner. Before noon a rabbi came and said *kaddish* over the body. He spoke only a few words about greed leading to the grave.

Jude then led the procession of his fellow Sparrows out to the Potter's Field, where Eizel the Fool was buried in a shallow trench. Jude supposed he was the only witness who would long remember Eizel's short life . . . and the only one to whom Eizel's life would matter.

A forest of broken bits of clay jars sprouted over the nameless dead. Eizel's grave and brief life would be commemorated by a headstone made from a shard of broken earthenware stuck in the ground. His name, scratched on its surface with a bit of charcoal, would wash away in the first rain.

And drops were falling even now.

Despite Yosef's confident prediction that today would be better for travel than later in the week, the steep slide down from Jerusalem to Jericho was not easy. The volume of rain increased until it was bucketing. The clay of the slope was treacherous and the footing difficult.

Yosef, leading Rabbi Mazzar's donkey, struggled to keep his footing as the weight of his pack threatened to pull him sideways. He remarked to Mary, "I hope Zachariah and Elisheba have already gotten out of this canyon."

"I'm certain they're fine," Mary returned. "Two fine young men to assist with the animals."

Yosef nodded absently. "If this weather worsens, we may need to aid Zachariah and Elisheba all the way to Heshbon."

Mary squeezed his arm. "Don't try to have everything planned so far ahead. Tonight, Jericho, the Lord willing. Tomorrow will take care of itself."

26 CHAPTER

The rain had fallen steadily since midafternoon. It was nearly sunset before Yosef and Mary and Rabbi Mazzar reached Jericho. It took most of another hour to erect their shelter, since all the rooms at the inn were already taken, and to scrounge enough dry brush to get a fire going. The elderly rabbi was soaked and chilled. Mary unpacked dry clothes for him to change into and put a kettle of broth on the fire.

Yosef was relieved they had not overtaken Zachariah and Elisheba on the trail. "I expect they got here plenty early. Probably already toasty warm and dry," he speculated. "I'll go get Yeshua and also borrow Yochanan. That amount of fuel isn't near enough for tonight; we'll go round up some more."

It took another quarter hour to locate Zachariah's space. Having arrived early enough, the priest had secured a cubicle under a wooden overhang. It was, as Yosef predicted, already comfortable. Mother, father, and muscular son were toasting bits of unleavened bread beside their own fire.

"So, Yosef," Zachariah said in greeting, "made it. Rough day, eh?"

Yosef smiled. "Later start than I planned, but no concern now. I see you're eating, so I won't ask for Yochanan's help gathering firewood, but I do need Yeshua to come with me. Where's he at?"

Consternation chased surprise across Zachariah's face. "Yeshua? Isn't he with you?"

Still not comprehending, Yosef said, "Did I miss him out there in the caravansary? Is he already out looking for us?"

Yochanan broke in before his father could explain. "But he wasn't with us, sir. He hasn't been with us all day. Isn't he with you?"

"No . . . no," Yosef returned uncertainly. "But I thought Mary said . . . two strong young men leading the . . . you," he said to Yochanan. "Not Yeshua?"

A bit of comprehension dawned. Zachariah explained, "Young Shim'on bar Jonah helped us. Not Yeshua," he added with another shake of his head. "We haven't seen him since last night."

Yosef's hand flew to his mouth. His eyes clouded and he rubbed his beard, pondering. "Well, no cause for alarm. He knew we were leaving Yerushalayim. He must be with one of the other families. I'll find him."

"May I go along, Father?" Yochanan asked.

The two split up, going in opposite directions and circling the caravansary, stopping to inquire of every single group they met.

Yosef encountered Beriah with his family. "Beriah, this morning, as we broke camp, did you tell Yeshua his mother needed him, like I asked?"

Beriah looked confused. "No, sir. You said when I saw him to tell him, so . . . but I didn't see him again, sir. Not since yesterday."

"But where can he be?" Mary said for the third time since hearing the news of her missing son. "He must be with some other family. He has to be."

Yosef stood in the doorway of the tent. He and Yochanan had already made several circuits of the Jericho caravansary, even popping in to ask the same clan the same question posed only moments earlier by the other searcher. Asa, Shim'on's relation, Beriah's father, and Nicolas' father had all joined the hunt, without result.

Nicolas and Beriah stood, heads bowed, in front of Yosef. Both felt guilty; neither was certain why.

"I never saw Yeshua this morning," Nicolas confirmed. "He wasn't by the Kidron Brook. But I just thought he'd gone up to the garden a different way. I'm . . . I'm very sorry."

Mary hugged the boys. "No need," she reassured them. "You didn't do anything wrong. Just a misunderstanding, that's all."

Relieved, Nicolas and Beriah bobbed their heads. Nicolas' father said in a guarded tone, "We'll be in our own tents if you need us, Yosef. You have only to call."

Call, yes . . . but what else was there to do? Where could Yeshua be?

There was only one conclusion: The boy had never gotten the message they were breaking camp. Yeshua was still somewhere in Jerusalem.

"He probably found out we were gone too late in the day to follow us," Yosef said. "Sensible choice, that. He'll know we'll miss him here in Jericho and wait for him here. He'll come with another family leaving tomorrow."

Nodding as if in agreement, Mary nevertheless said, "But we won't wait, will we, Yosef? We must go find him."

The rain drummed a constant rhythm on the canvas covering. The hillside in the direction of the Holy City was pitch-dark. No travelers were on the road this night.

"No," Yosef corrected. "Too dangerous. He's fine. You know how he is. By now he's telling stories around someone else's campfire. We'll go straight back tomorrow morning—probably meet him on the way down." Yosef spoke with far more confidence than he felt.

Nor did he sleep much that night. If ever he had needed a reassuring dream or an explanatory vision, now was the time . . . but no angelic assistance appeared.

Wrapped in the warmth of the Nazarene's coat, Jude shivered all the same. His back against the quarry wall, he stared at the empty place in the straw beside him. Eizel may have been a fool, but he was Jude's only friend.

The other boys who occupied the great cavern chattered like birds sharing a vast tree. Laughter punctuated conversations. It was as if Eizel had never existed, as if his death was of no more consequence to the flock than that of a tiny sparrow in a field.

Jude deeply missed Kerah. And Grandmother. And his papa. And his mama. His life before the Romans had destroyed everything dear to him. And . . . and . . . what would Papa do? Was this the destiny his father had seen for Jude as he hung on the cross? Was this why his father had told him to come to Jerusalem?

Jude buried his face in his arms and began to weep silently. He knew he was crying not for poor Eizel, but for himself. They were all worthless here in the quarry. While great men traversed the holy stones of the Temple Mount above them, the poor and the forgotten existed beneath their feet.

Did anyone notice the fall of a Jerusalem Sparrow? Jude wondered. Did anyone care? Would anyone be a witness for him that he had ever lived?

What was it that Grandmother had told him the night she flew away? *"Jude, you will need to pray. . . . Jude . . . say your prayers. . . ."*

But Jude did not know how to pray. And if he spoke to God from the depths of such a place as this, how could the Almighty God of Heaven and Earth hear the prayers of one so insignificant?

You . . . Adonai . . . you are so great. Grandmother said I should speak to you, and you would hear me. They tell me you made everything. The birds in the sky. Men, rich and poor alike. You made the lights in the heavens by your word, Grandmother said. But you've forgotten the sparrows. The starry cross I see rise each night in the heavens . . . its beauty mocks my sorrow for Papa's death. Where are you, Lord? You who made the Southern Cross . . . where can I go to speak to you? You . . . who live somewhere in the stars? While I am here, trapped in the grave of the living?

27 CHAPTER

Jude awakened from a restless sleep. The feet of a dozen Sparrows formed a semicircle around him. He sat up slowly, confused at their angry faces.

"What is it?" he asked.

"You." The reply was accompanied by spittle on his face.

"What? What's wrong?" Suddenly fearful of their unexplained rage, he spread his hands in innocence.

"Eizel was one of us," an older boy replied. "A Sparrow for as long as I lived here. Now he's dead."

"Well, sure," Jude answered. "My partner . . ."

A solid kick to his leg connected. He yelped. "What? What have I done?"

"He's dead because of you!"

The others joined in. Jude tried to shield himself as kicks and blows emphasized each accusation. "Because of you!"

"You could have sold the coat!"

"We all saw the shepherd give you money!"

"Something about the coat!"

"Eizel was killed because of that coat! You could have stayed to help him."

Jude tried to fend them off as blow after blow rained down on him. "No! No! It wasn't . . . he . . . told me to run!"

Blood spurted from his nose as a fist connected solidly with his face. Trapped against the stone like a wounded dog, he tried to fight back. Tried to hold on as the boys stripped his coat from him. Another solid hit to his head made the world spin around him. Would they kill him?

He cried for help as the frenzied rage of the pack increased at the sight of blood.

Then there was a shout that filled the cavern. "*Sheket!* Stop!"

Someone waded into the mob, throwing the leaders off Jude. They flew away, slamming into one another as they fell.

The silence of fear settled on them. Jude lay in his own blood, panting, unable to move or speak. A hand touched his forehead as someone . . . someone knelt beside him and said his name: "Jude?"

Jude's eyes fluttered open. After a moment he recognized the face of Yeshua of Nazareth, His eyes filled with concern and anger.

"They . . . stole . . . my coat."

Yeshua answered, "It's here. I saved it for you."

Behind Yeshua an accusing voice rang out. "What's this to you? Why do you meddle in our business?"

"This is my Father's business." Yeshua did not turn to answer His accuser but spoke directly to Jude. "Jude is my brother. The coat he wears was first mine."

Silence.

Yeshua wiped the blood from Jude's face.

Jude stammered, "I tried to pray . . . tried . . . Adonai . . . I said . . . and this is what I get."

Yeshua seemed undaunted as he helped Jude to sit upright. "Don't be afraid. Our Father is here. Even here in the depths of the earth. He heard you, Jude. It is written that Adonai makes his home among the poor and he knows when the smallest Sparrow of Yerushalayim falls."[64]

"What will I do? Where can I go now?"

"Come, Brother." Yeshua lifted him by the hand. "Follow me."

More than half a day was spent returning uphill, in the relentless rain, on the treacherous footing, before Yosef and Mary arrived back at the Mount of Olives just east of Jerusalem. The space in the Garden of Gethsemane was scarcely recognizable as the same campground from the day before. The Kidron, swollen with runoff, had caused the sudden relocation of many families to higher ground. Grateful to find such a prime spot unoccupied, there were now three families living where yesterday there had been only one.

And none of them had seen Yeshua.

"Is that the tall lad . . . rough appearing, like a prophet in the making?" one neighbor inquired.

"No, that's his cousin," Yosef corrected. "But the two were often together. Have you seen my boy?" The carpenter added a description of Yeshua.

The reply was an unconcerned shrug. "Don't think so, but he's bound to turn up. You know how newly bar mitzvahed boys are—eager to try their wings, so to speak."

Yosef was not so certain. This was so unlike Yeshua's normal behavior that a twinge of anxiety stabbed him, and the carpenter could not make it go completely away. Thanking the man, Yosef moved on to the next campfire and the next cluster of men, just as Mary was doing with the gaggles of women.

When they had completed their search, Yosef and Mary moved from the campground outside the city walls into Jerusalem.

It was a fearsome night. Though Mary and Yosef hired a pair of link boys to continue their search into the dark hours, no one they encountered had any notion where Yeshua might be.

"Likely knocked on the head and sold as a slave," one of the Sparrows offered helpfully.

Yosef pounded on every door in the Street of the Tinsmiths, in the Street of the Cheesemakers, in the Street of the Vegetable Sellers, and in the Street of the Spice Merchants.

Each merchant, apprentice, or family member who responded had the same negative answer. No one had seen a bar mitzvah–age boy, by himself, in Jerusalem.

But then, their grumpy attitudes suggested, who could be expected to remember one unremarkable boy out of so many thousands of shoppers?

When Yosef hammered on the door of a potter's shop, it was answered by a woman whose silhouette proclaimed her pregnancy. "Yes," she inquired. "Do you need to buy a lamp?" She did not invite them in out of the rain.

A child peeked around his mother's form. "Gershon," she scolded, "get back, now." Then she waited while Yosef patiently again described his quest. She shrugged but agreed to ask her husband, Yahtzar. The potter likewise had no assistance to offer, but as they turned away he suggested, pointing, "Why don't you ask the Temple guards?"

"Ask us what?" inquired a pair of soldiers tramping past.

Again, now wearily, Yosef explained.

"Tomorrow," one guardsman explained. "Come to Nicanor Gate. We keep a list. Yours isn't the only boy who's gone missing this week, let me tell you. May have been placed in a charity school till you showed up."

Mary said anxiously, "Does it have to wait until tomorrow? Can't we have the name of the place tonight?"

Patience clearly wearing thin, the guard repeated, "Tomorrow. There's more than one place he could be. The list is in Nicanor Gate and the scribes have left for the night."

"Thank you," Yosef said uncertainly. "But he's . . . he's not a small child to have wandered off. We'll keep looking."

The two soldiers exchanged a glance. Firmly, but not unkindly, the senior of the two replied, "Can't. Come midnight the legionaries will be patrolling the streets. Anyone they find out wandering about'll be locked up—meaning you. That wouldn't help matters, would it? Find someplace for the night and come up to Nicanor tomorrow."

In the last moments before curfew Jerusalem Sparrows cried out as Mary and Yosef passed them in the crooked lanes of the city: "Two Sparrows for a penny!"

"A light to link Yerushalayim!"

"Torches for hire! Two for a penny!"

A Roman soldier strode purposefully toward the towers of the Antonia Fortress. He glowered at the boys and growled a warning. "Get back to your cave! No more links tonight! Anyone caught in the streets will be arrested."

The cadre of torchbearers exchanged fearful glances. They extinguished their lights and started back toward their home.

Yosef brightened and took Mary's arm. What if Yeshua had taken shelter among the Jerusalem Sparrows?

"Sparrow!" he called.

The leader turned round and extended the smoking stub of his brand. "Sorry. You heard the guard . . . no more links."

"We are looking for two Sparrows and maybe a boy who is with them. One with bright red hair. His name . . . a funny name . . . Eizel. Fool, he is called."

The leader of the Sparrows spat. "Eizel? He's a fool all right. You'll find him where the potter finds his clay. He's worth less than a chamber pot now."

Yosef tried to decipher. "What do you mean?"

"To put it plainly, the fool is dead."

Mary gasped and put a hand to her heart. "But what happened? What . . . how did he die?"

The Sparrow replied, "Don't know all the facts. Something about a shearling coat his partner wore. Jude was the name. New boy. They cut Eizel's throat like a lamb and let him bleed out."

"And Jude?" Mary leaned heavily on Yosef. "What of him?"

"Almost dead, if not entirely. A great battle in the quarry between the Sparrows and Jude and a bandit—Galilean from the sound of him—he came out of nowhere to fight. All about the coat . . . then he came and took Jude away. Gone. Kidnapped, I would say. Maybe sold to a slaver."

All hope came crashing down. "Yeshua's old coat," Mary murmured.

Yosef extended a penny. "Never mind the torch. We need a place to sleep tonight. Caravansary."

The flock of boys raised their fingers in unison to point at the gate of the compound directly in front of them.

The leader snapped up Yosef's penny and pounded on the gate. "Open up! It's the Sparrows here! We've brought a link without a torch. Pilgrims in need of shelter."

28

Yosef and Mary were awake long before the blast of the shofar announced the opening of the Temple gates. Yosef wondered if Mary had slept at all. Dark circles were beneath her eyes. She had the haggard look of a woman in mourning.

It was already the third day since Yeshua had gone missing. He was buried somewhere in the depths of Jerusalem . . . nowhere to be found.

Yosef did not hold out much hope that the list at Nicanor Gate would help. Yeshua was not a five-year-old lost in the marketplace. Had He been arrested by the Romans? kidnapped by a slaver and sold? or worse, murdered in the street and left to bleed to death like Eizel?

Mary was ashen-faced as they emerged into the flow of pilgrim traffic. There was nowhere left to search, yet she frantically examined the faces of everyone in the street.

Yosef was angry. If the boy was still alive, why had He worried them so? Why take off like an unbroken colt at the moment of such danger?

"Where? Where has he gone? And why has he done this to us?"

Mary whispered. "Something has happened to him. He's never . . . worried us like this, Yosef."

Yosef tried to be reassuring, but his own heart felt like lead in his chest.

The lanes leading onto the Temple Mount were crammed with pilgrims, priests, thieves, rebels, and soldiers, all moving inevitably toward the Temple like the lambs being herded out of the animal pens and onto the holy mountain.

"Where could he be?" Mary murmured. "Why? Why has he done this to us?"

Yosef fumed as they pressed through the crowds. *Who does Yeshua think he is?*

"So, young man, you are back again?"

Jude was proud to hear Yeshua addressed by these obviously wealthy, brilliant scholars in such polite tones. The one speaking—Yeshua had said his name was Gamaliel—welcomed the carpenter's son from Nazareth with great warmth. Though Jude hung back, outside the fringes of the crowd, no one shouldered him aside or ordered him away, as if by being with Yeshua, he was welcome to witness the exchange.

Jude accompanied his friend Yeshua . . . his *brother*, Jude corrected himself happily. How magnificent, how comforting to have an older brother—someone at last to stick up for him.

Nor did Yeshua act concerned about His missing family. "They will come back for me," He said with assurance. "In the meantime, I must be about my Father's business."

Jude did not understand what that meant. Yeshua's father was a Galilean carpenter, wasn't he? What business could such an *am ha aretz* have with the sages of the Temples?

But the Sparrow shrugged and prepared to listen. Yeshua had said it as if He knew what He meant when He said it. That self-reliance satisfied Jude. Yeshua was both brave and trustworthy; He had plunged in to help Jude when he needed it. Who was Jude to question Yeshua now?

Gamaliel opened the discussion. "So, young Nazarean, Grandfather wants to know if you wish to continue the discussion in which he asked you this question: 'If we agree the Lawgiver and the Restorer both failed at least once, when did Mosheh and Elijah fail?'"

"Yes," Yeshua returned promptly. "I have been thinking about that. Mosheh failed *after* fasting on the Mount of Sinai. That is when he grew angry and threw down the tablets. Elijah failed *during* his fast in the wilderness at the Mount of Sinai, when he despaired because of Jezebel."

"And Messiah?" Gamaliel prompted.

"Messiah will also fast at the Mountain of the Lord . . . but he will not fail—neither by anger when his people do not know him nor by despair when his friends betray him."

This reply went far beyond the text of the question, and the circle of talmidim buzzed with the seeming arrogance of the reply.

"How can you say King Messiah will be unrecognized and betrayed?" one student demanded in a haughty voice.

"Have you not read the Prophet Isaias?" Yeshua asked, then quoted, *"He was despised and rejected by men; a man of sorrows and acquainted with grief. . . ."*[65]

"You take too much on yourself!" another student said in a hostile tone. "The prophet speaks of the nation of Israel as the servant of the Almighty . . . not of Messiah!"

In that instant Jude raised his eyes and caught a glimpse of Yosef edging through the crowd. The carpenter's face was set, grim and angry, as he entered the circle where Yeshua sat among the doctors of the Law.

Yosef seemed strangely out of place among the mighty, while his young son appeared relaxed and enjoying the interaction. "Yeshua!" Yosef shouted.

The heads of the talmidim swiveled to see who it was that shouted for Salvation.

Hillel's eyes widened at the approach of such a plain man.

Yeshua stood to embrace Yosef.

Yosef did not return the greeting. "Not here. Not now. Your mother is waiting in the Court of Women. She is sick with worry. Three days we've been looking for you. Get your things. Follow me."

Gamaliel inclined his chin and addressed Yosef. "You have raised a Torah scholar . . . perhaps one day a rabbi."

Yosef replied, "Perhaps one day. But today, honored sir, the boy has nearly killed his mother with worry. She's waiting in the Court of Women."

"Well then . . . well then . . . one cannot place the study of Torah over the suffering of one's mother, eh? Perhaps another time."

Ancient Hillel gave a slight wave, dismissing the Galilean youth. With visible effort Hillel lifted his head to watch Him leave.

Yeshua bowed to Hillel and Gamaliel, then followed His fuming father from the gathering as snickers of amusement erupted from the crowd.

Jude took up the rear, running to catch up as Yosef strode across the courtyard. Then the carpenter stopped abruptly. He turned back and embraced Yeshua before beckoning for Jude to join them.

Yosef, Jude, and Yeshua returned to Mary as she stood anxiously searching the faces of the multitudes who passed beneath the archway of the Eastern Gate. The sun was just above the Mount of Olives when she saw her son. Tears of relief moistened her face as she ran to enfold him.

Yosef stepped back, his calloused hands on Jude's shoulders as Mary held Yeshua for a time without speaking. He was so much taller than she was. He tucked her head beneath His chin and comforted her as if she were the child.

Mary managed a hoarse whisper. "Yeshua . . . son? Why have you treated us like this? Here your father and I have been anxiously looking for you."

Not unkindly, but with His countenance displaying the resolute expression Yosef knew so well, Yeshua replied, "Why did you have to search for me? Did you not know I would be here, in my Father's house . . . attending to my Father's business?"[66]

The memory of a long-ago dream echoed in Yosef's mind. *"Yosef, Son of David, do not be afraid to take Mary home as your wife, for what is conceived in her is from the Holy Spirit. . . ."*[67]

The angel had borne true witness to Yosef of God's great love for every person!

Yosef considered the mother and her son together. *Can he really understand? Can Yeshua know? Does Mary understand the meaning of the angel's words as her son holds her in his arms? "You will call Him Yeshua . . .*

Salvation . . . for He will save His people from their sins. . . . and they will call Him Immanuel—which means, 'God with us.'"[68]

Jude craned his head to look curiously at Yosef as if to ask what Yosef's carpentry business had to do with Yeshua remaining in the Temple.

Yosef remembered how the angel had whispered of salvation. *. . .Yeshua!* . . . to him and changed the course of his life forever. Yeshua was indeed about His Father's business—searching for the lost. Yeshua in His Father's House, bearing true testimony to the character of His Father's heart, seeking to comfort and save the poor and the outcasts and the orphans of Jerusalem.

And what of the other prophecies spoken in this very place twelve years before? Yosef studied the lines that creased Mary's brow and remembered again: *"And a sword will pierce your heart also. . . ."*[69]

It was in that moment Yosef saw Mary's expression change. She noticed the Sparrow near her son, wearing the lambskin jacket—the coat the grieving shepherd of Beth-lehem had sent for Yeshua to wear in place of the sons he had lost. Now Yeshua's treasured coat, made from the fleece of a sacrificial lamb, had been passed along to bless another child.

Suddenly it was clear! Yosef looked heavenward and thanked the Almighty Father for the witness this moment gave to his heart.

The business Yeshua's Father had sent Him to accomplish was not to argue the fine points of the Law with the learned rabbis in the Temple. Those religious hypocrites who lived in wealth and comfort, and who claimed the name and rank and privileges of Sons of the Covenant, broke the Ninth Commandment: While claiming to act in the name of God, they bore false witness against their neighbors and against the very nature and character of the God they claimed to serve.

Giving alms, they neglected to love the poor and the needy who cowered in their shadows. Walking in spiritual darkness, they purchased the light of the abandoned Sparrows of Jerusalem, two boys for a penny.

The Ninth Commandment declared, *You shall not bear false witness.*[70] Yet by rejecting love and compassion for others while proudly claiming to fulfill the Law of the Almighty, their actions bore false witness against the Truth declared in Scripture: *love your neighbor as yourself.*[71]

The Ninth Commandment was witness against them; they did not serve the business of God.

But as for Yeshua? *"Didn't you know I would be about my Father's business?"*

"You will call him Yeshua because He will save His people. . . ."[72]

Yosef understood then that Yeshua was called by His Father to live out true witness of God's nature. He could never be false to either God or man. The child in the manger had been born to seek and to find the lost and forgotten! Yeshua, both shepherd and lamb, had come to lead lambs like Jude home . . . home to safe pasture.

Yosef and Mary exchanged a glance of understanding.

Yeshua said, "Jude has a little sister too. Her name is Kerah. She lives in the orphanage." He nodded.

Mary asked the boy, "What do you think? You and Kerah . . . would you come home with us?"

Jude stepped into the shadow of Yeshua, who wrapped a protective arm around his shoulder. "I was lost," Jude said. "Everything lost from my life but his coat, which you gave to me. In the darkness I prayed that someone would love me enough to search for me . . . to bring me home. *YiSMaH!* Oh, Mother! And Kerah! How she longs for a mother to teach her . . . to sing her to sleep at night. " A look of wonder crossed his face. "I thought there was no one. But while you were searching everywhere for your son . . . he . . . found . . . me. And made me his brother."

Then He went down to Nazareth with them and was obedient to them. But His mother treasured all these things in her heart. And Yeshua grew in wisdom and stature, and in favor with God and men.

LUKE 2:51-52

Epilogue

The words of Mary and Yeshua's reunion that day are faithfully recorded in the Scriptures. Interestingly, Mary still called Him "child."

". . . why have you treated us like this? Here your father and I have been anxiously looking for you."[73]

The man of Israel replied, "Why did you have to search for me? Did you not know I would be here, attending to my Father's business?"

Bar mitzvah complete, Yeshua was no longer a child but counted among the men of Israel. He was also fully the age for apprenticeship in His father's business.

Nevertheless, from that day Yeshua returned home to Nazareth with His mother and Yosef, His brother, Jude, and their sister, Kerah. In the heavens that summer the planets Shabbatai and Ma'adim, having met in the Lion, moved back into the constellation of the Virgin. Yeshua was subject to His parents, fulfilling all righteousness.

Over the years of laughter and joy, Yeshua's coat was passed down through many other brothers and sisters who came to live at the house in Nazareth.

"You are my witnesses," declares the Lord,

"and My servant whom I have chosen,

that you may know and believe Me

and understand that I am He.

"Before Me no god was formed,

nor shall there be any after me.

I, I AM the Lord,

and besides Me there is no savior."

ISAIAH 43:10-11

Digging Deeper into
NINTH WITNESS

Dear Reader,

Have you ever wondered if God *really* cares about you? After all, if He did, wouldn't He intervene in your difficult circumstances? And what about all the evil in the world? Why do evil people seem to win, and honest folks get hurt? Sometimes life just doesn't seem fair. Justice is too long in coming.

If you've had these questions and thoughts, you're not alone.

In *Ninth Witness*, the Jews read the story of Esther, the queen who came into the limelight "for just such a time as this" (Esther 4:14). She and her uncle Mordechai were instrumental in the miraculous deliverance of the Jews of Persia from the clutches of the evil Haman, who wanted to annihilate them. (Interesting, isn't it, that throughout history other "Hamans" have arisen, including Haj Amin el-Husseini, the Grand Mufti of Jerusalem, who collaborated with Adolf Hitler during World War II to try again to annihilate the Jews? Yet a remnant always remains.) But now, in the first century, it seems that God has forgotten the people He created. No Esther, no Mordechai, has arisen to right the present wrongs. Is there no justice? No hope?

Jude has seen far too much suffering in his young life.

No wonder he longs to turn back the clock to when he, his mama, his papa, and his sister were all a happy family . . . before the barbarity of Roman rule shattered their lives.

Zachai, the most hated man in Jericho, has had a wake-up call because of his meeting with Yeshua of Nazareth. Now is his time to take action. He must right the wrongs he has done . . . and face those he has terribly hurt. Yeshua has shown him mercy, but will anyone else?

People like Rabbi Mazzar, Zachariah, Nakdimon, and Gamaliel wait and watch for justice to be done in the land of Israel. They are convinced God will provide, but hope seems so distant at times. Yet God's promises of His watchful care are evident all throughout the Scriptures.

Yosef and Mary are convinced that the Almighty has sheltered them for a reason. What plan might be unfolding in their lives? in Yeshua's life?

And, dear reader, what plan might be unfolding in your life?

If you are feeling discouraged, here's a secret we want you to know: Facts and Truth are not one and the same. The fact is, life *is* difficult; at times it can be overwhelming. The Truth? God never leaves us nor forsakes us. That Truth you can count on, in the midst of hard facts.

Following are six studies. You may wish to delve into them on your own or share them with a friend or a discussion group. They are designed to take you deeper into the answers to these questions:

- How can you hang on in the midst of hard circumstances?
- What if . . . your life were different?
- Why is it crucial for you to identify what facts are, what Truth is, and to know the difference?
- Why is mercy—receiving it, giving it—such a high calling?
- Can you *really* believe God's promises in Scripture?
- What might God be doing in your life?

What are you longing for? searching for? Why not come home, as Jude did, to Yeshua? In *Ninth Witness*, may the promised Messiah come alive to you . . . in more brilliance than ever before.

1 WAITING FOR JUSTICE

> These was no justice in the world—none at all.
> —P. 5

> Looking around the congregation, Rabbi Mazzar saw strained
> hopefulness on each face: Would the Almighty ever intervene again in
> Jewish affairs?
> —P. 7

If you could wave a magic wand and fix two things about the world, what
would you change and why?

_____

_____

_____

Have you ever wondered if God would intervene in your life—or in the
circumstances of those you love? If so, tell the story.

_____

_____

_____

Many people know the story of Queen Esther in the Bible. It's a most
satisfying story, filled with the excitement of a dastardly plot, a villain we can
love to hate, and two unassuming heroes who rescue an entire nation. Even

better, the villain is not only stopped in his tracks, he receives a swift and just punishment . . . the kind most of us, if we're honest, would like to see visited upon our enemies.

When the evil Haman plots to annihilate the Jews, he has no idea that he will end up dying on the very gallows he's constructing for his enemy. And all because of the courage of a young queen, who could have died for daring to approach the king without him requesting her, and the determination of her uncle, Mordechai, who chose to *act* once he heard about the plot rather than wait for someone else to change the situation.

In *Ninth Witness*, it's been almost five hundred years since the events recording in Esther took place. Once again, evil reigns. . . .

READ

Tonight a Roman governor ruled the land. Though the empire had held sway over Judea for close to a hundred years, now, for the first time, Rome ruled Jewish affairs directly, instead of through a puppet king. . . .

Herod's death, coming at the end of a string of murders, persecutions, and tortures, was acknowledged each year throughout Jewry. In the Galil they rejoiced quietly, for Antipas, son of the Butcher King, ruled here.

The rabbi shook his head sadly and peered out at the gathering darkness. Recent futile attempts to reestablish Jewish independence had failed miserably. After some initial success, including surprising the Roman garrison at Sepphoris, the Zealots had been defeated. Even now they were being hunted down. Like pinching out candle flames, the remaining pockets of Jewish resistance were being crushed.

All day today Roman legionaries, recruited from hereditary Jewish enemies like Idumeans and Samaritans, wielded hammers. They were not widening the Imperial highways or building another aqueduct or even repairing fortifications damaged in the revolt. They were crucifying the latest batch of captured rebels.

Though the executions were conducted along the main roads and not beside Nazareth's winding lane, the rhythmic thump of mallets, punctuated by anguished shrieks, echoed up and down the hillsides of the town.

The families would come to the synagogue tonight because it was their custom to do so. Mazzar would supervise the reading of Esther, because it was the right thing to do. What no one could instill in the occasion was any feeling of celebration. Where was the provision of the Almighty on this night? Where was there a Mordecai for this age? Where an Esther?

—P. 4

ASK

Imagine yourself in this scene—sitting in the synagogue on such a night, hearing the story of Esther and the rescue of the Jews while trying to close your ears to the shrieks of the masses of crucified Jews all around you. What thoughts would go through your mind?

_____

_____

_____

What questions would you have for God in such circumstances?

_____

_____

_____

READ

>*Justice is far from us. . . . We look for light, but all is darkness; for brightness, but we walk in deep shadows.*
>—Isaiah 59:9

ASK

When do you feel that justice is far from you? When have you desperately hoped to see light at the end of a long tunnel but seen only continued darkness?

_____

_____

_____

What has happened in your life since that time of walking in deep shadows?

_____

_____

_____

READ

Looking around the congregation, Rabbi Mazzar saw strained hopefulness on each face: Would the Almighty ever intervene again in Jewish affairs? Haman's plan to slaughter Jews had failed, yet just out of sight—around the bend, down the canyon—Jews were being slaughtered.

True, some of the crucified were brigands and bandits, but some were patriots, eager for Israel to live again.

The story had passed its climactic moment: Esther had triumphed; Haman was dealt with; the rest was a song of victory.

Mazzar's eye lighted on the screen of the gallery where the women and children sat. What had attracted his attention was the face of his student Yeshua. It was pressed into a gap in the lattice, eager to hear every word.

The cantor arrived at another Scripture portion to be spoken in chorus and the audience took up the refrain:

> *"Then Mordechai went out from the presence of the king in royal robes of blue and white, with a great golden crown and a robe of fine linen and purple, and the city of Susa shouted and rejoiced."*

Mazzar saw Yeshua's face beaming as He chanted . . . as if He were viewing the story as a present reality—not an oft-repeated legend, or a far-off promise . . . but a contemporary truth. . . .

The Jews had light and gladness and joy and honor.

—P. 7

ASK

At what point in the story did Rabbi Mazzar see Yeshua's face? Why do you think this timing is important?

_____

_____

_____

What do you think the sentence "The Jews had light and gladness and joy and honor" could mean?

_____

_____

_____

Do you tend to see the promises of Scripture as present realities or oft-repeated legends? Why? What in your life experience has led you to that conclusion?

_____

_____

_____

What would change in your life if you began to see the ancient promises as contemporary truths?

_____

_____

_____

READ

The Lord looked and was displeased
that there was no justice.
He saw that there was no one,
He was appalled that there was no one to intervene;
so His own arm worked salvation for Him,
and His own righteousness sustained Him. . . .
According to what they have done,
so will He repay
wrath to His enemies
and retribution to his foes.
—Isaiah 59:15-18

ASK

What does this Scripture passage say about God's response to the lack of justice?

_____

_____

_____

What will happen, in the long run, to evil people?

_____

_____

_____

WONDER . . .

Arise, shine, for your light has come,
  and the glory of the Lord rises upon you.
See, darkness covers the earth
  and thick darkness is over the peoples,
but the Lord rises upon you
and His glory appears over you.
Nations will come to your light,
and kings to the brightness of your dawn.
—Isaiah 60:1-3

How can you adjust your perspective as you wait for the Lord's justice?

_____

_____

_____

2 | WHAT IF . . . ?

What Jude knew for certain was that he was destined to now always be simply a witness—on the outside looking in. Never a part of a family or joy such as this. His life was just as it was. Not much of a life, but at least a life. His sister was safe and cared for. He had food and a place with the Jerusalem Sparrows. But he would always remember those moments in Mary's house . . . and wish life could be different. . . . What must it be like to live in a house like that in Nazareth? to have a mother and a father and a room of his own?

—PP. 17, 18

Have you ever played the "what if . . ." game?

- "What if I hadn't . . . ?"
- "What if he/she hadn't . . . ?"
- "What if that hadn't happened?"
- "What if I had been born in a different family? at a different time?"

When? What circumstances did you wish could be different?

_____

_____

_____

Looking back now, do you see any reason(s) for why that event happened to you or why you did what you did? What have you learned since then?

_____

_____

_____

Which of us hasn't played the "what if . . ." game sometime in life? Young Jude is no different from you or me. His circumstances aren't what he would have chosen either. He remembers back to a time when his mother was alive, when he and his family lived together in their own home, when food was warm and cooked with love . . . before the Romans killed his mother and hunted his father. How can he help longing for a return to such a peaceful life? Now Jude and his sister walk between the rows of executed Jews, looking for their father. Jude has seen many crucifixions in the nine years of his life. But now the crucifixion becomes personal—Jude finds his dying father among the victims.

READ

The old woman . . . squinted at the distorted features of a criminal tortured in the most prominent position at the junction of two highways. "Oh, where is he? Our champion? Judah of Galilee?"

The dying man's eyelid fluttered. The mouth contorted in a desperate attempt to speak.

Could it be?

Jude's head jerked up. His eyes widened with horror as he spotted an old scar on the victim's shinbone, now outlined with dried blood.

Grandmother cried, "Look, boy! Is that him?"

Jude clasped his sister's hand. Blossoms spilled from her fingers. She dropped to her knees to retrieve them from the dust.

The old woman declared with certainty, "Yes. It's him. Your father. He was the most important of the rebels. So they've executed him here, where everyone will see him."

Jude staggered and wailed. He reached out toward the twisted feet nailed to the post and shook his head violently. "Papa!" He stumbled, fell to hands and knees, then crawled to the side of the road.

Kerah, oblivious, picked up flowers one by one.

No! Please! Not Papa! Couldn't be! . . . Jude struggled to sit up, to look up. His father's eyes, clear for an instant, locked on his. Still here. Somehow aware of his children beyond the agony of the cross. . . .

Raising his gaze, Jude called, "Papa! Papa!"

The gore of days of suffering congealed on the wooden cross. Vultures circled slowly above them. There was no coming back.

"Oh, Papa! Don't die. Papa!"

Papa struggled to raise himself and draw a final breath to speak one word of comfort to his son. . . . A single cry of agony escaped his lips.

Kerah leapt to her feet and proudly extended her bouquet to Jude.

The body sagged forward, suspended by the spikes in grotesque surrender.

—PP. 18–19

ASK

If you were Jude, what thoughts and emotions would you experience as you watched your father die?

_____

_____

_____

What are the differences between Jude's reactions and Kerah's reactions to this scene? Explain.

_____

_____

_____

Which perspective—Jude's or Kerah's—is most like yours when difficult things happen in your life? Why?

_____

_____

_____

READ

Nudging a half empty rucksack with his toe, he spilled out its remaining contents. A single, shiny silver denarius bearing the image of Augustus Caesar gleamed in the dirt.

Jude whooped and snapped it up. "They left one behind! One is enough!" It lay in his palm. The rising sun glinted on Caesar's face. "Enough. Enough to get us to Yerushalayim if . . ."

Then his words faded at the realization that this single coin was all that remained of the blood money received for his father's life.

A wave of rage swept over him. His fist clamped down hard around the coin. With a shout he threw it away. Wavering a moment, he marked the place where the hated thing fell, then charged after it. Throwing himself to the ground, he clawed the dust until he found the coin.

"They killed Papa for this! For this!" Clutching it to his heart, he howled like a wounded dog and beat the ground.

—PP. 63–64

Jude considered the many ways it had been a good thing the children had not been welcomed into the warmth of the [Galilean rebels'] camp. And how fortuitous it was that their hiding place had not been found.

So, Jude thought, he had not needed a sword to avenge his father after all. Those who had betrayed Jude's father were dead now. Their blood money had been taken and their bodies left to rot in the open just like those of the men they had helped destroy. Corpses lay askew on the ground like dolls stuffed with straw. Mouths wide, and eyes frozen in horror, their expressions told Jude that in dying they had seen the demons rush in to take their souls.

Jude was glad for their terror. . . .

Staring fiercely at the wide, gaping eyes of a traitor, Jude murmured, "So, the Evil One lured you into his snare. In the end, you die too. You will not meet my father or your comrades in hell." . . .

Jude spoke aloud as if his father were in the burrow with them. "Papa, your true enemies are dead. Your true enemies who called you brother. It is a small thing, this stolen fire, but what warmed them now warms us. Providence and justice have saved our lives tonight. You must be watching over us." He stretched his hands to the warmth. "So, Papa. Yerushalayim, you said. Go there. Take Kerah there. I promise I will watch over her. We will find our way to Yerushalayim."

—PP. 60–61

ASK

What strong emotions does Jude experience when:

- he finds the silver denarius?
- he sees the dead traitors?
- he thinks of what his papa told him to do?

_____

_____

_____

Think about the times in your life when you have grieved. What role have these same emotions played in your own cycle of grief?

_____

_____

_____

READ

Jude could not remember the time when his father had owned an almond grove of his own. He only vaguely recalled his father's fight with the Roman mercenary in the street of Sepphoris.

The knife.

The blood.

The man dead on the pavement.

Jude only vaguely remembered them all running away. . . .

Mama refusing to leave Papa, even though she was pregnant.

Hiding in caves in the mountains overlooking the Jordan.

The night Kerah was born.

And the day Mama died by the sword of a Herodian soldier. . . . Kerah had not spoken a word since then. Before all that, what had their farm been like? Jude wished he could remember. Had there been lavender drying in the rafters? A stone wall around the garden? Washing drying in the sun while Mama sang and planted vegetables?

What would their lives have been like if only Papa had accepted the insults from the soldier? If he had not fought the man and won? Would they still own the almond grove outside of Sepphoris? Would Mama and Papa still be alive? . . .

Jude looked up and saw the stars winking on like candle flames. Were his mother and father now among the lights? In the southern sky the stars seemed to form the image of a cross rising on the horizon.

The image of Papa on the cross reared up in his mind. He closed his eyes tight and groaned. He tried not to think of it. Burying his face in the sleeve of the tunic, he pretended for a moment that Mary was his mother and that he lived in the white stone house in Nazareth. She set a place for him at the table and called him, "My son . . ."

What was that blessed family doing now as the darkness thickened? What would it be like to be always safe and warm and loved? to never wonder if a Roman gladius was drawn and poised to take your life? To never live in the shadow of a cross?

Jude's shoulders shook as he silently wept for the home of his imagination. "Mama, I can't remember now what your voice sounded like. Papa, I see you with blood spilling from your lips!"

—PP. 28–29

ASK
What changes did Jude long for?

_____

_____

_____

What images could Jude not get out of his mind?

_____

_____

_____

What images from your own circumstances do you struggle to forget? How do these past images affect your responses to what happens to you in the present?

_____

_____

_____

READ

Grandmother whispered, breaking his gloomy reverie. "Jude?"

He inhaled deeply. "I'm here."

"I didn't hear you . . . say your prayers tonight."

"I . . . said them to myself," he lied.

"You will need to pray, boy." She coughed, a hollow rattle from deep in her lungs. . . .

"I am dying, boy," she rasped. . . ."Jude . . . don't forget. . . . Be a good boy. . . . Remember to . . . say your prayers."

She fell silent. No matter how he begged, she would not answer him. . . .

The old woman . . . dying? How could Jude ever pray again if she died?

—PP. 40–41

Jude thought of Grandmother's admonishment: *"Remember to say your prayers."*

He had already forgotten the words. How could he know what to say to the Almighty? How could any human know what to say to He who was so high above the Sparrows that their small voices were lost in the vast gulf of creation?

—P. 140

He wished again that he knew how to pray. What to pray. He wished he believed Adonai could hear his words and love away the ache in his heart. But if his young life had taught him anything, it was that Adonai did not seem to notice the likes of him.

—PP. 137–138

ASK

When have you found it difficult to pray?

_____

_____

_____

When have you not known what to pray for?

_____

_____

_____

Do you believe that God notices the likes of you? Why or why not?

_____

_____

_____

READ

Just then Jude recognized the woman from Nazareth. The woman with the kind eyes who had fed him, clothed him, then sent him away with food and the lambskin coat he now wore. The woman whose simple home held the aroma of lavender; the woman whose compassion at his time of great need he would always remember. . . . Mary! Jude breathed in the lingering aroma of the lavender from the collar of the lambskin coat. The scent reminded him of the kindness of her embrace.

—P. 137

Kerah lay warm and comfortable, wrapped in the coat of the Nazarene boy and the woolen blanket. She opened her eyes and smiled back at Jude's indignation. "I am hungry."

He was unable to remain angry. The sound of her voice reminded him of Mama. What had happened to make Kerah speak again? She had only been managing to utter single words. His name. *Yes. No. Go. Hurry.*

Now here she was, actually speaking complete sentences and thinking clever thoughts like how to escape the tinsmith's prison! Perhaps the pilgrimage to Jerusalem had brought on this miraculous change in Jude's sister. He could not say what had caused this wondrous change to erupt from her mouth.

—P. 102

Turning round, he discovered he could not see the way out from the labyrinth. A sense of panic nearly overwhelmed him. The two stumbled forward a few dozen steps, only to find they had come to a dead end. A row of dark holes identified the homes of Gehenna's residents.

At Jude's feet lay an old man without legs. He peered up at Jude through a tangle of gray hair. "Boy! What is your name?"

Startled by the question, Jude cringed. "Sir, I am Jude. This is my sister, Kerah."

"My name is Sekhel Tov." . . .

Jude stammered, "We . . . my sister and I . . . we were looking for . . . something."

"You will not find it here," the creature wheezed. "Take her out."

"Where? How?"

"Look to the light." The old man pointed up at a patch of cloudy sky shining through the bridge. "There is an orphanage for girls. It is run by the charity of the school of Hillel. It is in the Street of the Weavers. Take your sister there to stay."

"And where shall I go afterwards? For myself?"

Sekhel Tov lowered his voice to a whisper. "You are no bigger than a Sparrow, boy. That has some meaning if you understand my words."

"Please, sir. No riddles for me now. I am too afraid to understand."

Sekhel Tov smiled. . . . "Leave your sister in the care of the good wives of Rabbi Hillel's talmidim. Then fly quickly to the quarry beneath Solomon's Temple. You must be the link. You must carry the light of the Rabbi among the Sparrows of Yerushalayim. . . . Ask the good wives of Hillel's shelter where the Jerusalem Sparrows roost. They will tell you the way." He raised a trembling hand to point over Jude's shoulder. "Take her now! Go quickly. Do not speak to anyone until you are out of this place."

—PP. 113–114

Children's laughter drifted over the high wall of the orphanage where Kerah was safe and happy.

"*YiSMaH.*" Jude spoke the word aloud as he leaned against the wall opposite the great gate. "He will rejoice."

Clearly there was rejoicing inside Jerusalem's haven for homeless girls.

—P. 139

ASK

How did God provide for Jude and Kerah in each of these circumstances?

- Through Mary of Nazareth
- In Kerah's speech/lack of speech
- Through Sekhel Tov, the beggar
- Through the girls' orphanage

_____

_____

_____

When you look back at your own difficult circumstances, how has God provided for you?

_____

_____

_____

WONDER . . .

The sun dipped below the horizon as Jude reached the verge of the almond orchard.

Shaqed, whispered the wind passing through the blossoms, "God is watching."

Jude felt safe and warm inside the coat. . . .

The fabric of his new tunic felt clean against his skin. He felt washed, as though he had bathed in a fresh stream.

—P. 28

As you become aware of God working in your life, how does your perspective change?

_____

_____

_____

Why not allow the Lord to wrap His safety and warmth around you like a coat? Why not let Him wash you in a fresh stream of His love?

3 | FACTS . . . OR TRUTH?

Never confuse facts with Truth! Regardless of a myriad of things that cannot be comprehended, trust in He Who Knows the End from before the Beginning. Look beyond the facts of this world by trusting in The One who held the universe in the palm of his hand.
Rabbi Mazzar, p. 32

What, to you, is a fact?

_____

_____

_____

What, to you, is truth?

_____

_____

_____

Can facts change? Can truth change? Why or why not? Give an example of a situation from your own life when *facts* and *the Truth* were very different things.

_____

_____

_____

READ

Perhaps it was time to speak again to his students of not confusing facts with Truth. The book of the Exodus taught as fact that the Israelites fleeing from Pharaoh were trapped between the pursuing Egyptian army and an uncrossable sea. The fact was, their situation was hopeless.

The Greater Truth was that the Almighty was perfectly capable not only of opening a way through the waters but of closing them over the heads of the enemies.

The fact was that the men hung on the crosses were dead, dead, dead.

The Greater Truth was that He Who Is Faithful was capable of raising them back to life again.

The fact was that the crucified had suffered horribly.

The Greater Truth was that HaShem committed Himself to keep account of suffering. Better to suffer a little while in this life than to fall into the hands of angry Elohim! . . .

When would The One come who could ascend the Mountain of the Lord in Jerusalem and cleanse the Temple once and for all? When? It seemed impossible against the entrenched power of Rome.

But the Almighty does not count time as men count time, Mazzar reminded himself. *Never confuse facts with Truth! Regardless of a myriad of things that cannot be comprehended, trust in He Who Knows the End from before the Beginning. Look beyond the facts of this world by trusting in The One who held the universe in the palm of his hand.*

"But a little help with our trusting," Mazzar muttered aloud, "a little reminder you are paying attention would also help, eh?"

—P. 32

ASK

What are the facts and truths in the passage above?

- Fact:

_____

- Truth:

_____

- Fact:

_____

- Truth:

_____

- Fact:

_____

- Truth:

_____

- Fact:

_____

- Truth:

_____

What do these facts and truths reveal about why we should trust God, even in the midst of circumstances we don't understand?

_____

_____

_____

READ

"Ezra didn't tell the priests to just read the Law. He told them to explain it."

[Shim'on's] comment came from so unexpected a source that the others turned and stared at him.

"Er . . . something I heard," Shim'on muttered.

"Well said, Shim'on," Yeshua praised. "But the issue wasn't, what does the Almighty want from people? It was, what does the Almighty like? What pleases him?"

"How can we know that?" Nicolas challenged.

"How about by looking around," Yeshua returned, gesturing at the field carpeted in greenery and studded with pinks and yellows and blues. "The

Almighty values beauty . . . that seems clear enough. He likes variety . . . He likes green a lot, but not only green, yes? . . . He likes orderliness, too," Yeshua added.

Shim'on waved his hand over the tangled thicket of grass and wildflowers. "What's orderly about that?" he argued.

Yeshua smiled. "Perhaps it's a matter of how you look at things. Take that purple flower there. How many petals to its blossoms?"

"Three," Beriah answered instantly, sensing this was a game he could win.

"And that yellow one just there?"

"Five!"

"The blue one here? No, Shim'on, you're looking too far out. Right here—beside the fence."

"Eight," Nicolas said hastily before Beriah finished counting.

"And the white ones over there with the yellow centers?"

Shim'on beat Nicolas and Beriah to the nearest clump of daisies while Yochanan contented himself with looking on from a distance.

"Thirteen?" Yeshua said before the others had returned with the same answer. "Knew that one already," He confessed.

"So?" Shim'on retorted. "We were talking about how the Almighty likes order. What's all this counting prove? They're all different numbers."

"Try thinking about them in order, from small to large."

Each face took on a different expression of study, from Yochanan's stare into the distant olive trees to Shim'on's tight-lipped concentration.

In the end it was Nicolas who replied, "I see it! Three and five make eight, and five and eight make thirteen! Each new pattern is the sum of the two that came before."

"Order, even where none seems to appear," Yeshua concluded. "The Almighty cherishes orderliness, even in the midst of variety, but the two ideas are not opposed to each other. Everything in creation sings together—a hymn to the name of The One who created it."

—PP. 116–117

ASK

What facts did Yeshua point out about the wildflowers?

_____

_____

_____

What do these facts reveal about The One who created them?

_____

_____

_____

How do the facts of your life sing a hymn to the Truth of The One who created you?

_____

_____

_____

READ

Above their heads a raven cawed in fear and flew away, pursued by a brave sparrow.

Grandmother caught Jude's gaze and somehow read his mind. "A brave little fellow . . . that sparrow is."

From the knoll, Jude observed the ensuing battle. The tiny bird protected its nest, diving on the black-winged menace again and again. "The raven is afraid."

"Remember him." Grandmother gasped the admonition. "Courage . . . little sparrow."

Jude nodded as the small warrior chased his enemy out of sight over the hill.

—P. 35

ASK

Why would a little sparrow chase away a larger bird?

_____

_____

_____

In what area(s) of your life do you need to be like that sparrow? Explain.

_____

_____

_____

WONDER . . .

> *I lift up my eyes to the hills—*
> *where does my help come from?*
> *My help comes from the Lord,*
> *the Maker of heaven and earth.*
> —PSALM 121:1-2

When you're tempted to confuse fact and Truth in your life, remember where your help comes from.

4 | A HEART OF MERCY

Do good, O Lord, to those who are good, and to those who are upright in their hearts!
—Psalm 125:4

How do you respond when someone "mighty" has fallen (a public leader is caught doing something illegal, a religious leader is disgraced, etc.)?

_____

_____

_____

When you see a poor person on the streets, how do you act toward that person? When you see a man, woman, or child who is disabled physically and/or mentally, what do you think? When you become aware of a lonely elderly neighbor, how do you respond?

_____

_____

_____

People had reason to hate Zachai. Not only did he collect taxes for the hated Romans, taking coins out of the pockets of the already poor to make them more destitute, he did it all with a superior, callous attitude. Then, in one night, everything about his life changed because he met Yeshua of Nazareth.

Then there's young Jude, who is without food, shelter, even warm clothes—all because of events not of his making or choosing. Worse, he has to care for his innocent, disabled sister, who doesn't seem to understand the evil in the world or the desperation of their circumstances.

Two people—at opposite ends of the spectrum—yet both are longing for acceptance, love, and mercy to be extended to them. Do you long for mercy too?

READ

Zachai sighed with contentment. Forgiven, fixed in his resolve to make restitution, eager to begin atoning for his sins against others, the once-most-hated man in Judea sat on the broad railing of the fountain. He leaned his back against a stone lion and began to make a mental list of what he must repay: a confiscated vineyard that had to be restored to its rightful owner; a slave, sold to satisfy a debt, who must be redeemed and set free . . . so many others.

Zachai was determined to fulfill his pledge to right every wrong he had done.

Dawn was only hours away. How dramatically Zachai's life had changed between yesterday's first light and now. Was it only yesterday the despised tax collector of Jericho had climbed the sukomore fig tree in order to catch a glimpse of the passing Prophet from Nazareth? Zachai had caught much more than he had bargained for. Yeshua had passed the synagogue, then stopped beneath the tree. Looking up, He had called Zachai by name: "Come down! I'm coming to your house today!"

And so Yeshua had shocked and angered the religious rulers of the city by entering the home of a publican. But Zachai's heart had been transformed from darkness to light, from sorrow to joy, from disgrace to honor.

Zachai felt truly happy for the first time in his life.

—PP. VII–VIII

ASK

If you were Zachai, what would you be thinking? feeling? Why?

_____

_____

_____

What steps was Zachai taking as a result of his encounter with Yeshua—and why?

_____

_____

_____

READ

Rabbinic law declared that if a Pharisee entered the gates of a publican's house he would become unclean. Yet for this meeting with Yeshua [the Jewish leaders] had come by night into defilement.

Zachai smiled ruefully at what deeds could be accomplished by night. "Ah, well. Don't hold it against them, God. They're only in my garden. Not technically beneath my roof, eh? The branches of the fig tree are the roof over their heads."

—PP. VIII–IX

Peniel, the man born blind, now sighted and among Yeshua's followers, raised his hand in greeting and approached the fountain with Yeshua's younger brother and His mother. Peniel saluted Zachai. "Shalom be with you."

"And also with you." Zachai held his hands palms up in greeting.

Yeshua's mother added, "May the name of Zachai of Jericho be blessed for his kindness to my son and all of us. May Zachai have peace at his going out and coming in."

Yeshua's younger brother, a short, swarthy man in his late twenties, scowled at Zachai as if he were an intruder instead of master of the estate.

—P. IX

Zachai inhaled deeply. "Until today I would have argued that Righteousness could not enter the gates of a publican like myself. Not in my home."

"We all heard what Yeshua said: 'Today _Yeshua_, Salvation, has come to your home, Zachai," Peniel countered. "As for seeing a vision of three Pharisees planted there beneath your fig tree, the part that might be mistaken for a Pharisee is only their outward bark."

—P. X

ASK

How did the following people respond to the "new" Zachai? Why do you think they responded the way they did?

- The three Jewish leaders
- Peniel
- Yeshua's mother
- Yeshua's younger brother

_____

_____

_____

If you had been among the crowd that night, how would you have responded?

_____

_____

_____

READ

Jude, all spindly arms and legs and wild, uncombed hair, trudged up the rutted road into Nazareth. He saw a woman watch his slow progress as she churned butter beneath the sukomore fig tree in front of the house.

Unwashed, ragged, and alone, he knew he had the look of grief and hunger and poverty about him. But Jude kept his jaw set and his eyes defiant as he neared the stone fence. He felt himself anger personified—the hatred of a Zealot living inside the body of a little boy.

The woman smiled at him and nodded. . . . She left her churn to gather in the washing that lay across the fence. Clasping the clean, dry, boy-sized tunic, she folded it over her arm and approached the gate as he drew near. "Shalom!" she greeted him.

Her voice startled him. He heard her clearly but did not respond. His pace faltered and slowed. Then, as if she were a menacing dog, he moved to the center of the road.

She tried again. "Are you hungry?"

He stopped and stared down at his feet. Both hands went to his belly. *Hungry. Yes.* That was a question the woman did not need to repeat.

She stepped aside, opening the path to the house for him. "Come on, then. And welcome. There's plenty for you to eat."

He hesitated, then nodded. Placing two fingers over his lips, he gave the beggar's sign that he was mute, then showed her a coin to prove he could pay for food.

"A coin. You're not a beggar."

He shook his head emphatically from side to side. Not a beggar! He could and would pay.

"Where is your family?"

Jude shrugged. His eyes brimmed.

"Your mother?"

He shrugged.

"Your father?"

He could feel his lower lip trembling as the facade of toughness dissolved. Involuntarily he looked away across the pink cloud of almond orchards, beyond which Roman crosses bloomed.

So, his secret was known in an instant. He was the proud child of a fallen Zealot. Yes. But he still could not speak out in the open. Someone might hear him. Someone might see them talking together and ask what was said. The woman seemed to comprehend this unspoken need for caution.

She led the way to the house. Removing her shoes beside the door, the woman offered him water and the two washed their feet. He imitated her actions, leaving the basin black with mud.

Touching the mezuzah on the doorpost as she entered, she blessed her guest: "May Adonai bless your going out and your coming in. . . ."

A cauldron of lentil soup simmered over the fire. Lavender dried in the rafters, filling the tidy space with a clean, welcoming aroma. Loaves of bread cooled on the window ledge. At the sight of such wholesome ordinariness, Jude's hard edge softened into wild desperation and longing.

The woman put her hand on Jude's head. "What is your name?"

He blurted, "Jude. But I'm not supposed to tell!" Then he began to cry. "Not . . . supposed to speak."

"I won't tell." She folded him into her arms. Like a mother, she held him close until his sobs subsided. "Jude. A good strong name."

"I wasn't supposed to . . . speak. It was the plan. Just buy bread and get back."

"You're not traveling alone?"

"Yes. I mean . . . no! I mean . . . please . . . I'm not supposed to . . ."

"I see. Then no more questions, Jude. So sit. Eat." She poured a bowl of soup and made him sit in front of the fire. Tearing a loaf in half, she put a dollop of fresh butter on it and slid it across to the boy.

As he slurped down his meal, she packed a leather satchel with bread and cheese and dried figs. Enough provisions to last one person a few days but not so much that he would have difficulty carrying it back.

Watching her every move, Jude saw her frown at his filthy, ragged tunic, then fetch clean clothes from a chest. Scraping the bowl with a crust of bread to get every last drop, Jude finished the stew and held out his bowl for more. The woman filled it twice more before sending him to change into the boy's clothes.

She stood watch in the doorway as if half afraid a troop of Romans would ride up the highway in search of fugitives. . . .

The boy expected the woman to ask how many of their band had survived the attack. And how many were in hiding? Where would they go now?

But she asked nothing. Jude was grateful, because he knew he would have told her . . . everything. . . .

He held out his coin.

She refused it with a single shake of her head. "Almost dark. It will be cold tonight in the Galil."

"No one will see me."

"I have something for you." She returned to the trunk and took out a fleece-lined coat made of lambskin. "My son wore this when he was your age. He has outgrown it. I'm sure he would want you to have it."

Jude had never seen such a fine coat. The leather was tanned to withstand moisture. The inside fleece was golden and soft. . . . Jude embraced the coat, buying his face in the wool. It smelled of lavender, like the house. "I . . . will. I mean . . . thank you. And your son. A thousand times."

"I know we will meet again."

He felt foolish and ungrateful. He had taken everything and had never even asked her name. "What are you called?" He wavered in the doorway, leaning against one doorpost as he donned his shoes.

"Mary."

"Shalom, Mary. Maybe . . . someday I'll come back."

"You will be most welcome. Shalom. Adonai go with you." She embraced him and caressed his cheek.

—PP. 23–26

ASK

List the many ways in which this woman of Nazareth, Mary (revealed later in the story as Yeshua's mother), showed mercy to the orphan Jude.

_____

_____

_____

How did Mary allow Jude to keep his pride intact while extending mercy to him? What details did she ask for—and not ask for? Why?

_____

_____

_____

READ

"She looks sick." The innkeeper of Nain spat and wiped his mouth with the back of his hand as he eyed Grandmother. "Gray as that stone wall she be. Ain't goin' to die are ye, old woman?" . . .

Grandmother pulled herself erect and managed a scowl, though she did look terribly ill to Jude. "I'll be here long after ye're gone!"

The innkeeper looked doubtful. "Aye. If y' die, ye'll be here 'til Judgment Day. Someone dies here, it'll be bad for business. . . . Ye can pay? . . . Lemme see your money first."

Jude produced a denarius. The landlord's eyes brightened. He plucked the coin from Jude's fingers.

"I got a room." The landlord jerked his thumb toward the opening of a tiny cubicle at the end of a row of curtains along a shabby portico. Shrieks of laughter and a coarse oath came from one of the nearby alcoves. "It'll suit an old woman and two kids. One denarius tonight. Water there in the well for washin'. Bread in the mornin'."

—P. 36

The landlord locked Jude and Kerah in the room with the body lest the lodgers see them cry and know the old woman had died. *Unclean* was a word religious Jews proclaimed loud enough when someone died inside a house.

Grinning, pale, and blinking rapidly, he sought to conceal the death of the aged lodger from his other guests. He wrung his hands, willing the crowd of pilgrims to depart so he could deal with the human refuse and change the straw. . . .

"What am I supposed to do now?" The landlord grasped the neck of Jude's tunic and gave him a shake. "I told you! I said she was too sick to stay. She swore she wouldn't die. Now this! . . . Now what am I to do? Eh? Call the rabbi? Say *kaddish*? He hates me enough as it is. He'll put me out of business over this. Unclean, he'll say. Some'll blame it on the plague and my reputation will be ruined!'

—P. 43–44

"Come on, boy!" Pergamon the slave glowered and snapped at Jude. "Hurry, before I beat you!" He led the burdened donkey toward the back gate—the rubbish gate—lest anyone see. . . .

"Maybe your family like to say *kaddish*. Family maybe pays if we dig a grave in a nicer place than the rubbish heap, eh? . . . You two got no family? Two children. No family at all? No one knowing you gone?"

A glint shone in the man's eye, warning Jude of danger. The slave of a caravansary would know well enough the price of slaves. What were two children worth to the passing Arab drover? How easy it would be to sell two orphaned children into servitude!

—PP. 45–46

In the darkness of their shelter, the two children huddled together, sharing the fleece coat, borrowing one another's warmth as the temperature continued to plummet. . . .

What would be the harm if Jude snuck into their camp and warmed himself for a few minutes? They would welcome him, would they not? He was the son of the rebel leader, after all. They had followed his father in war against the Roman garrison in the Galil and fought beside him when the rebel outpost was discovered and attacked. Would they not honor Jude, son of Judah the Galilean Zealot?

Gruff voices interrupted his reverie. . . .

"The boy and his sister. Simpleminded girl."

"Recognized 'em right off as belongin' to Judah. In spite of the layer of dirt. I says to myself when I sees 'em . . . them two are Judah's brats, all right."

"Why'd you send them away?"

"Didn't think of it. Not until later. Then the idea come to me sudden-like."

"Hostages."

Jude stiffened with fear as their plot unfolded.

"Aye. Roman garrison might take the brats of Judah of Galilee in exchange for . . . somethin'."

"Money."

"We got plenty for pointin' out where the Zealots was hidin' out."

"Always use more."

"Hostages. Now that's worth a few denarii."

"It's done among the highborn all the time."

"But the Romans might just as well kill them. They're just kids. Ain't highborn."

"Even so. We hand 'em over. A gesture of goodwill to the new governor, y' might say. Demonstration of our loyalty."

—PP. 52–53

ASK

What are the motives of the following people for taking in, helping, or finding Jude and Kerah?

- The landlord
- Pergamon
- The rebels

_____

_____

_____

Contrast the motives of these people with the actions of Mary. Who had a heart of mercy, and who did not—and how can you tell?

_____

_____

_____

READ

Jude sat a distance from Kerah beneath the outcropping of rock. . . .

"Oh, Kerah! Don't . . ." He did not finish the thought. He wanted to ask her not to leave him alone, but he had no right to keep her alive any longer.

Jude closed his eyes, not wanting to see her suffering. . . .

If only Kerah would open her eyes and look at him. If only he could have some hope that she would live. His empty stomach felt as if it would claw a hole in his backbone. He needed food, but he dared not leave her to forage. What if she awakened and he was not there? What if he came back and found she had tried to find him and collapsed in the rain?

"Papa," Jude said quietly, "I failed. She's dying, Papa. Soon enough she'll fly away to be with you." . . .

Jude wondered what he had to live for. First Mama. Then Papa. Now Kerah.

Jude would be alone.

"Oh, you! God . . . God of Israel. Take me instead. She is so innocent. She don't know anything. She don't even really understand she's not supposed to suffer. Please God, take me!"

Jude knew this was a selfish prayer. The God would never answer such a prayer. Better Kerah fly away and leave Jude down here to suffer. She could not take care of herself. She could not so much as find her next meal.

He sighed and tucked his head against his knees. "All right, then. Take her. But don't leave me long behind."

PP. 81–82

How long had Jude and Kerah huddled in the cave? Jude had lost count of the hours . . . or was it days? Still, Kerah clung to life.

Would Kerah die before morning?

Jude, wrapped snuggly in his new coat, observed her from the opposite side of the fire pit, afraid to go closer; afraid to share his warmth with her.

She shuddered and sighed in misery. Not even the warmth of the blaze seemed to help. Her clothes were damp and caked with filth.

How to help? If Grandmother were here, she would know what to do. Jude tucked his chin deeper into the collar of the shepherd's coat and inhaled the clean fragrance. Visions of dried bundles of lavender in the rafters of the Nazarene house came to his mind. The gentle face of the woman there seemed to smile back at him, urging him to do something for Kerah. He fingered the cuffs and remembered how much it had meant to him to receive such a gift. It had given him a will to live. Would such a gift give Kerah hope as well? If he put his new coat on Kerah, perhaps she could get warm.

In an impulse of pity he wrapped her in the fleece covering of the boy from Nazareth. The size of it swallowed her up, covering her chin to the sole of her foot.

"Kerah! Live!" He towered over her, expecting some miracle in that instant. But nothing changed.

He plunked down to watch and wait. Her frail form heaved, shuddering with each exhale.

Soon it would be over. Such suffering must end! And then what would he do? Here in the wilderness without a spade to dig a hole, how would he bury her?

Now he regretted giving her his coat. He had nothing to keep himself warm. Surely his beautiful new coat would be Kerah's shroud.

How to pray? What to say as Kerah lay dying?

Jude whispered, "Kerah. I've not been a very good brother to you. Oh . . . Kerah! If you will only live!"

But this was not a prayer. He was begging her; begging her to get well so he would not be alone. She could not understand his entreaty.

He tried again. "Adonai . . . if only . . . sir, if you will let my sister live. Let her get well . . ."

If only what? What use was it to bargain? Jude had nothing of value to offer to the great Eternal One God of Israel in exchange for his sister's life.

"Sir . . . I will . . . do whatever you ask of me . . . if only you would let my little sister live. . . ."

—PP. 84–85

A shadow fell over Jude, blocking the light.

Jude's eyes snapped open. He gasped.

Kerah stood, smiling, above him. Morning light framed her like a halo. The sleeves of the Nazarene's coat hung below her hands. Was she an angel?

"Kerah?" he asked. "Are you dead?"

She put a hand to her rumbling stomach.

No. Jude was fairly certain the stomachs of angelic beings did not growl. Kerah was not dead. She was alive. She was awake.

And she was hungry.

—P. 85

[Jude] held Kerah's hand and walked her to the imposing front gate of the orphanage. The squeals and laughter of girls drifted over the high wall.

Kerah smiled as though imagining other children and an afternoon of play in such a grand courtyard.

"You'll be safe here." Jude frowned and tried not to show his emotion.

"But you? Jude?"

"You heard the cripple. Only girls here. I am to be a Sparrow in the charity of the School of Rabbi Shammai."

Kerah spotted a flock of sparrows flying above their heads. Two of the little birds lit on the top of the compound wall. She sighed. "You'll fly here to visit me?"

"If they let me."

"Then you'll sit on the wall so I can see you?"

He banged on the wooden gate with his fist. "Yes. I can do that easy enough."

His promise satisfied her. . . .

He kissed his sister and bade her farewell with some relief. He could take care of himself well enough now that the burden of worry over Kerah was lifted.

—PP. 117, 119

ASK

How do Jude's emotions change during the story, as evidenced in these passages?

_____

_____

_____

How did Mary's heart of mercy toward Jude influence Jude's actions toward Kerah?

_____

_____

_____

In what way(s) can you show a heart of mercy toward others?

_____

_____

_____

In what situation(s) do you wish to have a heart of mercy extended to you?

_____

_____

_____

WONDER . . .
Do you long to be shown mercy?

Rabbi Mazzar explained how . . . the Spirit-inspired Word convicts a sinner of the presence of evil in his life. Yet, once aware of his guilt, at that same moment he may recall that a sacrifice has already been made. . . . And if he repents, turns from his sin and confesses his guilt, then he is, at that moment, cleansed and restored to fellowship with the Almighty. . . .

"But it is all by the *Chesed*, the Mercy of the Almighty," he said. "Not because of good works, for no one is righteous enough for that."
   —P. 135

Why not allow Yeshua, Salvation, to come into your home and extend mercy to you—and give you a heart of mercy toward others?

5 | A TIME TO BE WATCHFUL

"A time to be watchful," Mazzar murmured to himself. . . . "*Shaqad . . . watchful. . . . The Almighty is here, though you may not see Him. . . . His promises are forever. His promises are true and righteous altogether. . . . But how very hard it is to see past the suffering sometimes.*
—PP. 39, 31–32

Has the beauty of creation ever made you marvel and think about the Creator? Tell the story.

_____

_____

_____

Do you believe that God can reveal His Truth through signs in the heavens? Why or why not?

_____

_____

_____

Just take a look in any grocery store and you'll see that the tabloid section trumpets the claim that astrology can reveal truth about your life. But astrology—the belief that cosmic forces affect our lives, for good or ill—and the revelation of God's truth about Himself and creation are two entirely different matters. Since God is the Creator of the universe, does it not make sense that He would use His creation to unveil more about Himself and His promises?

READ

The full moon rose in the constellation of The Virgin. Its bright gleam illuminated a colorless landscape. It created a ring in the sky from which all the other nearby lights, save The Lord of the Sabbath, were banished.

The reading of Esther proceeded as planned. Despite the unavoidably somber tone of the evening, the Scripture portions designed to be spoken in unison by the assembly and the roaring and hissing that accompanied each mention of the villain Haman's name were louder than Rabbi Mazzar had ever heard. . . .

Mazzar turned to look out the window of the synagogue. A frown of surprise added to the wrinkles on his lined face. A shadow crept across the moon . . . but there were no clouds in the sky.

By the time the cantor sang, *"The Jews struck all their enemies with the sword, killing and destroying them,"* others in the assembly also noticed the celestial event.

It was impossible to miss: The eclipse was turning the moon to blood.

"Exactly what occurred just before the death of Herod eleven years ago," Mazzar murmured aloud.

—PP. 6, 8

Elisheba asked, "What does it mean, Husband?"

Zachariah remained silent as recollections of other such celestial events flipped through his mind. Days and dates and times, all tangled up with prophecies, and the rising and falling of the great men of the world. "Remember . . . we saw this very sight before the death of old Herod the Butcher King."

Elisheba nodded and grunted. "And now his evil son—twin soul, they say—Archelaus . . ."

". . . has fallen." Zachariah completed her sentence.

"But Papa," Yochanan asked, his voice cracking with the change to manhood, "we knew this. What is this sight? And on the night of Purim too?" . . .

Zachariah's eyes snapped open as the penumbra began to slide from the face of the moon. "It means . . . the end of all as we have known it . . . is near, my dear. He who shall oppose them all is among us. . . ."

The tint of crimson moved slowly from the face of the moon. At last the bright orb stood directly over the place where the city of David was planted.

—PP. 12–13

Glimpsed through the almond's boughs was the pale yellow wandering star known to the Gentiles as Saturn and to Hebrew speakers as Shabbatai, The Lord of the Sabbath. The moon's glare made it impossible to see details this night, but for several previous months Shabbatai had been rising away from the constellation of The Virgin, emerging from her nurturing grasp. In the months ahead it appeared that The Lord of the Sabbath would join Ma'Adim, The Adam, reddish-hued Mars, within the figure of The Lion of Judah.

A time to be watchful indeed!

—P. 39

ASK

What connection do Zachariah and Rabbi Mazzar make between the current Purim celebration and the death of Herod the Butcher King? Why would this make such a big impact on them and on the Jews who are hearing the story of Esther?

_____

_____

_____

Whom do you think "He who shall oppose them all" is? Do you believe that He was among the people of that day? Why or why not?

_____

_____

_____

What do you think the sign of The Lord of the Sabbath rising away from The Virgin and moving to within The Lion of Judah means? What could this foretell about a coming time of change?

_____

_____

_____

READ

High, icy streaks of cloud flowed across the heavens from the direction of Mount Hermon. The moon, long since out of its eclipse, now bored a yellow-tinged hole through the curtain of vapors overhead. The Lord of the Sabbath kept close company with it. The star of The Virgin's heart, The Star of Atonement, winked fitfully nearby. . . .

"Tonight's moon . . . so dark, so red . . . it means something, doesn't it?"

"Perhaps," Yosef said, noncommittally, hoping to spare her his own anxiety.

"And it is in the sign of The Virgin . . . isn't that right? You taught me so much about the wonders of the sky."

For the first time in his married life Yosef regretted having shared his fascination with the stars with Mary. This remorse was reinforced by the next words she spoke. "I can't help but remember what Old Simeon said to me: 'And a sword will pierce your heart as well.' Is that what we saw tonight, Yosef? Blood on the heart of the virgin?" . . .

As Yosef escorted Mary down the steps a new constellation rising in the east caught his eye—one he was grateful Mary appeared not to notice.

It was the sign of the swan winging upwards . . . the form of a cross splayed over the darkest part of the sky.

—PP. 14–15

ASK

What responses do Yosef and Mary have to the wonders of the sky?

_____

_____

_____

Why would Yosef worry about the sign of the swan?

_____

_____

_____

_____

READ

Just now the moon blazed in at the window. Its cheerful brilliance only
served to emphasize the shadows on the Holy City and its would-be king.
Antipas had heard excited reports about an eclipse of the moon during the
Purim festivities, but he had not seen it himself. He told himself he had
no interest in omens and such. Old Herod, his father, had spent way too
much time and energy worrying about such things. Everything in life had
a practical—usually political—explanation. Once understood, the only
questions remaining were what outcome was most desirable, what action
was more expedient, and by what means was the result most to Antipas'
advantage.

Take the numerous slaughters committed by Papa Herod. In the end
he was still dead, most of his sons were dead, and his dream of a dynasty
was practically dead. And Augustus, who had once called Herod "friend,"
so distrusted all things Jewish that independence was more a remote dream
than ever.

So much for Herod the Butcher's attempt to eliminate all rivals,
real and imaginary. The midnight massacre of babies in Beth-lehem had
accomplished no more than to make Herod the most reviled ruler since
Pharaoh treated Jewish babies the same way more than a thousand years
earlier.

Had it been a night like this? Antipas could not recall. There was
something about a sign in the sky . . . a mystic star . . . foreign soothsayers
talking nonsense about a newborn Jewish king.

Antipas considered that thought for a moment. There had never been
any proof that the murdered children had been special. Once dead, all babies
were much the same.

But what if the Butcher's extreme strategy had failed? What if there *was*
such a child . . . a rallying point for fanatical Jews to gather around? What if
he had survived?

Antipas squinted at where Mars, the Roman god of war, hovered just outside the moon's glare, beneath the outline of The Lion. His pudgy lips moved in and out with calculations. How old would such a phantom menace be? About thirteen, if Antipas' headache-plagued memory served.

A man, or almost one.

Perhaps ripe to be proclaimed, announced to the nation as the rightful heir to the throne of David.

Antipas snorted and a fit of wheezing seized him.

There was a Roman in David's capital at the moment, and David's throne was held hostage to the servility of the Jews.

Antipas formed a new resolve. If Rome could ever be dislodged from Judea—and the vision, while remote, was never far from Antipas' thinking—no one except the rightful heir, Antipas himself, would ever occupy David's throne. There would only be one king of the Jews, no matter what the cost, and it would never be some religious madman born to *am ha aretz* in a smelly village like Beth-lehem.

—PP. 94–95

What about that twelve- or thirteen-year-old rumor of a miraculous child . . . or was it two children?

A cross shape of stars stood perfectly upright on the southern horizon. The vertical line of the figure drew Antipas' eyes upward. Directly above the cross, the same vertical line pierced the heart of the figure called The Virgin.

Antipas had heard the prophecy; he knew the rumors. All nonsense, of course. But it was not important whether Antipas believed them. What if the Zealots used the same old Jewish desire for a divine king to fan the flames of rebellion?

A cross loomed large for the mythical child of the virgin, or for any child who pretended to be king without Rome's permission.

The question was, how soon might that child reappear?

It was time to restore his father's network of spies.

Thirteen years? The child, if indeed he still lived, might be in Jerusalem this year. The imposter might even have journeyed to the Holy City to celebrate his coming of age. He might be proclaimed as the true prince at a time when hundreds of thousands of potential supporters were already in Jerusalem.

Antipas would see what more he could learn—and quickly.

—PP. 140–141

ASK

Does Antipas believe in signs and omens? Why or why not? How does he act (or not act) on that belief?

_____

_____

_____

What is his response to these signs in the sky?

- the eclipse
- Mars and The Lion of Judah
- the cross shape of stars

_____

_____

_____

What were the long-term results of old Herod's slaughter of the children of Beth-lehem?

_____

_____

_____

READ

At the meeting of two roads hung the Zealot chief, Judah the Galilean. Just as the Romans displayed his torment as an example, so the men of the Galil wanted to remove his body first.

Above him in the air and perching on boulders beside the cross were the ravens . . . like eager demons.

Yeshua struck the air with the back of His hand in a gesture of command. *Be gone from here!*

The scavenging flock took flight, winging off toward the south.

—P. 27

Yosef volunteered that he and Yeshua would retrieve Judah's body. Planting the feet of the ladder firmly in the dusty soil, he was ready to ascend before Yeshua spoke.

"Let me go. I'll go. I knew this man, Papa. I met him once in Sepphoris before the revolt. He was always sad, I think. Now his children are alone. Let me do this for him and for them."

Yosef studied the boy. The carpenter read firm resolve in Yeshua's gold-flecked eyes, saw determination in the set of the jaw and the muscular shoulders. . . .

Yeshua of Nazareth rose past the pierced feet, the tortured limbs, and the slumping chest till he drew near the agonized features. . . .

A single bird, a sparrow, remained on the beam beside Judah's outstretched clawlike right hand. It spoke softly as Yeshua arranged the rope.

With Yosef and another man grasping the ends of the rope, Yeshua worked at freeing the right hand from the piercing nail.

When it was clear He could not loosen the clinched nail that went all the way through flesh and wood, He used the pincers to clip off the head of the spike protruding from Judah's crushed palm.

It took all the boy's strength, working from what was an awkward position, but the iron parted finally with a snap. Yeshua gently touched the dead man's hand, palm to palm, as if apologizing for causing him pain.

To Yosef, gazing up from below, it seemed the boy measured His own hand against the crucified fingers. The image made him shudder and caused the world to spin.

With a yank on the wrist, Judah's right arm sprang free of the nail. Even though Yosef and the other helper were ready for the weight, the sudden movement allowed the arm to drop, falling across Yeshua's shoulder in an embrace.

And the bird spoke softly to Yeshua alone.

—PP. 27–28

Yeshua looked up at Yosef's approach. "It's time," the boy said matter-of-factly.

Yochanan's face was grim, Yeshua's set with focused determination. It was the same visage that Yosef had noticed Yeshua used with every difficult emotional situation.

The lamb did not need to be dragged or even led. It trotted ahead of Yeshua as if going eagerly.

Lambs were always chosen at least four days ahead of the feast and kept as pets before being slain, but this time was harder than ever. Grief was important to a full understanding of the holy day. Everyone had to understand Passover had only been accomplished at a great price.

Only the death of the Egyptian firstborn had set Israel free; only the lamb's blood on the doorposts had kept the firstborn of Israel safe that night. A sacrifice was necessary. The depth of the sacrifice could not be appreciated without a personal sense of the cost.

Now Jews from all over the world were going up to the place where the Almighty had demanded that Abraham sacrifice his only son, then had provided a substitute at the last moment. The concept of a substitute sacrifice was deeply engrained in all Jewish belief.

—P. 149

What could the signs in these three passages mean?

- Yeshua banishing the ravens
- Yeshua measuring His hand against the crucified Judah's hand
- the sparrow
- the lamb eagerly moving toward sacrifice

_____

_____

_____

How do these signs deepen your understanding of Yeshua—who He was and why He was sent to earth?

_____

_____

_____

READ

"YiSMaH speaks to you of the day when MaShiYaH will come for you! He will search for you like a shepherd. He will be the Elder Brother who will protect you. In the day Messiah finds you, then you will rejoice! And this is your reward!" . . .

"Where can we find him?" Jude asked [Rabbi Mazzar], gazing at the flickering flame of his torch as they came at last to the rabbi's house.

The old man fished pennies from his money pouch and counted out the treasure into each boy's open palm. "We will not find him, I think . . . but rather, the Son of David will come here to find us. Wait for him! Look for him! For the darkness is so dark now that he must surely come soon! . . ."

But when will the Son of David come? Jude wondered. *If only he would find me soon!*

—PP. 132–133

ASK

Do you, like Jude, long for the Messiah to come? In what way(s) do you long for Him to search for you like a shepherd? protect you like an elder brother?

_____

_____

_____

_____

What can you do in the meanwhile, as you wait for Him to come?

_____

_____

_____

_____

_____

READ

"It says the Lord called to Mosheh from the Tent of Meeting and told Mosheh to give these instructions to the people. Why didn't HaShem just give the instructions himself?"

Abiram the Goatherd suggested, "Because being the one chosen to relay the message increased Mosheh's authority?"

Mazzar stroked his beard thoughtfully. "This is a good answer. Anything else?"

No others seemed inclined to speak, so Yosef noted, "Because no one else could hear HaShem's voice?"

"Ah!" Mazzar concurred, smiling. "So say some of the sages. Not that HaShem whispered or spoke in an unknown language, but perhaps only Mosheh heard because . . . only Mosheh was listening. See what the psalmist says: *For He is our God, and we are the people of His pasture, and the sheep of His hand. Today, if you hear His voice, do not harden your hearts . . . .* So we *can* hear his voice, but we do not always chose to do so."

"And how do we hear the voice of the Almighty?" demanded Abiram, perhaps emboldened by the shepherd imagery of the psalm.

"It is said the Almighty has written his word in Torah, in the wonders of nature, and on the hearts of those who seek him."

—PP. 73–74

The old rabbi clucked his tongue. "YiSMaH, you say? Eh? Only one small word? Nay! YiSMaH is much more than that! It is the mystery of all the ages. It is the blessing the Almighty One promised to our Father Avraham! Do you not know what else the four letters of YiSMaH spell?"

Jude cocked his head at the mystery. "Tell us. We don't want another penny. Just the answer!"

The rabbi cast his rheumy eyes heavenward. "Those same letters point to the One who is coming to reign as King in Yerushalayim! Rearrange the letters of Yismah, and you have the reason we will rejoice! Mem, Sheen, Yod, Heh . . . can you say the word now, boy? For all the treasure of heaven and earth is yours when you call that name!"

Jude skipped and shouted the meaning. "MaShiYah! Messiah! The Anointed One!"

—P. 132

ASK

In what way(s) are you preparing for the Lord's coming? Through listening for the Lord's voice? reading His Word? prayer? watching His signs in nature? Explain.

_____

_____

_____

Do you believe that all the treasure of heaven and earth is yours when you call on the name of Messiah? Why or why not?

_____

_____

_____

WONDER . . .

> The Lord watches over you—
>   the Lord is your shade at your right hand;
>   the sun will not harm you by day,
>   nor the moon by night.
>
> The Lord will keep you from all harm—
>   He will watch over your life;
>   the Lord will watch over your coming and going
>   both now and forevermore.
>   —PSALM 121:5-8

It is time to be watchful, indeed!

6 | SHELTERED BY THE ALMIGHTY

"The Almighty has kept us safe, hasn't he? . . . He has never failed to keep us sheltered, eh?"
—YOSEF TO MARY, P. 15

When you hear the word *shelter,* what images arise in your mind?

_____

_____

_____

When in your life have you felt sheltered? What were the circumstances? Who were you with? Why did that event make you feel safe?

_____

_____

_____

Who of us doesn't long for shelter from the storms that so often seem to rage around us? Mary and Yosef had experienced the storms of life. The beautiful picture of the crèche that we often see and think of at Christmastime is only one snapshot of their lives (although a very important one). Their faith in God was not an easy faith, because their life was far from easy. They had wrestled with deep questions, faced the gossip of neighbors, undergone a harrowing journey while Mary was pregnant, experienced great joy in Yeshua's birth, escaped from Herod's soldiers, and, finally, returned to their home after the death of the wicked Herod, who had slaughtered so many innocent children.

Even more, disgrace had somehow become honor in their lives. How did such a thing happen?

READ

And the child grew and became strong; He was filled with wisdom, and the grace of God was upon Him.
—LUKE 2:40

What a contrast this life of Yeshua was now, compared to the gloomy expectations Rabbi Mazzar had when he'd first learned Yeshua's mother, Mary, was pregnant while still only bethrothed to Yosef. The dark thoughts and gossip of the villagers of Nazareth had been turned to light by Yeshua's kindness as He was growing up. The sorrow of His grandparents had been transformed to gladness and joy in the presence of Yeshua's laughter. The disgrace predicted for Mary had instead become honor through the virtue and wisdom of her son.

It seemed like few even remembered now the questions that had swirled around Yeshua's conception. The villagers simply accepted Him as one of them.
—PP. 7–8

ASK

What made Yeshua unique as a child?

_____

_____

_____

_____

What happened, over the years, to the gossip and disgrace that Mary and
Yosef suffered?

_____

_____

_____

What does this say to you about taking the long view when you face the barb
of gossip?

_____

_____

_____

READ

Take Yeshua back to Jerusalem, that hotbed of political turmoil and
religious intrigue? The last twelve years had all been about living quietly . . .
protecting Mary and Yeshua . . . establishing a normal life in Nazareth . . .
avoiding the attentions of all forms of authority, civil or religious.

Casting his thoughts back across the intervening time, Yosef shivered.
Only a divine warning had set the family on the road out of Beth-lehem,
mere steps ahead of Herod's murderers. Nor had that angelic alert prevented
the massacre of all the other boy babies in Beth-lehem.

That horrifying event, along with Herod's other atrocities, was still
whispered throughout Jewish lands. The tragedy fulfilled ancient prophecy:
"A voice was heard in Ramah . . . Rachel weeping for her children. It was said the
anguished cries of the mothers of Beth-lehem that fearful night had indeed
been heard in Ramah, some ten miles away.

Nor had the angelic warnings ceased then. When news reached the
Jewish colony in Alexandria that Herod the Butcher King had died, there
were spontaneous celebrations in the streets. Yet Yosef was still directed to
avoid Judea and go instead back to Nazareth.

Once again events proved the timeliness of the counsel: Herod's son
Archelaus ruled Judea in his father's place. As ruthless as his father but even

less subtle, Archelaus had quickly proven himself a tyrant . . . and every bit as likely to assassinate anyone proclaimed as "the true King of the Jews."

While Yosef had been apprehensive about how his family would be treated in Nazareth, given the way they had been shunned by gossipy villagers, none of his fears were realized. The months of their absence in Beth-lehem and Egypt had allowed scandal-serving neighbors to move on to other topics, other victims. By the time of their return to the Galil, the area was fully embroiled in the behavior of Archelaus. There was little time for barely remembered rumors.

Arrests, torture, and executions mounted each upon the other throughout the nine-year span of Archelaus' reign. Revolts real and imaginary plagued the last decade. Archelaus' oppressive cruelty only ended when delegations of Jews and Samaritans, agreeing on something for almost the first time ever, protested his brutality to the aging Emperor Augustus.

And just like that, Archelaus was gone.

In his place the Romans brought in their new governor with his new census to impose a new round of taxes. The Romans had quickly and ruthlessly suppressed one more rebellion . . . and now an uneasy peace lay across Judea and the Galil.

True, Antipas, another of Herod's sons, ruled in Galilee, but so far he had shown himself more interested in pleasure-seeking than in spies and secret tribunals. Still, he had responded with inherited ferocity to the rebel attack on his pleasure city of Sepphoris, concurring with the Romans that rebels should be crucified and many innocent inhabitants sold into slavery.

Perhaps this was a good time to get out of the Galil after all.

Live quietly and unobtrusively.

Go or stay? Which was the safer course?

The lone flame gnawing at the twisted wick slurped up a final drop of oil and began to sputter.

Yosef's forehead bounced gently against the words of Isaiah 9: *The people who walked in darkness have seen a great light. . . .*

For to us a son is born, to us a son is given and the government shall be upon His shoulder, and His name shall be called Wonderful, Counselor, Mighty God, Everlasting Father, Prince of Peace.

Nor did the prophet's utterance about the coming Messiah stop there. Though the scroll required turning to reveal the next lines, Yosef heard an almost audible voice continue: *Of the increase of His government and of peace there will be no end, on the throne of David and over his kingdom. . . .*

The throne of David was in Jerusalem. David's birthplace was Bethlehem, but his kingdom was centered in the Holy City.

—PP. 55–57

ASK

If you were Yosef, what concerns would you weigh in your decision?

_____

_____

_____

What would help you make your decision?

_____

_____

_____

What were the end results of Herod the Butcher King and Archelaus? What kind of leader was Antipas proving himself to be?

_____

_____

READ

"Elisheba, you must remember what the angel said to me. Yochanan is a miracle. He will be called a prophet of the Most High. He will make the road straight for the one to come after him. For the Son of Mary . . . the Son of the Almighty! If these things are true and we believe them, then I tell you, like Avraham, we will take our son up and offer him to the Most High where Avraham offered Yitz'chak. And remember, Elisheba! We will come down again alive from Mount Zion!"
—P. 72

There shall come forth a shoot from the stump of Jesse, and a Branch from his roots shall bear fruit. And the Spirit of the Lord shall rest upon Him, the Spirit of wisdom and understanding, the Spirit of counsel and might, the Spirit of knowledge and fear of the Lord. And His delight shall be in the fear of the Lord.

Reverence for the work of HaShem will consume Him, the angel interpreted. *A shoot from the stump of Jesse. A* Netzer . . . *a fresh, green Branch among King David's descendants. . . . will be eager to be in the House of HaShem.*

"And none too soon, either!" Yosef agreed. "Even here in little Nazareth, friends and neighbors, who by Judeans are derided as 'ignorant Nazareans,' know the need for a new David. And Yeshua will be he?"

The angel bowed his head at the utterance of the name *Yeshua* . . . *Salvation.*

"But he's still so young. Only twelve. Must he go to David's capital already?"

From Nazareth . . . the Nazarean . . . He who is the Netzer . . . *must already be about His Father's business. But have no fear, Yosef of Nazareth. . . . Have no fear. Remember: He will be full of wisdom and understanding, counsel and might, knowledge and the fear of the Lord. You yourself will bear witness.*

—PP. 57–58

Yosef was not worried about the trip. He and Mary had made the Passover pilgrimage to Jerusalem every year, even while Archelaus ruled Judea.

Some went every few years; some once in a lifetime.

For Yeshua this was a first. Because of Yosef's concern for His safety, the boy had been left with Mary's parents each spring. This year, for the first time since His appearance at the Temple when He was an infant, Yeshua would once again be in the Holy City.

—PP. 77–78

Yes, Mazzar had high hopes for Yeshua, the carpenter's son . . . Mazzar saw in Yeshua one who would continue to immerse Himself in Scripture all His days. Already the boy was the first to ask, "Why does it say that? Why does Torah include that story, that phrase, that particular word?"

The scholar had hopes this boy would be his crowning achievement as a teacher . . . that perhaps the boy would even become a rabbi someday. No rabbi out of Nazareth had ever achieved great fame in the rest of the Jewish world. Galilean rabbis were not reputed to be pious like those educated in Jerusalem or brilliant like those from Babylon or creative thinkers like those from Alexandria.

But Yeshua . . . here was a penetrating, insightful mind to be reckoned with. Good-natured, not aloof or arrogant, Yeshua seemed to study people as well as Torah.

Such a one could make a great rabbi . . . perhaps even the founder of an enduring school like Shammai or Hillel.

—P. 34

ASK

What was Yochanan's purpose? And why should knowing his purpose help Elisheba not to worry about Yochanan going to Jerusalem?

_____

_____

_____

What does the angel say that Yeshua's purpose is? Why must Yosef have no fear of taking his young son to Jerusalem?

_____

_____

_____

Why does Mazzar have high hopes for Yeshua in particular?

_____

_____

_____

READ

Mary glanced up at the moon, then peered toward the south as if she could see through the hills to the parade of crosses marching into the distance. "So much cruelty in the world," she murmured. . . .

Yosef tucked her head beneath his chin. "The Almighty has kept us safe, hasn't he? Twelve years, and he has never failed to keep us sheltered, eh?"

"It's not that," Mary responded, peering up into Yosef's worried frown. "The Lord is faithful and trustworthy at all times. I can't help but think that something's happening . . . or about to. It just seems that something is about to change; some new corner of a plan we don't yet understand is unfolding even now."

—P. 15

A frown crossed her face, and Yosef suspected she remembered the terrors of giving birth and the flight from murderous Herod that came after.

"Yosef," she said, confirming his concern, "were we right to bring him on this trip? Is it safe? I know Archelaus is gone and we're away from where the Romans . . ." She shuddered.

Mary had seen the forest of crosses. The same horrifying image was emblazoned in Yosef's mind.

"So this is a good time to go to Yerushalayim," he maintained stoutly. "To see Zachariah and Elisheba and cousin Yochanan. He was such a big, lusty baby. Must be a strapping big youth by now."

"And that bloodred moon?" Mary wondered. "Who was it for? What did it mean?"

Yosef scanned the sky. A half-moon was sinking in the west, followed by Mars, The Adam. The Lord of the Sabbath was nearly directly overhead, between the constellations of The Virgin and The Lion. "Remember that the angel told me to not be afraid," he reminded Mary. "This is right for us to do. Yeshua may be from Nazareth, but his future lies in Yerushalayim."

Mary nodded. "I know, but I can't stop thinking about how pleasant the last years have been. I trust Adonai and . . . I trust you, Yosef. But there's so much I don't understand. I heard Rabbi Mazzar speaking about the Anointed One liberating the captives, and it sounds so good and so right. Then I think about what the prophet also says of him: *Surely He has borne our griefs and carried our sorrows; yet we esteemed Him stricken, smitten by God, and afflicted.* I don't understand!"

Leaning toward her, Yosef kissed her forehead and tucked her close beneath his chin. "Nor do I," he admitted. "But I remember a young girl who trusted Adonai for something very great she had no way to understand. If everything made sense and we understood every reason, what place would there be for trust?"

"You're so strong," Mary murmured. "So good and so strong."

"And so needy to hear the same words spoken to me! But there is the sign of The Virgin and The Lord of the Sabbath." He pointed upward. "*The heavens declare the glory of the Almighty,*" he quoted. "And there—" he angled his chin toward the circle of laughing boys and indicated Yeshua—"there is the proof of his faithfulness. It is enough for right now; we will go on trusting."

—PP. 105–106

ASK

What does Mary think about? worry about?

_____

_____

_____

How does knowing that the Lord has a plan help her when she doesn't understand?

_____

_____

_____

How can knowing that the Lord is faithful and trustworthy help you when you don't understand?

_____

_____

_____

READ

"What do you think, Yeshua?" Nicolas piped up. "Will it be this year? Will Messiah appear in Yerushalayim this year?"

"That would be amazing," Beriah commented. "To be in Zion when Messiah arrives. To watch him destroy the enemies of Israel. To have a king again on David's throne."

"But you didn't answer the question, Yeshua," Nicolas persisted. "You're the best student of all of us. Even Shim'on admits that."

"Fishermen have no time for nonsense about books," Shim'on blustered. "I know how to cipher and I can read . . . mostly."

"Not the point," Nicolas honed in. "However much we may want him to come, he can't come until all the signs are right. What do you say, Rabbi? This year?"

Yeshua measured His words carefully. "The prophet Dani'el gives signals that bring us very near this year. His message also agrees with the number of years calculated from the Redemption of the Firstborn of the Levites that started during the Exodus. But I don't think he will be revealed this year."

"Not this year? So you do think he's alive, then?" Shim'on challenged.

"Oh yes," Yeshua agreed. "I'm very certain he's alive."

A lamb bleated in the distance.

—P. 107

ASK

Do you believe that Messiah could appear soon? Why or why not? What signs do you see of His imminent coming?

_____

_____

_____

Why is the symbol of the lamb important to this scene?

_____

_____

_____

READ

Jude buried his face in his arms and began to weep silently. He knew he was crying not for poor Eizel but for himself. They were all worthless here in the Quarry. While great men traversed the holy stones of the Temple Mount above them, the poor and the forgotten existed beneath their feet.

Did anyone notice the fall of a Jerusalem Sparrow? Jude wondered. Did anyone care? Would anyone be a witness for him that he had ever lived?

What was it that Grandmother had told him the night she flew away? *"Jude, you will need to pray. . . . Jude . . . say your prayers. . . ."*

But Jude did not know how to pray. And if he spoke to God from the depths of such a place as this, how could the Almighty God of Heaven and Earth hear the prayers of one so insignificant?

You . . . Adonai . . . you are so great. Grandmother said I should speak to you, and you would hear me. They tell me you made everything. The birds in the sky. Men, rich and poor alike. You made the lights in the heavens by your word, Grandmother said. But you've forgotten the sparrows. The starry cross I see rise each night in the heavens . . . its beauty mocks my sorrow for Papa's death. Where are you, Lord? You who made the Southern Cross . . . where can I go to speak to you? You . . . who live somewhere in the stars? While I am here, trapped in the grave of the living?

—P. 168

Yeshua seemed undaunted as he helped Jude to sit upright. "Don't be afraid. Our Father is here. Even here in the depths of the earth. He heard you, Jude. It is written that Adonai makes his home among the poor and he knows when the smallest Sparrow of Yerushalayim falls."

"What will I do? Where can I go now?"

"Come, Brother." Yeshua lifted him by the hand. "Follow me."

P. 170

ASK
Why does Jude grieve? What does he think of himself? of God?

_____

_____

_____

Have you ever felt like Jude? If so, when? Tell the story.

_____

_____

_____

How does the coming of Yeshua make a difference in Jude's life and thinking?

_____

_____

_____

Why do you think *Ninth Witness* comes full circle back to the story of Jude?

_____

_____

_____

READ

Yosef remembered how the angel had whispered of salvation . . . *Yeshua!*
. . . to him and changed the course of his life forever. Yeshua was indeed
about His Father's business . . . searching for the lost. Yeshua in His Father's
House . . . bearing true testimony to the character of His Father's heart . . .
seeking to comfort and save the poor and the outcasts and the orphans of
Jerusalem.

And what of the other prophecies spoken in this very place twelve years
before? Yosef studied the lines that creased Mary's brow and remembered
again: "*And a sword will pierce your heart also. . . .*"

It was in that moment Yosef saw Mary's expression change. She noticed
the Sparrow near her son, wearing the lambskin jacket—the coat the
grieving shepherd of Beth-lehem had sent for Yeshua to wear in place of the
sons he had lost. Now Yeshua's treasured coat, made from the fleece of a
sacrificial lamb, had been passed along to bless another child.

Suddenly it was clear! Yosef looked heavenward and thanked the Almighty Father for the witness this moment gave to his heart.

The business Yeshua's Father had sent Him to accomplish was not to argue the fine points of the Law with the learned rabbis in the Temple. Those religious hypocrites who lived in wealth and comfort, and who claimed the name and rank and privileges of Sons of the Covenant, broke the Ninth Commandment: While claiming to act in the name of God, they bore false witness against their neighbors and against the very nature and character of the God they claimed to serve.

Giving alms, they neglected to love the poor and the needy who cowered in their shadows. Walking in spiritual darkness, they purchased the light of the abandoned Sparrows of Jerusalem, two boys for a penny.

The Ninth Commandment declared, *You shall not bear false witness.* Yet by rejecting love and compassion for others while proudly claiming to fulfill the Law of the Almighty, their actions bore false witness against the Truth declared in Scripture: *love your neighbor as yourself.*

The Ninth Commandment was witness against them; they did not serve the business of God.

But as for Yeshua? *"Didn't you know I would be about my Father's business?"* *"You will call him Yeshua because He will save His people. . . ."*

Yosef understood then that Yeshua was called by His Father to live out true witness of God's nature. He could never be false to either God or man. The child in the manger had been born to seek and to find the lost and forgotten! Yeshua, both shepherd and lamb, had come to lead lambs like Jude home . . . home to safe pasture.

Yosef and Mary exchanged a glance of understanding.

Yeshua said, "Jude has a little sister too. Her name is Kerah. She lives in the orphanage." He nodded.

Mary asked the boy, "What do you think? You and Kerah . . . would you come home with us?"

Jude stepped into the shadow of Yeshua, who wrapped a protective arm around his shoulder. "I was lost," Jude said. "Everything lost from my life but his coat, which you gave to me. In the darkness I prayed that someone would love me enough to search for me . . . to bring me home. *YiSMaH!* Oh, Mother! And Kerah! How she longs for a mother to teach her . . . to sing her to sleep at night. " A look of wonder crossed his face. "I thought there was no one. But while you were searching everywhere for your son . . . he . . . found . . . me. And made me his brother."

—PP. 179–180

Mary managed a hoarse whisper. "Yeshua. . . . son? Why have you treated us like this? Here your father and I have been anxiously looking for you."

Not unkindly, but with His countenance displaying the resolute expression Yosef knew so well, Yeshua replied, "Why did you have to search for me? Did you not know I would be here, in my Father's house . . . attending to my Father's business?"

The memory of a long-ago dream echoed in Yosef's mind. *"Yosef, Son of David, do not be afraid to take Mary home as your wife, for what is conceived in her is from the Holy Spirit. . . ."*

The angel had borne true witness to Yosef of God's great love for every person!

Yosef considered the mother and her son together. *Can he really understand? Can Yeshua know? Does Mary understand the meaning of the angel's words as her son holds her in his arms? "You will call Him Yeshua . . . Salvation . . . for He will save His people from their sins. . . . and they will call Him Immanuel— which means, "God with us."*

—PP. 178–179

Jesus said to him, "Today salvation has come to this house, because this man, too, is a son of Abraham. For the Son of Man came to seek and to save what was lost."

—LUKE 19:9

ASK

What does the questioning Yosef at last realize about Yeshua? And about why He must be about His Father's business?

_____

_____

_____

Once Yosef and Mary understand why Yeshua had to stay behind in Jerusalem, how do they act on that understanding?

_____

_____

_____

In what ways can you step out of your comfort zone and act to help those who are lost?

_____

_____

_____

WONDER . . .

"The Lord is faithful and trustworthy at all times. I can't help but think that something's happening . . . or about to. It just seems that something is about to change; some new corner of a plan we don't yet understand is unfolding even now."

—P. 15

What plan might God be unfolding in your life right now? Why not accept the shelter of His love?

_____

_____

_____

"The Lord bless you and keep you; the Lord make His face to shine upon you and be gracious to you; the Lord lift up His countenance upon you and give you Shalom! Amen!"

—P. 78

Dear Reader,

You are so important to us. We have prayed for you as we wrote this book and also as we receive your letters and hear your soul cries. We hope that *Ninth Witness* has encouraged you to go deeper. To get to know Yeshua better. To fill your soul hunger by examining Scripture's truths for yourself.

We are convinced that if you do so, you will find this promise true: *"If you seek Him, He will be found by you."* — 1 CHRONICLES 28:9

Bodie & Brock Thoene

Scripture References

1. Luke 19:4-6
2. Luke 19:9
3. Luke 9:51
4. Esth. 7:9-10
5. Esth. 8:15
6. Esth. 8:16
7. Esth. 9:5
8. Esth. 10:3
9. Isa. 59:3-4
10. Isa. 59:9
11. Isa. 60:1-3
12. Luke 2:35
13. Ps. 121:8
14. Ezek. 43:26
15. Ezek. 43:27
16. Jer. 31:15
17. Isa. 9:2
18. Isa. 9:1
19. Isa. 9:6
20. Isa. 9:7
21. Isa. 11:1-3
22. Gen. 22:5
23. See Luke 1:13-17.
24. Lev. 1:1-2ff.
25. Ps. 95:7-8
26. Num 6:24-26
27. Exod. 3:5
28. Exod. 3:6; Matt. 22:32
29. Ps. 121:1
30. Ps. 121:2
31. Ps. 121:3
32. Ps. 121:4
33. Ps. 121:8
34. Ps. 131
35. Ps. 129:1-2
36. Ps. 129:3-4
37. Ps. 129:5
38. Ps. 129:8
39. Ps. 134:1
40. Ps. 130:1
41. Ps. 127:1
42. Ps. 134:2-3
43. 1 Kings 9:3
44. Isa. 53:4
45. Ps. 19:1
46. Zech. 9:9
47. Ps. 125:1
48. Ps. 125:2
49. Ps. 125:4
50. Ps. 122:1, 3-4
51. Ps. 126:1-3
52. Num. 19:1-2
53. See Rom. 3
54. Mal. 3:1
55. Isa. 60:1
56. See Isa. 25:8
57. Ps. 91:12
58. Deut. 18:15
59. Ps. 113:1
60. Ps. 114:1-2
61. Ps. 116:12-16
62. John 18:11
63. Mal. 4:5-6
64. See Matt. 10:29-31
65. Isa. 53:3
66. Luke 2:48-49
67. Matt. 1:20
68. Matt. 1:21, 23
69. Luke 2:35
70. Exod. 20:16
71. Lev. 19:18
72. Matt. 1:21
73. Luke 2:48

Authors' Note

The following sources have been helpful in our research for this book.

- *The Complete Jewish Bible*. Translated by David H. Stern. Baltimore, MD: Jewish New Testament Publications, Inc., 1998.

- *iLumina*, a digitally animated Bible and encyclopedia suite. Carol Stream, IL: Tyndale House Publishers, 2002.

- *The International Standard Bible Encyclopaedia*. George Bromiley, ed. 5 vols. Grand Rapids, MI: Eerdmans, 1979.

- *The Life and Times of Jesus the Messiah*. Alfred Edersheim. Peabody, MA: Hendrickson Publishers, Inc., 1995.

- Starry Night™ Enthusiast Version 5.0, publishing by Imaginova™ Corp.

About the Authors

BODIE AND BROCK THOENE (pronounced *Tay-nee*) have written over 50 works of historical fiction. That these best sellers have sold more than 10 million copies and won eight ECPA Gold Medallion Awards affirms what millions of readers have already discovered—the Thoenes are not only master stylists but experts at capturing readers' minds and hearts.

In their timeless classic series about Israel (The Zion Chronicles, The Zion Covenant, and The Zion Legacy), the Thoenes' love for both story and research shines.

With The Shiloh Legacy and *Shiloh Autumn* (poignant portrayals of the American Depression), The Galway Chronicles (dramatic stories of the 1840s famine in Ireland), and the Legends of the West (gripping tales of adventure and danger in a land without law), the Thoenes have made their mark in modern history.

In the A.D. Chronicles they step seamlessly into the world of Jerusalem and Rome, in the days when Yeshua walked the earth and transformed lives with His touch.

Bodie began her writing career as a teen journalist for her local newspaper. Eventually her byline appeared in prestigious periodicals such as *U.S. News and World Report*, *The American West*, and *The Saturday Evening Post*. She also worked for John Wayne's Batjac Productions (she's best known as author of *The Fall Guy*) and ABC Circle Films as a writer and researcher. John Wayne described her as "a writer with talent that captures the people and the times!" She has degrees in journalism and communications.

Brock has often been described by Bodie as "an essential half of this writing team." With degrees in both history and education, Brock has, in his role as researcher and story-line consultant, added the vital dimension of historical accuracy. Due to such careful research, the Zion Covenant and Zion Chronicles series are recognized by the American Library Association, as well as Zionist libraries around the world, as classic historical novels and are used to teach history in college classrooms.

Bodie and Brock have four grown children—Rachel, Jake, Luke, and Ellie—and seven grandchildren. Their children are carrying on the Thoene family talent as the next generation of writers, and Luke produces the Thoene audiobooks. Bodie and Brock divide their time between London and Nevada.

For more information visit:
www.thoenebooks.com
www.familyaudiolibrary.com

Discover where it all began. . . .

Turn the page for an excerpt
from the first book in the
A.D. Chronicles series.

I

In a tiny, unpretentious house in the village known as Beth-lehem, "House of Bread," bunches of lavender dried in the rafters of the main room, filling the place with sweet aroma. The seder supper was finished. The stories of Israel's deliverance from bondage in Egypt had all been sung. The clutter of empty dishes remained stacked on the table.

Three boys and a sheepdog shared a bed made of soft fleece. Avel, aged nine, lay between five-year-old Emet and eleven-year-old Ha-or Tov.

Emet and Ha-or Tov were drowsy, nearly asleep. Avel, eyes heavy, listened to the soft voices of two men engaged in conversation. Red Dog blinked at the firelight.

Zadok, Chief Shepherd of the flocks and herds of Israel, was old. A patch covered one eye. Skin was like leather, face split by the scar of an ancient wound. His voice and that of his Passover guest, Yeshua of Nazareth, drifted into the bedchamber.

"But if not now, when?" Zadok inquired of Yeshua.

Avel strained to hear Yeshua's reply.

When?

In the history of the world, had there ever been a more important question? So many things depended on the answer. Redemption. Freedom. Vengeance against Roman oppressors and corrupt religious rulers.

Avel rested his cheek on his hand. Zadok was not asking one question, but many.

When?

When would Yeshua openly declare His right to the throne of David?

When would He take His place at the head of an army to drive the Romans from Jerusalem and Israel?

When would He avenge the blood of those who had fallen victim to Roman swords within the Temple courts only today in Jerusalem?

"If not now, Lord, when?"

And who had more right to know than Zadok? Zadok, who as a young man had been among the first shepherds to see the angels and hear their heavenly proclamation that the Messiah had been born in a lambing barn at Beth-lehem.

Zadok, who had brought first word of the miraculous event to the elders of the Temple as he delivered the young lambs of Beth-lehem and Migdal Eder for the daily sacrifice.

Zadok, who had made room in his own home for the young mother, her husband, and the newborn baby king.

Zadok, who had secretly sent the family on their way to safety as the soldiers of the old butcher king, Herod, had come by night to kill every male child under the age of two in the village.

Zadok, whose face had been ripped open by a Roman gladius in his battle to save his children.

Zadok, who had buried three tiny boys while the keening of his wife, Rachel, echoed across the pastures of Migdal Eder to be heard as far away as Ramah.

Zadok, who had kept his holy vow of silence about the whereabouts of the promised King of Israel for thirty-two years until tonight.

Did a man who suffered so much not deserve to know why? What had it all been for?

When?

Yeshua, His gaze fixed intently on the old man, did not answer at first. Then He grasped Zadok's hand. "You were the first to hear. The first to believe. The first to suffer loss for my sake. Your babies are the first martyrs. Surely you've known, old friend, that it was no accident that the Son of David was born in a stable among the lambs set apart for sacrifice in the Temple of Yerushalayim. That same child born thirty-two years ago in Beth-lehem is *korban*, that which is holy and set apart for the purposes of the heavenly Father."

"But what can it mean?" Zadok's voice was intense.

"Zadok? You're Chief Shepherd of the Temple flock. You tend the lambs for sacrifice. Can it be that you've forgotten the words spoken by the prophet Isaias about the Messiah?"

Zadok waved a hand. Evidently, Avel thought, the old man did not want to be reminded of that part of the Scripture. "So much written about what is *korban*. How can an old man be expected to remember it all?"

Yeshua stroked His beard. Without taking His eyes from the shepherd He said, *"He was oppressed and afflicted, yet he did not open his mouth; he was led as a lamb to slaughter."*[4]

That was all. As if it explained anything!

Ha-or Tov, now wide awake, whispered to Avel, "What does Yeshua mean? What do the sacrificial lambs raised here in the fields of Beth-lehem have to do with Messiah, the Redeemer?"

"I think he's talking about the riots today," Avel replied.

"The penalty for breaking the commands of the Almighty," Yeshua continued, "is death. That curse now rests on every human soul. Redemption costs something, Zadok, my old friend. It is written by Isaias about the Son of Man, *'Surely he took up our infirmities and carried our sorrows. . . . He was pierced for our transgressions, he was crushed for our iniquities. . . . the punishment that brought us peace was upon him, and by his wounds we are healed.'"*[5]

Zadok leaned close. Firelight glowed golden on his face. "Can the cost of our salvation be so high?"

"Tomorrow I'll be teaching in Beth-Anyah."

"So close to Yerushalayim! You'll draw the wolves out along with the sheep. You put yourself at their mercy."

"A day is coming when they will understand God's Mercy."

"But not that way, Lord! Tell me it won't be!"

"God's love for each person is that profound."

"There must be another way! Crush our enemies! Call down fire from heaven! Destroy the wicked! Set up a kingdom in Yerushalayim like our shepherd-king, David! Like you, he was born here in Beth-lehem!"

"Zadok, when the soldiers of Herod came to Beth-lehem to kill every baby boy, you sought to save your three sons." Yeshua touched the scar on Zadok's cheek. Avel fixed his eyes on the scene, remembering his own healing. But this time Yeshua did not make the jagged line smooth again or restore the eye lost in the battle, though Avel knew He could have done so. "This scar is proof of your love for your children."

"I failed. I am alive and my babies are in their graves."

"Not for want of effort. You would have died to save your little ones. I know you. Even now you'd face a lion and lay down your life to save your flocks. Can the Son sent by the Father do any less for the flock given to him? Would you deny the Lord the honor of wounds and scars that will be eternal proof of how much he loves you?"

"I will die for you, Lord."

"He was led like a lamb to slaughter."[6]

"But I am more ready to give up my own life! Gladly!"

"One day it may be so. Anyone who lays down his life for my sake will find it.[7] God so loved the world that whoever believes in his Son will never die but will inherit eternal life.[8] But first, the good shepherd will lay down his life to save his flock. That price must be paid to redeem those the Father has given to me. The prophecy of what will happen is all there, recorded by Moses and the prophets. They longed to see what you see, to hear what you have heard.[9] The battle for mankind will be won."

"Rabbi, will we fight the enemy then? Together?"

"Don't misunderstand, old friend . . . *by his wounds we are healed.*"[10]

The prophecy hung like the scent of lavender on the air. Then, inex-plicably, Avel saw a tangible sorrow grip the old man, as if he remem-bered something. What was the meaning of it? Avel wondered. What had that fragment of verse awakened in the old man's understanding?

Shoulders sagged. With a groan Zadok bowed his head. Ran crooked fingers through his thatch of white hair. What did Zadok hear that Avel did not?

After a long time the aged shepherd pleaded, "Ah! No! And after such a fine beginning. I looked up! Saw the stars shinin' there above us in the field. Such joy we felt. What a beautiful baby boy! Such hope! What's it for? It can't be meant to end so ill!"

Silence descended. Then, finally, Yeshua replied, "It can't be any other way."

"But when?"

"Next year in Yerushalayim. Passover."

"I won't attend." Zadok raised his chin defiantly. But Avel knew the truth of it: Yes, Zadok would be there.

Yeshua stood and smiled. "Never mind, old friend. I'll see you again. Soon." He glanced at Red Dog. "The faithful ones are gone. Wolves lead the flock of Israel. They won't let you rest."

Zadok's lower lip shot out. "Get yourself out of Judea! Y' know what they'll do! The office of high priest is bought and paid for. They fear you. And after today? What happened in the Temple? They'll find some way to blame you for it."

"It isn't yet my time."

"Y' must leave! Thirty years ago I warned your mother and Joseph to leave. Go to Egypt. To Alexandria. There are true Israelites in Alexandria. They have a temple there where some might listen. Them that hold the power in Yerushalayim now will use their might against you as Herod, the great butcher, once tried. Caiaphas as high priest is in league with the Romans. Up to the neck. Herod Antipas depends on Roman soldiers to keep the people from revolution and the Nabatean king from attacking. It's a dangerous time for us all."

"Men's souls have a fiercer enemy than Rome. More terrible than Herod Antipas. Don't be afraid of those who have power to kill the body. Beware of one who will destroy your soul if he can." Yeshua glanced toward Avel, Emet, and Ha-or Tov. "Follow the shepherd," he said to the boys. "Learn from him. Listen to no other voice and you will live!" Then He placed His hand on Zadok's shoulder in farewell. "Teach them Torah as the Lord commands a father to teach his children. Zadok! Take care of my lambs!"

Zadok nodded, unable to speak.

The two clasped hands. "I'll see you soon. Won't I?" A flash of understanding appeared to pass between them.

Avel fought the urge to run to Yeshua, to wrap his arms around Him and beg Him not to leave them unprotected.

Yeshua touched His finger to the mezuzah, the small rectangular case containing a fragment of Scripture. This was the covenant-mark placed on the doorpost of every Jewish house in remembrance of the blood of the Passover lamb.

In a gentle voice Yeshua whispered the blessing: *"The Lord will watch over your coming and going both now and forevermore."*[11]

Yeshua's benediction seemed a promise that the Lord Himself would watch over them, Avel thought. Why then was Avel afraid to see Him go? Even with hope that the Lord would preserve them, death felt very close. Wolves were stalking the flock, nipping at the heels of the Good Shepherd and all who followed Him.

The two men embraced. Without a backward glance, Yeshua strode into the night.

THOENE FAMILY CLASSICS™

✪ ✪ ✪

THOENE FAMILY CLASSIC HISTORICALS
by Bodie and Brock Thoene

*Gold Medallion Winners**

THE ZION COVENANT
*Vienna Prelude**
Prague Counterpoint
Munich Signature
Jerusalem Interlude
Danzig Passage
*Warsaw Requiem**
London Refrain
Paris Encore
Dunkirk Crescendo

THE ZION CHRONICLES
*The Gates of Zion**
A Daughter of Zion
The Return to Zion
A Light in Zion
*The Key to Zion**

THE SHILOH LEGACY
*In My Father's House**
A Thousand Shall Fall
Say to This Mountain

SHILOH AUTUMN

THE GALWAY CHRONICLES
*Only the River Runs Free**
Of Men and of Angels
*Ashes of Remembrance**
All Rivers to the Sea

THE ZION LEGACY
Jerusalem Vigil
Thunder from Jerusalem
Jerusalem's Heart
Jerusalem Scrolls
Stones of Jerusalem
Jerusalem's Hope

A.D. CHRONICLES
First Light
Second Touch
Third Watch
Fourth Dawn
Fifth Seal
Sixth Covenant
Seventh Day
Eighth Shepherd
Ninth Witness
Tenth Stone
and more to come!

CP0064

THOENE FAMILY CLASSICS™

✪ ✪ ✪

THOENE FAMILY CLASSIC AMERICAN LEGENDS

LEGENDS OF THE WEST
by Bodie and Brock Thoene

Legends of the West, Volume One
   Sequoia Scout
   The Year of the Grizzly
   Shooting Star
Legends of the West, Volume Two
   Gold Rush Prodigal
   Delta Passage
   Hangtown Lawman
Legends of the West, Volume Three
   Hope Valley War
   The Legend of Storey County
   Cumberland Crossing
Legends of the West, Volume Four
   The Man from Shadow Ridge
   Cannons of the Comstock
   Riders of the Silver Rim

LEGENDS OF VALOR
by Luke Thoene

Sons of Valor
Brothers of Valor
Fathers of Valor

✪ ✪ ✪

THOENE CLASSIC NONFICTION
by Bodie and Brock Thoene

Writer-to-Writer

THOENE FAMILY CLASSIC SUSPENSE
by Jake Thoene

CHAPTER 16 SERIES
   Shaiton's Fire
   Firefly Blue
   Fuel the Fire

✪ ✪ ✪

THOENE FAMILY CLASSICS FOR KIDS

BAKER STREET DETECTIVES
by Jake and Luke Thoene

The Mystery of the Yellow Hands
The Giant Rat of Sumatra
The Jeweled Peacock of Persia
The Thundering Underground

LAST CHANCE DETECTIVES
by Jake and Luke Thoene
Mystery Lights of Navajo Mesa
Legend of the Desert Bigfoot

THE VASE OF MANY COLORS
by Rachel Thoene (Illustrations by Christian Cinder)

✪ ✪ ✪

THOENE FAMILY CLASSIC AUDIOBOOKS

Available from
www.thoenebooks.com or
www.familyaudiolibrary.com

CP0064